Fight Like A Girl

Edited by
Joanne Hall and Roz Clarke

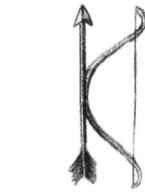

www.kristell-ink.com

Fight Like A Girl © 2015 Juliet McKenna
The Women's Song © 2015 Nadine Andie
Turn Of A Wheel © 2015 Fran Terminiello
Arrested Development © 2015 Joanne Hall
Asenath © 2015 Kim Lakin-Smith
The Coyote © 2015 K R Green
The Quality of Light © 2015 K T Davies
Silent Running © 2015 Sophie E Tallis
Unnatural History © 2015 Danie Ware
Vocho's Night Out © 2015 Julia Knight
The Cold Wind Oozes © 2015 Kelda Crich
Sword Dancer of Azmai © 2015 Roz Clarke
Archer 57 © 2015 Lou Morgan
The Runaway Warrior © 2015 Dolly Garland
Fire and Ash © 2015 Gaie Sebold

Paperback ISBN 978-1-909845-66-4
Epub ISBN 978-1-909845-67-1

Cover art by Sarah Anne Langton
Typesetting by Book Polishers
Edited by Joanne Hall and Roz Clarke

Kristell Ink
An Imprint of Grimbold Books
4 Woodhall Drive
Banbury
Oxon
OX16 9TY
United Kingdom
www.kristell-ink.com

Contents

Fight Like A Girl

Introduction

Anne Lyle

ROM A VERY young age I was a sucker for a good sword fight, and on Sunday afternoons the BBC fed this appetite with re-runs of classic Hollywood swashbucklers like *The Adventures of Robin Hood*, *The Crimson Pirate* and *Scaramouche*. Errol Flynn versus Basil Rathbone, Steward Granger versus Mel Ferrer; I lapped it up. At the time I didn't consciously register that the dudes with swords were all, well, dudes. Then in January 1977 the Doctor Who of my teenage years, Tom Baker, got a new companion: a knife-wielding but intelligent "savage" named Leela. I immediately developed a huge girl-crush on this character who was eager to fight first and ask questions later. In retrospect of course she was mainly designed to appeal to the dads in the audience, with her skimpy outfit showing off an awful lot of fake-tanned skin, but for me Leela was my first experience of what "fight like a girl" really meant.

It wasn't just Leela, though. The late seventies saw the rise of a new type of female character, one who was in the thick of the action instead of the damsel in distress. Or, if the princess did need rescuing, as often as not it was her own daring that had landed her in captivity in the first place, like *Star Wars'* Leia Organa. In one notable case a woman was cast in

7

a part – Ripley in *Alien* – originally written for a man, thus inadvertently creating an iconic female character.

Thankfully in the twenty-first century it's become less acceptable for female characters to be stripped down to their gold lamé bikinis for the male audience's titillation. From *Battlestar Galactica*'s Lieutenant Kara "Starbuck" Thrace to Katniss Everdeen in *The Hunger Games*, our modern heroines are more likely to be wearing sweat-stained coveralls and grime than sequins and lipstick. Which is not to say they can't be glamorous as well. Agent Peggy Carter manages to kick arse as easily in a sharp 1940s suit as she does in army fatigues!

Despite these advances, female characters who wield weapons are still a comparative rarity even four decades later, perhaps because war has traditionally been a male pursuit and violence a male preoccupation. Women who fight often do so in self-defence or self-preservation rather than any desire for aggression; a characteristic exploited in Frank Herbert's 1981 *God Emperor of Dune*, in which Leto II builds an all-female army to protect himself and his empire. "You fight like a girl" might be a taunt in the school playground, but our culture also acknowledges the idea of the "mamma bear" who will fight to the death to preserve her cubs.

In this anthology you'll find all kinds of women who know what to do with the pointy end, from soldiers and mercenaries to cage-fighters and duellists, to those who have no choice but to fight or die. There's more to each of these women, of course, than their fighting skills: some are mothers, some are sisters, or lovers, or perhaps they're all alone in the world. They may be fighting other humans, or monsters beyond our comprehension. Sometimes they win, sometimes they lose. Badly. But whatever their reason for fighting, it is always a compelling one.

Reading these stories I'm reminded once more that "you fight like a girl" is a compliment, not an insult. Or at least it should be. Anyone who thinks otherwise, well, I'm sure any of the ladies in these stories would be happy to give you a demonstration . . .

Anne Lyle
Cambridge, 2016

Coins, Fights and Stories Always Have Two Sides

Juliet McKenna

A S SHADOWS LENGTHENED across the camp ground, Erlin surveyed his fiefdom with satisfaction. Two tall tents of oiled leather were securely pitched at either end of a sturdy wagon, all embracing a sizeable hearth. A broad griddle and three lidded cookpots rested above the flames on an iron frame. To one side, a spit rested on its uprights above an oval pan. That wouldn't be empty long. Korose was approaching with a plump young sheep carcass over his shoulder.

The lanky lad grinned as he arrived. "We'll do well tonight."

"We will." Erlin set the last of the flatbreads he'd been cooking in their linen-lined basket and moved it a prudent distance from the hearth. "Get that fire stoked."

He secured the beast on the spit with interlocked skewers. Customers would appear once the aroma of roasting lamb drifted through this Lescari mercenary throng; customers with coin in their pockets, so soon after the end of the fighting season. Aft-Autumn's shifting colours had yet to subside into For-Winter's unchanging calm and the weather had been kind thus far.

The camp would be a different place come Aft-Winter. Once the frosts bit deep, Korose would have to forage ever further afield for firewood. Hungry mercenaries would grudge every copper spent on barley broth. Erlin would need all his guile to persuade the Caladhrian villages across the river to part with their jealously guarded stores. He was already buying sacks of flour, beans and onions from farmers gloating over well-stocked barns.

Each day, as hungry mercenaries came to his fire, Erlin discreetly looked for those most likely to try stealing from him after the solstice; sneaking up to the wagon at night like a rat after cheese or threatening him with a sword, demanding the leathery remnants of a side of bacon.

"I'll want you out of your blankets early tomorrow," he said as Korose fetched an armful of firewood. "To practise with your quarter staff."

"Maybe try some sword work?" the lad asked, hopeful.

Erlin smiled. "If you impress me."

He had every intention of getting his notched blades out from under the wagon's driving seat. These past ten days, this stretch of well-drained grassland between the river and a sprawl of coppices had been attracting ever more mercenaries seeking a winter haven. Time to show any covetous strangers that a grey-haired, weather-beaten old man was no easy prey.

Erlin had served his time in Lescar's interminable wars, as six rival dukes spent their silver and other men's blood on their ambition to be crowned High King. He still practised the skills that had seen him safe through countless battles.

He'd teach Korose, so the lad had some chance of surviving his first bloody season, once he'd put on enough muscle and height to catch a recruiting sergeant's eye.

Maybe the lad would come back years later, scarred and wealthy. Maybe Erlin would never hear of him again. No telling with such waifs and strays.

"Stir up the fire." He set the laden spit on its uprights.

Korose threw weathered wood onto the flames. "What news today?"

Erlin shrugged. "Quicksilvers took a beating when Sharlac's duke challenged His Grace of Triolle. Greenhawks scattered to the four winds after the battle at Chinel turned against Draximal."

"You reckon we'll see any of them here?"

Korose looked dubious. That particular bloody fight had soaked the soil on the far side of Lescar. But Erlin had tramped the length and breadth of this blighted country ten or more times in his youth, loyal to his scrawl on various mercenary companies' muster rolls.

"Stranger things have happened."

Korose tended the cook pots seething over the flames. Erlin turned the spit, making sure only the dull splat of fat dripped into the pan underneath, not the hiss of the meat's precious juices.

Dusk approached and more newcomers arrived. Some had laden horses or handcarts. Others had only the clothes and weapons they wore. Once they'd claimed a space, late arrivals wandered towards the cook fire in search of supper.

Korose served turnip pottage to a hungry warrior and replaced the pot lid. "He'd be useful in a fight."

A broad-shouldered and warmly-cloaked man with swords on each hip and carrying a bulky leather bag passed by their hearth.

"I'd say so." Noting the lithe walk of an alert swordsman, Erlin fixed the man's face in his memory. If he wasn't hungry tonight, sooner or later their paths would cross and Erlin would learn his story.

The man's fine clothing and better weapons indicated that he had no trouble filling his purse. So why come to this lesser camp instead of wintering in a larger stockade with some wealthy mercenary company?

Had he fallen out with the captain he'd mustered with last spring? Some quarrel over a wench or a wager? Never mind. Once the year had turned and For-Spring was on the horizon, Erlin would offer the stranger some introductions. By then the cook would know which warbands would welcome a swordsman who knew a rival company's secrets. Grateful coin would chink in the coffer Erlin kept well-hidden in his wagon's recesses.

Such profitable opportunities were merely one reason he liked to winter in these lesser camps. That, and the big mercenary company quartermasters ruled their cold-season stockades with an iron hand. Free spirits like Erlin paid extortionate sums just to breathe the same air.

"That smells good." Two leather-armoured men approached. One was tall and broad in a long jerkin with tarnished brass studs. He had a close-cropped head and eyes as dull as a dead trout.

The other was lithe as a snake in a short cuirass of oiled hide. Curly black hair and his sallow complexion spoke of Tormalin blood. He reached out with his belt knife to cut a slice from the succulent meat on the spit.

Erlin knocked the blade aside with his meat-jointing knife, as quick as he ever had been with a sword. "I carve, and only once I'm paid."

The snake withdrew, raising hands in mock surrender. "I beg your pardon."

"Granted." Erlin made no move towards the spitted lamb.

A heartbeat later the snake reached for a purse tucked inside his leather breastplate. "How much for two?"

"A silver mark each." Erlin held out a hand. "Silver, not Lescari lead."

The snake cocked his head. "Caladhrian or Tormalin?"

Erlin shrugged. "Whatever you're carrying."

The snake handed over two Caladhrian coins. Erlin slipped them into the pouch laced tight to his belt. "Fat or lean?"

"Fat," the croppy head growled.

"Lean." His companion smiled.

Erlin trusted that like he'd trust a mantrap's grin but coin was coin. Korose offered a leathery flatbread in each hand. Erlin laid a generous helping of meat on each one and the lad handed them over.

"We'll see you again." The snake tore off a mouthful and went on his way.

The croppy-head lingered to stare at Erlin before he followed.

"He thinks a lot of himself." Apprehension undercut Korose's attempt at a laugh.

"He does." Erlin pursed his lips.

He knew the snake's attempt to help himself had little to do with meat. When that sort got away with acting as though they had every right to take what they wanted, soon everyone would yield for the sake of a quiet life. Newcomers wouldn't even ask what gave such men their spurious authority.

He'd also seen the croppy-head taking in every detail of their little encampment, including the dun carthorse picketed on the far side of the wagon. Good luck to him trying to steal the beast or sneaking past to rob the wagon. Erlin had trained Pipkin to attack as readily as any guard dog.

He greeted the next man approaching the fire. "What's your pleasure?"

"What's your price?" the Lescari countered.

Customers hurried up now they'd seen Erlin carving the lamb and plenty more wanted pottage. By the time the carcass was reduced to bones and gristle, all three cook pots were down to the dregs and the flatbread basket was long emptied.

"I'd say we're done." Erlin weighed the silver in the pouch against his thigh with satisfaction.

Korose was looking out into the darkness. "Do you–?"

He wasn't talking to Erlin. The cook saw a slender figure in the shadows, wrapped in a blanket doing duty as a cloak.

He beckoned. "If you don't want to eat, you're welcome to warmth."

"I'd like that." The girl's hesitating voice betrayed her nature.

"Do you have a bowl?" Erlin tilted one of the cook pots. "Otherwise I'll pour this away."

"Thank you." The girl's haste betrayed her hunger. As she rummaged in her bag and moved closer to the firelight, Erlin noted her shirt's ragged cuffs and her much-mended jerkin. Her purse must be as empty as her belly.

Erlin filled her age-darkened wooden bowl with the last splash of broth and snapped his fingers at Korose. "Get those bones into a pot with a good tight lid and stow it in the wagon before any dogs come sniffing around."

As Korose hurried to obey, the girl crouched down to drink her bowl dry.

Didn't even have a spoon to call her own, Erlin guessed. He scraped the drippings from the spit into an earthenware jar. As he stood up, he saw the girl look hungrily at the smeared pan.

He fetched one of the flatbreads he'd set aside for himself and the lad. Wiping up the savoury residue, he tossed it to the girl. "Here."

She caught it, deft as a pup leaping for a titbit and vanished into the darkness. Erlin saw Korose looking after her.

"Stir up that fire for one last blaze, lad." He fetched juicy beefsteaks from the wagon along with a cast iron frying pan. "Let's have an onion and those mushrooms from this morning."

Korose was still trying to see where the girl had gone. "Do you think she'll be all right?"

"What's it to us?" Erlin brushed windblown ash off the chopping block.

Though once they were fed, had tidied up and were settled in their blankets, his thoughts turned to the girl.

How old? Hard to say in the dying firelight. Not in the first bloom of maidenhood. That was some reassurance. If she'd been living around mercenary companies for a couple of years – and by her battered gear Erlin guessed she had – she must have learned a few tricks to save herself from rape or worse.

Not a whore. Skinny as she was, she'd worn a sword at her hip and made no offer to take his meat in her mouth in return for a meal. That was good to know. Satin Fantine's brothel tents were on the far side of the camp. The henchmen who guarded her girls would offer freelance trollops the choice of handing over half their earnings or taking a beating so bad that no man would come near them.

Maybe she was a scout, Erlin mused as he drifted off to sleep. He'd known a few such women in his day; nimble enough to spy out an enemy camp and get back alive to tell the tale.

*

KOROSE WAS UP with the first glimmer of dawn to rekindle the fire. Erlin fed himself and the lad, then began serving griddled pancakes and bacon to those with silver to spend and porridge to those with copper.

Erlin was assessing the batter in his green-glazed jug when the broad-shouldered warrior from the night before offered Korose a shiny mark. "Good day to you both."

"The lad's Korose and I'm Erlin." He mixed more ale and flour. "What do we call you, friend?"

"Triggen," the man said easily.

Young enough to still be friendly with strangers. Old enough and strong enough to stand his ground against anyone who tried to take liberties. Erlin wondered when he'd walked away from whatever plough or prentice bench he'd been born to. At least five years since, he guessed, maybe as long ago as ten.

"Looks like you had a good summer," he observed.

"Up in Sharlac with the Sundowners," Triggen agreed. "Looking after the townsfolk of Welland."

"Sundowners are a fine company." Honourable, for the most part, though that wouldn't have stopped them extorting safe-passage money from any merchants taking the Great West Road. Erlin poured batter onto the hot griddle. "What's your pleasure for breakfast?"

Triggen grinned. "A couple of those wrapped around bacon. Nice and crisp if you please."

As Korose served several bowls of porridge Erlin watched the swordsman wander off with his breakfast, stopping to chat with someone every few paces.

"Sundowners don't take just anyone," Korose breathed.

"True," Erlin agreed. "And they'd slap a cook's boy silly for letting bacon burn."

"Shit!" Korose hastily lifted the smoking pan from the grating.

"Good morning all!"

Erlin looked up as the snake greeted everyone present with an expansive gesture and a smile.

"Thank you for your attention! Now, I know Aft-Autumn's not even turned to For-Winter—" he held up self-deprecating hands although no one had said a word "— but a sensible man thinks two steps ahead. We'll need someone paying for our swords and skills before Spring Solstice. Better to have that agreement signed and sealed with a duke's ring sooner than later?"

He looked around but before anyone spoke, he nodded, as though satisfied with everyone's agreement.

"I'm Chellan, for those who don't know me. I've fought with the Shearlings, the Wheelwrights and the Red Dyed Men. My sergeant is Acuri." He gestured to the croppy-head at his side.

"Show us your skills if you want to sign up. That's all, for the moment. Carry on." The snake nodded at Erlin before strolling off, dead-eyed Acuri at his side.

Who was he to give Erlin permission to do anything? The cook gripped his ladle, wishing Chellan had come within reach of a hefty clout.

"Chellan?" A mercenary looked at his tent mate. "What's his company?"

"Who's to say there's a company?" Erlin scraped a burned pancake off the griddle with his knife. "A man swaggers like a captain, that doesn't make him one. If he's fought with those fine companies, why's he wintering here?"

But he could see several men were tempted. Learning to take orders, quick and unquestioned, was a skill which kept mercenaries alive. Following any obvious leader soon became a habit.

Erlin pondered as he cooked pancakes. Once their last customer was served, he hefted their biggest cauldron onto the grate's iron bars and filled it from the water butt by the wagon.

"Once this is hot, you wash the pots," he told Korose. "I'll take a turn around the camp before I scour the pans. See if anyone else is setting up a cook fire."

Strolling among the tents, he was pleased to find he had no rivals thus far. Though as he'd expected a good few mercenaries had dug small pits to cook for themselves. Along his way he noted Triggen falling into conversations. The burly swordsman must be a companionable fellow.

When Erlin spotted a familiar face re-sewing a boot seam, he raised a hand. "Marsis!"

The weathered warrior looked up, puzzled. His lined brow cleared. "Erlin? It must be three years, you dog!"

That was invitation enough. Erlin sat down. "What have you been doing?"

Marsis grinned. "That's a story and a half."

As he told it, Erlin learned some useful information. In return he shared a few insights to help Marsis secure a profitable hire for the next year's fighting.

"So what do you know of this Chellan?" he asked casually as their conversation wound to a close.

Marsis frowned. "Nothing, for all he acts like everyone should know his name."

"Wasn't there some trouble with the Red Dyed Men back at the start of the summer?" mused Erlin.

Marsis nodded. "Near split the company down the middle. Rankers whispering round the shit pits, stirring up any fools who'd listen. Refuse to fight unless they got more of the Duke of Draximal's coin."

Erlin raised astonished eyebrows. "What happened?"

Marsis shrugged. "The company didn't split. I guess the sergeants traced the stink to its source, beat those fools black and blue and slung them out on their arses."

"Reckon so." Erlin got to his feet. "Good to see you. Come over when you want a meal."

As he wandered back, Erlin wondered if Snake Chellan and Cropped Acuri still carried the scars of a Red Dyed sergeant's kicking. If he was a betting man, he'd wager on it. But Erlin took bets. He didn't lay them.

Back at the wagon, Korose was looking guilty. It wasn't hard to see why. The scrawny girl had scraps of scorched bacon in her bowl and the last crumbs of the burned pancake. As soon as she saw Erlin, she fled.

In the daylight she was definitely no poult. Past her twentieth year, by Erlin's guess, of an age to be wed with three or four brats if she'd stayed in whatever village bred her. Old enough to know her own mind if she chose to give Korose a thrill.

He looked up to check the sun. "I'll scour those pans and we can try some blade work before we make a start on this evening's meal."

*

SETTING ASIDE STAFFS and swords as the daylight faded, Erlin stirred and spiced while Korose chopped and sliced. A bull calf was on the spit this evening. Not worth costly fodder through the winter for a farmer but well worth fattening on summer grass to feed hungry mercenaries after autumn's slaughter.

Erlin noticed eager anticipation on the faces making their way to his fire. Though he soon learned it wasn't for his food.

"Thinking of trying your luck?" A scar-faced Caladhrian asked his Dalasorian friend.

"Depends what they're offering the winner." The hawk-nosed man looked tempted.

"I got through the summer without shedding blood," a solid Lescari said to no one in particular. "I won't risk a winter wound festering."

"Plenty of time to heal before spring," countered the man beside him.

"A bout will only be to first blood," a Carlusian agreed. "They won't want anyone badly injured, not looking to sign the best fighters onto their muster."

Erlin interrupted. "What's this?"

A handful of excited voices answered him.

"A sword tourney?" Korose looked over the fire, bright-eyed.

Erlin sucked his teeth. "At this Chellan's behest, and Acuri's?"

Before anyone answered, half the men by the fire turned as someone exclaimed.

"Here they come!"

The snake and his croppy pal approached, to be bombarded with questions.

"Will you make the winner a sergeant?"

"What about the runner up? You'll need more than one troop leader!"

Some seemed less confident of their prospects.

"You'll give everyone's skills a fair test?"

"You wouldn't write a man off for one unlucky slip?"

A vital question fell into one of those unaccountable silences that open up in the noisiest of crowds.

"How many days do we have to prepare?"

The snake squared his narrow shoulders, head tilted back as he surveyed the crowd like a rich man buying a horse. "Three days," he said tersely. "From tomorrow. We draw lots on the fourth morning from now and then we'll see what you're made of."

His last words were almost lost amid eager cheering. Chellan smiled thinly before he looked at Acuri, cold-eyed, and jerked his head towards the river. As Chellan turned and stalked away, the crop-headed man followed, scowling.

"What do you reckon?" Korose bit his lip as he looked at Erlin.

"No, I don't reckon you should try your luck," he said firmly. "You won't learn anything from a beating and you might be unlucky enough to catch a bad wound."

He smiled to soften the blow of his words, seeing Korose crestfallen.

"Watch how the skilled men practise these next few days. You'll learn a lot from that. Once the tourney starts, look for what loses a man the bout, not just how his opponent wins. Here, you take charge of the spit. I won't be long."

He handed the long meat knife to the lad and headed for the latrines. As soon as he was beyond the cookfire's light, Erlin changed direction. Cutting between tents and bivouacs, he headed straight towards the river.

As he saw his quarry ahead, he slowed and proceeded carefully. Thankfully the dusk was thickening and Chellan and Acuri were intent on their conversation.

"Why didn't you talk to me before telling half the camp your bright idea?"

"My idea?" Acuri growled. "Everyone was telling me you spread the word."

"Why?" spat Chellan. "We've no coin for a victory purse!"

"So the notion sprang up like a toadstool?" Acuri challenged.

"More like some fool mixed one rumour with another like a drunk with white brandy and ale." Chellan exhaled with a hiss. "Does it matter? If no one claims the notion, we can steal it. Has anyone definitely said there's a purse for the winner?"

"Not that I've heard," Acuri said cautiously.

"So we say for certain there isn't," Chellan mused. "Offer sergeants' rank for the last two standing? Banner sergeant for the winner?"

"Where does that leave me?" Acuri snarled.

"Lieutenant," Chellan said testily.

"Equal captain," Acuri snapped back.

Chellan drew a resolute breath. "We talked about that. Two captains means split loyalties and troublemakers always try to drive in a wedge."

"I—" Acuri broke off to stare into the darkness.

Erlin stood as still as a tent pole, sliding his eyes sideways. Somewhere to his off hand, he saw a shadow move. He blinked. Or had he imagined it?

"Let's get a drink." Chellan walked away along the river bank towards Jartan's wine wagon.

"We haven't agreed—" Acuri stood stubborn for a moment, before following with a muttered obscenity.

After waiting to be certain that neither glanced over his shoulder, Erlin took a roundabout path back to his hearth.

*

KOROSE WAS OUT of his blankets first the following morning and quick to do all his chores. He wasn't the only early riser. Clashing steel rang through the camp before they were halfway done serving breakfast, interspersed with angry shouts or startled yelps from someone caught unawares.

Erlin nodded when the lad asked for leave to watch the men practise for the tourney. Amiably resigned to doing the bulk of the day's work, he was surprised when Korose returned halfway through the afternoon, scowling.

Erlin stopped chopping cabbage. "Who stepped on your heel?"

"Me? No, I'm fine." Korose still looked troubled. "How many swordswomen have you known?" he asked abruptly. "How do they usually fare?"

"None so many, though more than a few." Erlin paused to consider the armed and armoured females he'd encountered in his time. Most mercenary companies had a handful on their roster.

"For the most part, they fare as well, or as badly, as any man. You don't last in this life without some talent for it. Some women rise to captain their own companies. You must have heard of Ridianne the Vixen?"

That was barely a question. Everyone had heard of her. Any man in this camp would clean her boots with his tongue if that was the cost of joining her roster.

"Do you know where she's camped?"

Erlin wasn't expecting that. "You're thinking of leaving?"

"No." Korose paused in his pacing. "Do you think she'd look more kindly on a woman asking for winter shelter?"

Erlin laid down his knife. "What's this about, lad?"

Korose dropped onto the turf and moodily poked the fire's ashy bed with a stick. "It's Letsis. She wants to hone her skills, to make a decent showing in the tourney. Half the men won't spar with her and those who will just want to beat her bloody."

Erlin guessed Korose meant the ragged girl. "If she chooses to set herself up, she must know she risks getting knocked down."

"It's not fair," Korose protested.

"It's not your business," Erlin pointed out. "Who was giving a good showing? Who could you learn from?" He lowered his voice. "Help me decide what odds to offer, when I take bets on the tourney and you'll earn a share of the profits."

Korose still looked inclined to argue on the girl's account. After a long moment, he capitulated. "That swordsman, Triggen is a wonder. Wonderful light on his feet for all he's so broad, and quick as lightning with his hands."

"Who else?" Erlin began chopping again. "Stir up that fire while you're telling me. We can both do two things at once."

By the time they had the evening meal ready, he was more than satisfied with Korose. The lad definitely had a good eye and a sound brain to go with it. Just as long as his head wasn't turned by that ragged lass Letsis.

Erlin caught a glimpse of her slinking past while Korose was fetching that evening's fat lamb from Rila Butcher. Looking for the lad, he guessed, and whatever scraps she could scrounge. He wasn't sorry to see her gone before Korose got back. The boy would be a danger around the fire, distracted by the sight of her battered face.

Seeing she carried herself stiff and careful, Erlin guessed she'd taken some hard falls, maybe even a kicking, leaving bruises hidden by her clothes. He hid his sympathy behind an impassive face. The sooner she learned this life showed no one mercy, the better for them all.

"I wonder—?" Triggen's voice broke into his thoughts. "Might I have a cup of hot water for a copper?"

"Have it and welcome." Erlin nodded towards the steaming cauldron. "No charge."

"My thanks." Triggen carefully dipped a silver cup into the roiling water and dropped in a knotted scrap of muslin.

Drinking herb tisane like a fine lady, Erlin noted. "Keeping clear of wine and ale until after the tourney?"

"Something like that." Triggen grinned. Then he stiffened like a hound sighting prey.

Erlin pretended not to notice, concentrating on his flatbreads. But as Triggen strolled away, he covertly watched where the swordsman was going.

Not obviously hurrying, Erlin approved. Not making too much of his apparent surprise. Not one man in a hundred would have guessed his path crossing Chellan's was anything but happenstance.

He glanced around the fire. What might be stolen if he wasn't there to keep watch? Nothing he couldn't afford to lose. Knowing what Chellan was thinking would be worth far more. Erlin slipped quickly between two tents, getting as close as he dared. To his relief, Triggen and Chellan were still exchanging pleasantries. Naturally the snake wanted to stay friends with such a promising recruit.

"I hear you'll be the man to watch, come the tourney."

"Don't believe all you hear." Triggen chuckled. "I'm just glad to know we'll see you fight. No better way for a captain to win a man's trust than showing his courage is equal to theirs."

"I haven't said I'd take part, just yet." Chellan cleared his throat. "Who told you so?"

Triggen's brow wrinkled. "The three-fingered man who fought with the Daybreakers? He was talking to Sergeant Acuri this morning?"

"Malhen?" Chellan forced a laugh. "He never could keep a secret."

"Everyone will be pleased to hear you'll show us your mettle," Triggen assured him.

"Quite so." Chellan nodded a brisk farewell and strode off through the camp.

Erlin glanced over his shoulder. He was still within sight of his fire and there was no one who shouldn't be prowling round his wagon. Though if he followed Chellan he wouldn't be able to see if a gang of robbers ransacked it. Where was Korose?

He yielded though, pursuing the snake through the camp. At first he was poised to duck behind any concealment. Then he realised Chellan was so intent that he wouldn't have noticed a troop of Dalasorian horsemen on his trail.

Acuri was taking his ease outside a tent Erlin guessed was his own. Chellan strode up and grabbed the crop-headed man's shoulder, all but dragging him inside. Erlin's grin widened. It never failed to amuse him how people assumed a canvas wall was as solid and soundproof as wood or stone. Especially when they were angry. He strolled casually up to the side of the tent and knelt, as though to retie a bootlace.

"Why tell folk I'll fight in this fucking tourney?" Chellan accused. "You're hoping I'll fall on my arse? Maybe get a knife in my ribs? So you'll end up captain?"

"I never said any such thing," Acuri protested.

"You expect me to believe that?" Chellan's voice turned ugly. "I remember Inchra."

The whole tent shook with the scuffle inside. Erlin didn't wait to see if they brought poles and canvas down. He hurried off, discreetly pleased. Better yet, he found Korose at their hearth, standing guard.

*

THE DAY OF the tourney dawned crisp and clear. Korose was up and about before the sun rose over the coppices. Erlin took his time preparing a modest pile of griddle cakes. No fighter would want a full belly and the rest wouldn't linger for fear of missing a good bout. He saw Chellan and Acuri approaching. The croppy-head carried a bucket while the snake's leather armour gleamed with fresh oil.

"First bouts!" Chellan shouted. "Stand forth or fight in your nightshirt!"

Acuri slapped a tent in passing. "I've got your token, Vendrish, so swap that cock in your hand for a sword hilt!"

"How many in that bucket?" Erlin asked Korose quietly.

"Near enough full, yesterday evening." The lad looked anxiously at the gathering mercenaries. Searching for the girl no doubt.

Erlin watched the crowd swell with mixed feelings. Having his fire become the camp's meeting place would be profitable but he didn't like Chellan and Acuri deciding that without a by-your-leave.

Still, Erlin could get a good look at the men he'd taken most bets on, as Acuri drew pottery shards from his bucket and shouted out the men's names scrawled on each one. Women were competing too. Letsis wasn't the only female fighter in the camp, though two others trying their luck and skills overtopped her by a head.

Several of the heavily backed men looked none too bright. Erlin had seen them over-indulge in ale last night. Over-confident.

Triggen had stuck to drinking his tisanes, always ready to chat by the cookfire with whoever might be passing. The young warrior looked formidable, shirtless in a leather jerkin.

The man called to fight him looked distinctly nervous. Unlike the warrior who'd face Letsis. He could barely restrain a laugh.

Acuri called out the rules of engagement. "Find clear and level ground. Square off and fight on the count of three. Best of three touches if nobody yields but I don't want anyone maimed. We'll call witnesses to agree on a victor if there's any dispute."

The crowd scattered into fighting pairs, eyeing each other warily, surrounded by knots of eager onlookers. Acuri took Erlin's chopping block for a stool. "I'll take a stack of those griddle cakes, and find some honey to go with them."

Erlin ignored him, watching Chellan stalk off. The snake was glancing sideways at a bull-necked bruiser from Ensaimin. Did he wonder if Acuri had palmed that particular token, setting him up against someone forewarned of his strengths and weaknesses? The two of them had barely exchanged a glance, still less a friendly word this morning.

"Did you hear me?" Acuri snapped.

Erlin looked levelly at him. "Did you pay me?"

Acuri's lip curled but after a breath, he tossed a silver mark onto the turf. Erlin made no move to fetch it. When Korose took a step, he stilled him with a glance. "You go see the bouts. Come tell me all the news."

He had been planning to watch at least some of the fights himself. Not now, and leave dead-eyed Acuri unwatched around his tents. Not with all the camp's gamblers' stake money hidden beneath his wagonload of sacks.

Erlin fetched more firewood from the stack by the water butt. When he returned, Acuri was holding out a silver mark. Erlin didn't need to look to know it was the one he'd thrown onto the grass.

He served the man a handful of griddle cakes, expressionless. "No honey."

He'd barely had time to wonder how Acuri would respond when the first roars indicated a sword bout was already over. The chagrined loser trailed back to the fire after the crowing victor, both surrounded by friends and strangers offering congratulations and commiseration.

Erlin left Acuri collecting the winner's potsherd while he went to the wagon to fetch his ledger of wagers. Soon they were both too busy to quarrel over cakes or honey.

The tourney was half done, by Erlin's reckoning, before Korose reappeared. Dismay and elation chased each other across the lad's face like clouds scudding across a bright sky.

"Triggen just took two wounds—" he began.

"Sorry to hear it." Erlin made sure not to show his elation. A lot of men had just lost their stakes.

"But Letsis has won again." Korose shook his head in wonderment. "Though barely," he allowed.

"Really?" Once again, Erlin kept his face impassive.

Though it wasn't long before he could express his amazement as openly as anyone else. The skinny girl came back time and again, to tell Acuri she'd won. Several times she had to shout to make herself heard above the men arguing over what they'd just seen.

"She's no skills. She's just lucky."

"She's quick and that counts for a lot."

"He slipped, that's all there was to it."

"Too soft-hearted to skewer a pigeon, the fool."

Korose was the first one back when the tourney was down to the final four. He raced up, barely stopping short of the hearth. "She did it!"

"Well, well." Erlin feigned astonishment, then concern. "What if she fights Chellan next?" Much as he disliked the snake, the man's formidable skills had seen him safe through the tourney.

"Will she—" Korose broke off as the horde of mercenaries surged through the tents to the fire.

A circle formed and Chellan faced the girl. So he had won his last bout. But Erlin noted the blood smeared on his arms. He'd taken a few flesh wounds on his way to victory.

To be fair, so had Letsis, from the stains on her shirtsleeves. But she looked a different girl to the timid waif who Erlin had seen cowering around the camp these past few days.

Not that Chellan had noticed. He took a rag from Acuri and wiped his arms clean, scowling. Whatever he said provoked his supposed ally into a hostile sneer.

Letsis had barely taken guard before Chellan launched a storm of blows. Not that any hammer-stroke touched her. Letsis didn't bother trying her strength against his with any show of locked hilts. Chellan barely made contact with her deftly parrying blade. She dodged, nimbly retaliating with thrusts to slice Chellan's wrists or knees.

Recoiling robbed Chellan's swordplay of power and rhythm. Now he was on the defensive. Darting ever quicker, Letsis forced him backwards, unbalanced. A cry rose from the crowd, somewhere between a groan and elation, as her questing blade sliced into his forearm.

"Yield?" She grinned.

Chellan didn't even answer before assailing her. He didn't even allow her to take a proper guard. The crowd's murmur turned concerned as everyone saw her forced back towards the fire. That was hardly fighting fair.

That wasn't the worst of it. Erlin guessed Chellan's plan an instant before the snake ducked low and snatched up a burning stick with his free hand. He threw the searing brand at Letsis, provoking a howl of protest.

Breath caught in Erlin's throat. But Letsis was quick enough. She dodged it. More than that, she denied any instinct to parry the flames with her blade. What threat was mindless wood, after all? Instead she lunged, her sword thrust at full stretch.

Chellan was caught unawares, already coming forward to follow up his advantage. He was an instant too slow to realise she wasn't cowed by his unexpected assault. Her blade bit deep into his thigh.

Now the crowd's cheer was all congratulation for Letsis. Chellan's dishonourable ploy had robbed him of all sympathy. She stood still for a moment, before turning to Acuri and winking at him.

Stooped, clutching his wound, Chellan gasped. "Shithead!"

"What?" Acuri spat.

"You're in it together, you and her?" Chellan staggered forward, sword raised.

Acuri drew a dagger, teeth bared.

The surging crowd closed around them before Erlin could see who landed the first blow. Then the throng parted just as quickly. Some were heading for their tents. More were escorting Letsis towards Jartan's wine wagon for a celebration. Chellan limped off in one direction, more bloodied than before. Acuri stalked towards the river, hand pressed to a wound in his side.

Someone tapped him on the shoulder. Erlin turned to see Triggen smiling at him.

"Come to collect your winnings?"

"Whenever suits you best."

Erlin cocked his head, contemplating the younger man. "So she's your lover?" He realised that was wrong before the words left his mouth. "Your sister?"

"Big sister." Triggen's grin widened. "Taught me everything I know."

Of course. Why else would he have wagered such a sum on her? Erlin chuckled despite himself. "Including how to fight like a girl? Precious few men can do that so well."

Triggen spread innocent hands. "I don't know what you mean."

Erlin nodded. "As you wish. Come and see me tomorrow morning and I'll pay you what I owe."

He watched Triggen stroll away. Would Letsis have won without her brother's aid? Perhaps, but it would have been a far closer thing without Chellan's suspicions distracting him.

"He fights as staunchly as any man." Korose was still defending Triggen.

Erlin briefly considered explaining. Maybe later, when Korose had some chance of understanding how devastating spreading calculated rumour and starting precisely targeted gossip could be. Those tactics could undermine the strongest men and their alliances, like a tunnel dug under a castle's foundations.

Erlin never underestimated women, with or without swords in their hands.

The Women's Song

Nadine Andie

THERE WAS A familiar scent hanging in the air. After training bouts, the arena always smelt like this: a little like skin, a little like the salt tang of bodies and blood, and a little like the throat-tickling char of newly burned magics. Tey'dor wiped his face and shoulders down with a rough rag. It reddened as he wiped. His breath was still coming heavily, in jags and heaves, and his flesh prickled with sand. He arched his back, bowed his head, and pressed the fingers of his empty hand into a sore spot, where a blow had taken him below the shoulder-blade and pushed the wind clean out of him. It was a pleasure-pain, this probing of injured flesh with still-trembling fingertips. But this queasy sensation of pushing against tenderness was familiar too, and as his breathing fell back into its old, easy rhythm he allowed himself the smallest of smiles. The smell, the ache, the blood-red rag knotted between his fingers: they all meant one thing.

He had survived another fight.

Tey'dor lifted his head. The low sun distorted things: for a moment, he could see only long, purple shadows spilling out across the yellow floor. Earth, sand, blood, and shadow. Then his eyes began to make sense of the scene; he saw the other recruits of the Ma'chek scattered across the arena, the Masters they had just fought alongside them, the newly-conscripted boys running barefooted across the hot ground, bearing their water-pails and wash-cloths. Precious few of the recruits were standing. One was vomiting, his agony plain for all to see as he knelt in the dust. His Master was bent over him, murmuring something, a hand placed on the boy's heaving shoulders. Another boy was being lifted and borne away: he wore the ashen look of one who had spent too much magic in the fight, and his eyes were glassy and hollow.

"Can you walk?" The voice came from behind him.

"I can." Tey'dor turned. He shielded his eyes against the sun.

From somewhere within the glare, a figure emerged. The calm movements of an elder. A strong body wrapped in the brown hide garments that the Masters wore, the uniform that protected and shielded the skin in battle. The dark, close-cropped head and flared cheekbones of his own Master, Vey. "Then you are stronger than some. Or more fortunate," the Master said. No smile, but one dark brow flickered. "And perhaps more than fortunate. It was a competent battle, and you have made my bones ache with your casting. Come."

Tey'dor scooped up his cloak from the floor, and handed his rag, heavy and blackened, to the small boy who stood alongside them, averting his eyes, holding out his pail. The boy's hands, he saw, were shaking as he took the thing. Vey dismissed him with a single gesture: two fingers, raised in the air. As the child ran from them, Tey'dor sighed.

"Yes, you were," the Master said.

Tey'dor felt, rather than saw, the Master's glance. "I was what, Master?"

"Once so young. And skittish, too. Nervy around your elders. Was it you who dropped the High Commander's goblet at dinner service, not five years ago?"

"And the High Commander whipped me well for it."

"As well you deserved. You left a stain on his cloak that looked like a bungled assassination attempt. But you learned. And grew." Master Vey paused, and gestured. Beyond them, seated above the tunnel that led down into the dark warrens of the training school, were four men, cloaked and hooded against the sun. Their green cloaks were huddled together, and they had paid scant attention to the Masters and boys who were passing from the arena into the darkness. But as they reached the archway, Master Vey made one, simple sign in the air. The casting hung before them for a moment, reddish and thickening, and Tey'dor felt a new pulse in his temples, hard and strong.

The green hoods turned.

Tey'dor stared into the hollows.

The casting blurred, shifted, and then vanished, and for a long moment he felt the pressure of the four against his mind. He had felt it before, long ago, on his recruitment day. The heat, even as the sun set and the air cooled around him. The sweat prickling on his brow. The questioning, like insects scurrying within his skull: *Are you grown strong?*

Have you learned humility?

Have you learned obedience?

And the last question, as full of fear as it was full of wonder.

Are you ready to be made a man?

Then, suddenly, gaspingly, the pressure was gone. It was withdrawn as quickly as it had come, and the four hoods turned from him and then there was only the pressure of the Master's hand on his shoulder, leading him into the mouth of the tunnel. In the sudden darkness, with his other senses sharpened, Tey'dor could hear the whispering of feet on sand and something else, soft but close: the sound of voices, singing, from behind the high wall that bounded the left side of the training school. It was a complex melody, in many parts. At dusk, if you found a still place and listened hard enough, you could always hear the song from the women's school that welcomed the night.

Aside from training rides into the surrounding country, Tey had not seen a woman or girl since his selection, five years before. He had taken time to listen to them, though, in still places. He wondered, for a moment, before the shadows of the tunnel opened again into the blaze and racket of the robing rooms, if he truly understood the ceremony that awaited him.

A cheer went up as they stepped into the light, and the soft music of the women was lost. The other boys had seen the assembled council, seen his strength in the arena and his power in the fight. The stamping of feet began, leather-soled combat boots drumming their respect and honour on the yellow stone of the floor. He lifted his head. It was a ritual that he had taken part in many times, and it always said the same thing without words.

You will achieve ascension.

The council has decided.

Tomorrow you will go out from here and go through the ceremony, and be made a man.

*

IT WAS NOT considered right to discuss the nature of the ceremony. Older boys shushed younger boys - the young ones newly recruited, with the bravado of selection still in their blood, and with their voices cracking and swooping- when they dared to make their crude jokes. Masters glanced at older boys – the older ones with just enough sense to turn their ribaldry into veiled suggestions – and quelled them with little more than a raised eyebrow and a heartbeat's shame. So the younger boys learned, and the older boys learned more, and the Masters kept their counsel.

Nonetheless, boys talked. They said, you go into a room with a girl. They said, they train them; that's what they do in the women's school, they train at it like we train at men's work. They said, there is nothing but a bed, in that room. They said, you have to prove that you are a real man, a complete man, that you can take her. They said, she wears no clothes, or, sometimes, they said she wears only a robe and nothing more, or they said that she comes dressed in fine women's garments: they could have said anything at all, boys as they were, who had not seen an unclothed female form since they had run bare-bodied around the edges of a watering-hole with their sisters and their neighbours' sisters, when they were small. The boys in the training school were not supposed to sully their bodies with anything that might detract from their training: poor food, smuggled wine from a bribed trader, poor hygiene, or the other, less savoury vices that can lead young men into temptation. Their bathing and sleeping arrangements, in shared rooms with ten boys splashing or sleeping side-by-side, and a Master always by the door, existed to guard against moments of private indulgence. Nevertheless, it was a rare boy indeed who did not at least conjure the image of the ceremony to mind in his own quiet moments, if only in the hopes that his imaginings would give him vivid, heated dreams.

As he walked through the hushed street, sun beating down on his hooded head, and the heat intensifying beneath the ceremonial robe he had been given before leaving the boys' compound, Tey'dor glanced left to right at the escorts in full military uniform who flanked him, at the few other people who passed them, and at the wooden doors and low-slung windows that punctuated the long, connecting avenue between the training schools of the boys, and the girls. His mind racing, he tried to remember Master Vey's words. What he must do, and what he must not do, and what he must say. The rules of the ceremony. His Master's tone had been sombre. Tey'dor muttered the formula to himself as they walked, until one of the escorts silenced him with a swift gesture: no speaking, not until he entered the chamber. More doors. An archway. A cool, shaded passageway. A quick, sharp smell of lemons.

Then, suddenly, the escorts came to an abrupt halt. One of them knocked three times, heavily, against a wide, wooden door. It opened, inwards. Behind it was another hooded figure, a dim vestibule, and another opening, this one covered by a rich, amber curtain. No one spoke, but the hooded figure gestured.

Tey'dor drew in the longest, deepest breath of his life.

*

HE RAISED ONE hand to the curtain, stepped out of the darkness, and over the threshold.

There she was, seated, cross-legged, on a raised platform in the centre of the room. She was cloaked. Hooded. Her hands and feet were tucked neatly away: only her eyes were visible, and only her eyes moved, and they danced over him rapidly as he pushed past the curtain and then let it fall, with only the softest of sounds, behind him. Her stillness unnerved him. He glanced away from her as his eyes adjusted. The chamber was broad and round, sparely furnished, cool, and dim, lit by oil lamps which hung from four high poles embedded into the walls. He had entered beside one, its shifting flame deforming the shadows that spread in dark pools around his feet. The floor underfoot was not stone. It was hard and dry, swept clean but with the gritty sense of dried earth that was familiar to him: it felt like the floor of the arena. Disorientated, he took another step. The long robe made him clumsy, and he clutched at it with both hands.

She lifted her head. She stood, stepped precisely and steadily across the platform, and descended three wooden steps until she was level with him. Her form was concealed completely by the robes, but he was aware that she matched him for height, and that she was barefoot. She paused, then put both of her hands to the cowl of the cloak, pushed at the heavy fabric, and then lifted her hands away. The hood fell slowly, moving under its own weight.

Somewhere distant, a song had begun.

Still, neither of them had spoken. Was it his task, to begin? Yes. He remembered. He opened and closed his lips, soundlessly, aware of the dryness in his mouth.

With the hood fallen, he could see her face. She was perhaps a little older than he; her jaw was strong and her bones broad, and there was a dark down of growth upon her shaved head which did not mask a strange series of patterns beneath. He tilted his head to see, and she tilted hers in response. For a moment, he felt the oddest of sensations, that she was moving in response to his mind, as she angled her head, birdlike, and turned it slowly. He saw, more clearly now, that upon her bare scalp were fine, black ink lines, scored into her skin, and beneath it. His eyes widened.

"Did it hurt?" he said, quietly, and then recoiled. He had made an error. The words he had practised with Master Vey burned in his mind.

Something of surprise played about her lips. "Yes," she answered, dipping her head slightly in acknowledgement. "It hurt very much." She rolled up one sleeve of her robe and extended one slender, pale wrist to him. His eyes traced the lines of similar black inks that wrapped around her arm and vanished into the crook of her elbow. "These hurt as well. They work with a needle, and the tender skin is the worst."

"How long does it take?"

"Years, in total. They begin when we are taken for service. And it is done piece by piece."

They both stared, for a moment, their eyes locked together on black ink and white skin. Then they glanced at each other, and smiled, a little bashfully. "This is not how we are supposed to begin, is it?" he asked.

"I think not," she said.

They took a step, each of them, backwards. She withdrew her arm, and he took a deep breath. He would begin again. He tried to recall the precise words.

"I am come by the command of the High Masters to . . . to request the completion of my training." She nodded a little, encouragingly. Emboldened, he went on. "For it has been determined that I am fit to stand with my brothers of the Ma'chek, shoulder to shoulder, and as each of them has done in his turn, according to the ritual, I have come to be fully . . ."

He broke off, suddenly fearful. She mouthed the final three words, slowly, noiselessly. Made. A. Man.

He repeated them. "Made a man."

"Then by the authority of the high masters and the will of the women's council, I accept you and bid you a warrior's welcome," she said, her voice richer than his, more certain. She pulled at her robe, then, untying the broad, dark belt and stepping out of the garment in one fluid movement. Beneath it she was clad in dark bands of skins, all secured with clasps of ornate metal. The intricate tattooing was all at once like a kind of clothing, and like a greater kind of nakedness: it drew his eyes across the plains of her shoulders, her strong arms and thighs, her belly. It demanded that he knew her body with his eyes. She did not shrink from his gaze.

"Do you fully understand what it is we must do?" she asked, extending one hand towards him.

"I think I do," he replied. A feeling that was both familiar and strange was growing upon him, like the wary arousal of the moments before a battle, when the senses sharpen and the body braces. He looked down, abashed, and fumbled with his robe.

"No. You don't," she said.

And then the air thickened and shimmered, and her first casting hit him with the power of a hundred weapons.

Blinded, almost, knocked onto the hard earth and against the stony walls of the chamber, he gasped for air and let out an involuntary cry. His first instinct was to look around for the man, the warrior who had crept up on him in this chamber and violated the ritual before it was complete. Lungs heaving, he raised his head and scanned the shadows.

When her second casting came, he stopped looking for a man. He saw her draw down power, saw the flare in her eyes, saw the body tense: saw all of this in the half-heartbeat it took her to hit him again with a blow that snapped back his head and ran a bright knife of pain down his spine.

His training took over. He rolled. He left his baffled mind alone and his body moved for him. Habits asserted themselves. He rolled for cover. Threw the robe from him in the opposite direction, drawing her eyes. Then, hidden behind the platform, crouched low, he stilled himself and hushed his hard breathing, and listened.

Nothing moves silently. A memory flickered, of long-ago desert training, of drawing the powerful sand cats with raw meat lures, so that they could listen for the smallest of noises that even sand cats made as they moved across the dry earth. And so it was that he could make out her footfalls, soft and pulled as they were – and she was good, very good, he realised, as the fear made another coil in his stomach – now approaching the platform, now ascending the wooden steps, now pausing.

He wondered if he could make himself hurt a girl.

Perhaps he did not have to. He made himself draw in power, and felt the beating of his heart speed up as he held it. He gestured softly with his left hand, and for a moment a half-transparent yellow line hung in the air. Hurting her could wait. When the line had arched its back and faded into the air, he listened again, and then stood, hands poised in front of him.

But it had worked. The paralytic cast held her, poised at the platform's edge with her intricately patterned legs bent, ready to jump. Her eyes were wild, moving furiously as she fought the spell that had frozen her. He backed away, looking about the chamber for anything he could use as a weapon. Hurriedly, horribly aware of the small handful of minutes a paralysing cast would last, he grabbed at a lantern, and fumbled the cord from his discarded robe which lay crumpled on the ground. He passed the curtain which marked the chamber door, but resisted the urge to flee: shame, yes, there was shame pressing on him, but also something inside him that itched to understand the attack, a desire stronger than the desire for safety. He circled back. Her head was already beginning to move, eyes blinking, lips parting. He kept the distance between them.

"I do not understand," he said, his voice low. "Do you not wish to perform the ritual?" Her lips parted and closed again. He frowned. "I have done only as I was instructed. I thought . . . I believed . . . If you are unwilling, I will not hurt you. I will leave." He watched the convulsions of her face as she struggled to speak, her eyes widening, fear written on her brow. Her body still looked frozen, and suddenly he felt barbaric. He took a step towards her and lowered his hands.

And then he was on his back, body slamming, dust rising, her legs and hands gripping him with an overwhelming pressure. Her leap had come from nowhere. She took his left hand and hit it against the floor, and the lantern skittered out of his grasp and rolled as he felt his knuckles begin to bleed. "It wore off as you picked up the robe," she muttered in his ear. She pressed her knee into the side of his belly, where the flesh was softer, where the organs were vulnerable, and as the pain mounted in his side he began to care less about hurting her. Gathering his strength, he braced his lower back against the floor and began to use his hips. He had fought off Master Vey and the other recruits time and time again in the arena. He had not been beaten and bloodied by an opponent since his fifteenth summer. If it was hand to hand combat she wanted, then he could provide, without understanding her reasons; he could fight her if fighting was what she wanted.

Pressing his weight and hers, using the floor beneath him to leverage them, he summoned all his strength and turned her. She flailed angrily, her hands reaching towards his face, and as he struggled to brace himself on his toes, to pin her, she used one foot to drive into the skin behind his knee, once, twice. He flinched. Her painted hand twitched, a cold cast washed over him in a shade of grey, and he found himself chilled, shivering so hard that she was able to crawl from his grasp and escape him. The shaking cast began to wane, and he drew himself up onto the balls of his feet.

Her combat magic is outstanding, he thought, as he steadied himself. He began to wheel the heavy rope that had belted his robe, still clenched in his right hand, making it describe blurred circles in the air. Now there was anger in his voice, as he shouted. "I came here in good faith. You welcomed me. You made an oath. We made an oath, your words and mine!"

She circled with him, body low, feet sure. "And I keep my oath!" she returned, before trying to slide beneath the rope and take out his feet with her own. For a moment he was elated as he leapt sideways and evaded her, but then his spinning rope hit hard against one of the narrow lantern poles, tangled, and yanked at his arms and his shoulders as its speed became a weapon against him. He released it, palms burning. He sighed, and turned to face her once again.

When Tey'dor reflected on it later, it was not a long bout. No more than a quarter hour, no more than twenty or thirty further passes exchanged. No more than a good bout in the training ring, and yet harder, more breathless, more bloody a fight than he had endured before. It wore both of them down. And at the end, when his strength faded and her agility waned, and when her speed lessened and his casting fumbled, it came down to two simple things. First, that he dropped a half-broken lantern pole from his sweat-slickened hands, and, second, that he stopped in his tracks, with his spirit as shattered as the pole, to stare at its dull length in the dirt. So when, from behind, she softly wound the length of fabric from her own robe around his throat, and began to exert slow but mounting pressure, he dropped to his knees and struck his own chest thrice, and then the floor thrice, and then bowed his head.

Submission.

*

WHEN THE CHAMBER curtain moved behind him, and he heard footsteps, he had just enough strength left to feel shame, and not enough to turn his head. His opponent moved from him, back into the room, and conducted the low, humble bow of the champion. She stepped forward, offered him her hand, and clasped his own in hers. She took his forearm in her other hand, and they rested there, for a moment, and her touch was warm, and not unkind.

"My dear," came the deep voice from behind him.

"Master," she replied, and bowed again, and bowed lower.

"You have fulfilled your duty, and you were . . ." Master Vey's voice broke off for a moment's silence. Tey'dor could sense words being weighed. Master Vey did not complement lightly. "And you were quite dazzling."

"I hope always to serve." The girl looked, for a moment, very serious. Then a smile broke the line of her mouth and lit up her face.

Tey'dor allowed his body to sag again. He arched his back, bowed his head, and pressed the fingers of his empty hand into a sore spot, where one of her blows had taken him below the shoulder-blade and pushed the wind clean out of him. It had always been a pleasure-pain, this probing of injured flesh with still-trembling fingertips, but now it was coloured with fear and confusion. With his head still sunken, he muttered, "My Master. I have failed in the ritual. I have failed you, and I am sorry."

Tey'dor felt himself being lifted. He planted his feet beneath him on the cool earth, determined not to shame himself further by falling. Vey's eyes were frank and half-amused. "Tell me, then. Why do you think you have failed?"

Tey'dor gestured helplessly with his raw and swollen hand at the chamber, and at the broken poles and shattered lanterns that littered the ground. "Do you mock me? I entered to complete my training, to be made . . ." For one final time, his voice stumbled on the words. "To be made a man." His hand lingered, pointing at the girl who still stood before him, arms behind her back, head dipped. "She consented. She said I was welcome. We said the words as you instructed me. She bade me a *warrior's* welcome!" He knew his voice was rising, uncontrolled, and that he was close to weeping.

"Of course she did. And you believed, I presume, that you were the warrior."

Tey'dor blinked. "I . . . I . . . Yes, Master. I did."

Vey nodded. "And if I asked you now?"

"I would say that . . ." He watched as the girl raised her head, and pulled neatly into full attention, feet together, hands by her sides, wide shoulders set firm. "That she . . . was the warrior?"

"Very good. And now, tell me. What did I tell you of the ritual?"

"That it was the final part of my training. That I would come to the chamber and meet a woman there, and that I must honourably and respectfully perform the ritual, as my brother Ma'chek had done before me, to truly become men."

"And one thing else?"

He paused. Racked his memory. "That I should never speak afterward, to any boy or recruit, of the ritual, and only ever speak of what happened in the chamber to men who had achieved their full ascension."

"Quite." The Master moved slowly, quietly around the chamber, with its round, swept floor and four lantern poles, one broken in the dust. One gentle hand rested on the girl's bare, patterned shoulder for a moment. "So tell me. What was the ritual?"

Somewhere, beyond the walls, but close this time, and more stirringly, the song of the women resumed.

When realisation came, it was as the singing, warm and swelling in his head and all around him, and it made him gasp. "*This* was the ritual?"

Beside him, the chamber curtain opened, and light and song flooded in. Tey'dor could see, beyond the doorway, a line of people saluting, and waiting for them to pass. He shook his head and looked helplessly from his Master, to the honour line, and back to his Master and the girl again.

"Come," Master Vey said. "Let us walk out together, and greet the others, and then you will both clean yourselves and clothe yourselves, and I will explain."

They passed on, into the sudden light.

*

LATER, WHEN WOUNDS had been dressed and food had been taken, Master Vey and Tey'dor walked the high walls of the compound together. The wall patrol was a privilege reserved for men of the company: despite his aching body and exhausted mind, Tey'dor still felt a thrilling rush as he ascended the carved stone stair for the first time and took his place beside his Master. From this vantage point, he could see the whole vast compound laid out before him, the dunes and mountains beyond, and the sun setting bloodily behind them. He gazed at the adults' section, where men and women lived side by side, where he would sleep for the first time this very night; he could see figures in gowns and hoods going about their evening tasks, in busy streets, bringing water, leading dogs or livestock, carrying garments or pushing barrows, and it occurred to him that he could not tell which were men and which were women.

Master Vey had told him many things, as they walked. Told him how the council demanded that every warrior must first learn to be the strongest and best in his cohort, and then must learn to be beaten in combat, and beaten hard. How they themselves had learned, the hard way, that great warriors who have never known what it is to fail, who have never learned submission, were not only a liability in battle but were also cruel and tyrannical in victory.

"And you felt it, did you not? What it is to be bested, and to feel weak, and to set your mind and body to a great task and – as you believed it then – to fail?"

"I did, Master."

Master Vey paused, dark brow raised once more, eyes knowing. "Then you can remember that moment, and know humility, and that is a great thing. But you have another question for me, I think. You should ask it."

Tey'dor turned his head, gripped the wall, and watched the sun. "Why the pretence? You know the things that are said about the ceremony. You must know what the boys believe. You chastise us for it, and so we talk of it in secret and think that the initiation is conducted with a woman because it is a matter of . . ."

"Sex."

"Yes."

"We know."

"Then why are we not told?"

Master Vey sighed. "Tell me, Tey'dor. What does your heart say about women, now, tonight?"

He laughed, a little. "That I was beaten to a standstill by one, this day! And that she was a warrior, and . . . and I liked her, Master. We spoke, a little, beforehand, and she was thoughtful, and wise."

"And what did your heart say of women when you were laughing with boys, in secret places, on other days?"

Tey'dor thought, and was silent. The silence grew for a while, alongside the shadows. Eventually, as the red back of the sun arched for a final moment above the horizon, he said, "She truly was a warrior."

"Yes."

"What was her name?"

"Ahn'mey."

"Are all women trained as warriors?"

"Not all."

"But she was a great fighter."

"One of the finest. The best of the women always are."

"And do they fight alongside us, then? Those women?"

Master Vey did not speak. Only, with strong hands and gentle movements, rolled back the sleeves of the long Masters' robe, very slowly and deliberately, and in the half-light Tey'dor could see, for the first time, the uncovered skin, the dark brown arms that had always been wrapped in protective hide-strips in the battle arena. Each arm was covered, to the wrist, in coiling, swimming patterns of black ink, faded somewhat with age, more subtle on the dark skin, but spinning and twining upwards, towards the crooks of the elbows. Tey'dor looked up at the close-cropped hair and wise, broad-cheeked face, so familiar, of his Master.

"Yes," she said. "We most certainly do." Tey'dor gazed at her in wonder. And she smiled, just a little, as the sun slid behind the mountains, and the sound of the women's song marked the closing of the day.

The Turn of A Wheel

Fran Terminiello

T HAD BEEN a year. Winter's chill hung crisp in the air but the sun shone bright among the headstones. One stood out. Gleaming, smooth.

Here lies Jorvan Travin, brother of Jermond, husband of Fera.

The woman laid flowers on the cushion of grass, dewdrops glistening on petals. Her dress, still red in mourning, was the finest brocade silk; hem damp and darkened, sleeves fashionably long with plenty to spare. She let them drape over her hands for a moment, as she stood, silent thoughts passing through the air, into earth and stone.

Derin watched her all the while, taking in the dress, the hair artfully piled and pinned, the veil, sheer and short as a whisper now that the long year had ended. It suited her, she decided, and she felt a smile pull at the corners of her mouth.

Others had passed this way all morning. Dutifully paying respects and shedding modest tears in this calm quiet. Birdsong chorused to their work, but they were all as dull as the stones that stood about them, compared to the widow.

Derin's hand rested on the pommel of the sword at her hip, the one that had created the widow who stood twelve heartbeats away. Carved out a new life, as it had ended another. She watched as the woman gathered the folds of her skirts about her, eyes still on the polished stone before she made the sign of three fingers, turned and followed the mourners down the gravelled path.

ONE YEAR AGO

THE BLADE BIT into the rim of the buckler gripped hard in her fist. Pain shot through Derin's joints at the impact but she knew it was nothing compared to the oblivion she'd have faced if the buckler had not been there. As her opponent pulled the sword back it nearly tugged the small shield out of her hand and she followed the movement, striding forwards as her own blade cut down at his head.

But he was fast, and strong. His blade parried her cut, turned and the point thrust at her chest.

A slipping step back, and once more she circled with him. Their ragged breath came in unison as their eyes met over the shields in their fists. A flap of skin hung down one side of his head, blood dribbled in and out of the creases of his nose, mouth, into his ear in a red network. She could feel warmth inside her sleeve, more than the sweat that drenched her back, stung her eyes. The sword was heavier by the second, but she gripped and released the familiar leather in her hand. Breath hissed through her teeth.

"There's nothing for you here. Crawl back to your master." Her voice was low, but she could not keep the fear from it. Instead of laughing, he just shook his head, resigned. Sweat and blood sprayed from him.

"I can't do that. There's nothing for me to go back to. I'm doing this for me."

The thuds of her heart against her ribs grew more insistent, her head swam, teetered between the fight before her and the vengeance that was to come. And he saw her hesitation, and he took his chance.

"Ah!"

She leaned into the cut, sword edge met sword edge, steel rang out in the dark. He grunted, turning his point towards her eye as they drew closer to one another. She was running out of room. As he moved to slide the sword through her skull she stepped to her left, raised her buckler and smashed the rim into the side of his head, the side where the flap of skin hung. He screamed at the pain and tripped on something, scurried back, finding his feet as he hissed curses through his teeth.

"Bitch!"

"I'll give you that, but why want me dead?"

"For my brother."

She gazed at the half shadowed, bloody face, searching her memory.

"Nope, sorry, you'll have to be more specific." He bared his teeth. "As if you'd recall. His name was Jermond Travin, we worked together for Sedgewick."

"So?"

"You slit his leg after stealing two thousand wheels and Mistress Sedgewick's jewels." Their breath rasped, and she felt herself stepping away from him. "He just kept bleeding, bled to death."

She remembered the fists in her back, the fingers squeezing her throat.

"Good."

And her snarl matched his as they came together, swords clashing with anger and defiance. Momentarily her fear left her as she raged against this idiot trying to steal her life; she'd make him pay for daring to raise her anger. What was his dead brother to her anyway? She was glad.

He ducked low. His leg shot out sweeping her aside and she tumbled, head hitting hard on the cold cobbles. White flashed at the edges of her vision, a tightness in her nostrils as she reeled.

A boot, hard in the softness of her belly, kicked the wind from her chest and she doubled onto her side. Another – and she felt something snap. All she could focus on was trying to keep a grip on the sword; the buckler clattered clumsily to the ground and rolled away into the dark.

"Whore! I'll kill you slow."

His voice was far away, faint, drowned under the blood pounding through her head . . . but his boots thudding into her confirmed he was still right there.

She would die here in this cold alley among the litter and the shit of Sondim. Another forgotten soul to be dropped in the sea and never spoken of again. She heard him spit, and felt warm spatter against her cheek.

"It's not right you know," said the man, sniffing "Me doing this. I've never hit a woman in my life, even my wife, when she clawed at me. Just couldn't do it, stood there and took it. But you . . . you need to suffer."

His boot ground into her hand and she screamed as her fingers were crushed amid the steel in her grip, the weight of him above, and the stone beneath her. When he took his foot off he kicked the sword away. Her ears rang and she rolled from side to side, clutching her hand with the other. His voice was close to her ear.

"Does it hurt?"

Air hissed between her teeth as she huffed, trying to regain control, grip onto her milling thoughts. Memories and fears jostled for attention as he stepped around her. Who was he? What would he do next? How could she stop him?

She kept her hand to her chest, the pain matched only by the pain in her belly and ribs.

"Listen," she croaked, she felt warm breath in her ear, smelt sourness. He was still close. "I will give you everything, just . . . let me live."

A low, cold chuckle. But when he spoke, she heard pain at the edges of his voice. "Oh you stupid bitch, I don't want anything from you. Just your life."

"Thousands, I've thousands of wheels at the house of Culdass locked up there. I can get it to you, I'll take you there."

He paused, and she turned onto her back, breathing breathing quick with the pain. Maybe some things were stronger than brotherly love. She tried to find his eyes but they were hidden in shadow as he crouched over her, only his jaw was visible, stubbled and slick with dark blood down one side. His lips pulled back revealing yellowed teeth.

"Dog shit. You'll say anything to save your scrawny arse. Keep begging, it's funny."

"Please!" She opened her eyes wide, awaiting the thrust of a sword through her neck, raising a palm in supplication, in protection.

Now his laugh was genuine, and he pressed his face closer, she could see it.

"I'm going to enjoy this."

Her outstretched hand reached up and snatched the flap of skin on his cheek, tearing it down hard.

"Aaaaargh!" He screamed, pulling away, but she put all her weight into it, the skin stretched taut into a string. He dropped his weapons, pushed her away, grabbed at his face, and she felt fresh blood run down her forearm. She released, rolling away as he danced in pain, head tipped back with his screams.

Her sword was in her reach, she grabbed it with her left hand, heard his boots scuff the ground. Jumping up into a crouch she turned, and thrust it into his thigh. He screamed again and she jerked the blade out of his leg.

"Does it hurt?"

He released his face and both his hands went to his leg, she could see the meat beneath the skin. Blood gushed down his neck and shoulder, darkened his clothes. The sounds he made were unintelligible; the screams would only bring people out of their houses. She moved a little closer, her voice soft.

"Keep begging, it's funny."

Reaching down she drew the blade against the back of his knee. His eyes grew wide, darting from side to side, before turning on hers, incredulous. She wasn't smiling. In the dim light she saw the dark puddle grow beneath him, spreading into the cobbles like spider legs stretching. Still close, she whispered.

"Your brother was in it with me, he let me in."

His eyes widened further still.

"He got greedy, wanted half for doing nothing. I didn't want to kill him. I didn't want to kill you."

She felt the weight of guilt shifting in her chest, though it had simply moved to another place where in time it would grow uncomfortable once more.

"I'll leave the half in your house. If you can make it there, it's yours. If not, your widow will be well provided for."

ONE YEAR LATER

THE CRIMSON DRESS lay spilled across the floor, wine splashed and rumpled. Fire crackled in the hearth and softness lay in the bed. Fera sighed.

"You really shouldn't be here you know, I'm still in mourning."

The sword rested in a corner, leaned against a wall. Derin looked up at the portrait of Jorvan, his face grim with disapproval, before turning her attention to the face on the pillow beside hers. She brushed a stray lock of hair, loose now, from Fera's cheek, running her fingers lightly down the side of her neck, tracing the curve of her shoulder.

"You seem content enough to me, and doesn't a widow need a bit of comfort now and then?"

Fera smiled, though Derin could see the pain at the corners of her eyes. She brushed the damp away from one with a thumb tip, kissed her lips once more.

"You're safe now. I'll be here as long as you need me."

"Thank you. It's a dangerous world."

They kissed again, longer this time. Derin opened her eyes as they came apart, pushing that brick of guilt to another compartment in her chest.

"It certainly is."

Arrested Development

Joanne Hall

CAY'S BACK SLAMMED into the canvas and bounced once, twice, before coming to rest. The air burst from her lungs, sending up a fine spray of blood from her nostrils. The blurred face of the referee loomed over her. He raised his eyebrows in question or concern, his hand already beating out the countdown.

She allowed herself seven seconds. Seven blissful seconds where she could have been lying on the softest bed in the most palatial Grondhaus, before she forced herself up on her elbows, shaking her head. The murmur of people exchanging bets intensified.

The referee stepped back. He wasn't permitted to help her to her feet. She had to stand on her own. It was one of the few rules.

Cay's opponent had retreated to the corner and was glaring at her, yellow eyes beetling beneath her lowered brow-shield. The wire mesh of the cage threw patterned shadows across her green skin. One of her incisors was loose and bloody, and she wobbled it with her forked tongue as she stared. Cay didn't know her name. The Grond didn't share their names with humans, and it didn't matter to Cay anyway. She was just another fight.

"Are you ready?" the referee asked.

Cay wiped the blood from her nose and her eyebrow with the back of her bandaged hand, and bounced on the balls of her feet. "Bring it on," she said thickly.

The lithe Grond flicked her loose tooth with her tongue in a final gesture of contempt and rose to her feet. Her spine cracked, audible even over the rustles of the crowd. Grond in the front rows, humans pushed to the back and the sides. At full stretch, she was a head taller than Cay, and her tail lashed back and forth as she prowled, waiting for the signal.

At the whistle, the Grond lunged forward. Cay bounced back, leaping high over that lashing tail that thickened to a club at the tip. She had seen other fighters go down with broken ribs or legs after a blow from a Grond tail. Cay had toyed with the idea of getting the enhancement; it was better for balance, an extra weapon. But it would cost every credit she had and more, and she needed to save her cash. There was a trade; there was always a trade. She could add the enhancement, fight better now, and make more money in the short term. Or she could do what she had been doing for the better part of a decade, and invest in the future. A better future. And not just for her.

The Grond stumbled, momentarily thrown by the force of the blow that didn't connect. Cay was on her in an instant, raining punches against the hard carapace of her barrel chest. The Grond pushed at her with stout arms, seeking an opening. She jabbed in hard against Cay's ribcage, a series of sharp explosions that left her reeling and drooling.

The crowd roared, or it could just have been the blood rushing in her ears. Her foot slipped on the canvas and she lurched forward. Recovering from the slip, she caught the Grond around the waist, barrelling into her and pushing her back against the wire of the cage. The Grond's feet scraped against the canvas as she tried to lift one leg to claw Cay's stomach. Talons raked her bare thigh, scoring twin lines of fire from groin to knee.

Cay pressed harder, breathing in her opponent's sweat, her musty lizard scent. The fingers of her left hand dug into the flesh of the Grond's back, slick now with loose scales as she shed in fear. Cay was inside her grip now, pressed tight as a lover, shifting so her elbow ground against the Grond's exposed throat. She pushed the Grond back, her yellow eyes bulging, feet skittering for purchase as the metal of the cage dug into the flesh of Cay's wrist.

Cay clenched her teeth and hung on, muscles burning from the strain.

The Grond made a choking sound. Drool hung in strings from her lipless mouth, and her eyes popped red as thousands of tiny blood vessels burst. Cay pushed harder, crushing her windpipe, willing her to break.

The Grond was as tense as wire and then all at once Cay felt her snap, muscles falling into slackness. She stepped back and the Grond slumped forward, like a tree toppling. Cay slammed a fist into the back of her head as she went down, just to make sure.

Cay held her breath for the long ten seconds it took the referee to count the Grond out, exhaling only as he took her arm and raised it high above her head. The hordes of Grond in the pricey seats hissed and flicked their tongues, the humans in the cheap seats cheered, money changed hands and Cay accepted the applause. She felt no particular joy, only satisfaction at another job survived without serious injury, another day lived through.

"Still lucky," she breathed.

By the time the referee released her, the defeated Grond had crawled away, back to her own team and the nurture of her people. Cay had no people in the arena. As she lowered herself out of the cage, wincing as the adrenaline wore off and the pain kicked in, the hall was emptying fast. The punters had paid their entrance fee, placed their bets and won or lost, and now they were streaming out into the afternoon, back to their

Grondhaus or to their own towns. Not to the Delphi. No one who lived in the Delphi could afford to watch fights.

She crunched across the debris, the sticky floor and discarded plasteen cups still holding dregs of brew. They dug into her bare feet, bloodied from the wound in her thigh. There was no-one waiting in the changing rooms to greet her, no-one to take her gum shield and wipe down her wounds with astringent, or congratulate her on her win. She didn't need them. She was used to acting alone. Rumour had it the Grond changing room had hot water, but in here she was lucky to be able to thump a lukewarm trickle from the taps. Still, it beat her capsule in the Delphi, and the stanchion pipes on the street outside that were often dry.

Cay showered as best she was able, scraping the sweat and blood from her skin with a sliver of hardened soap and drying herself down with a rough gym towel that smelled like the inside of her shoes. Her trousers and vest lay on the bench where she had abandoned them before the fight and she pulled them on, wrinkling her nose as she caught a whiff of the ingrained stench in the armpits and the groin.

She stood up, brushing herself down, running her hands over hair cropped close to her scalp, to dry off the last of the water. Then she headed upstairs to the booth to get her money.

The female Grond had reached the booth before her, so Cay hung back until she left, the door almost closing on her club tail. There was no point taunting a defeated opponent. The Grond would most likely be back. So would Cay.

Sheeny sat in the booth, thick fingers flicking though the take, bottom lip pushed out in eternal petulance. He looked up as Cay's shadow fell across him, and grunted.

"You did OK out there today."

"Thanks." She didn't want to stay and chat with him. The smell of grease rising from his skin coated her tongue and made her long for a drink to wash it away.

"Always nice to see someone get one up on a Grond. Even a little one like that."

"I'd take on a big one if I had to." The Grond pitted their fiercest male fighters against each other. They didn't waste them on humans. The fights would be over too quickly.

Sheeny chuckled, his crooked eye swivelling away from her. "I've no doubt you would. Here's your money."

He handed over a tatty brown envelope. Cay made a point of opening it right there in the foyer.

"What's the matter? You don't trust me?" His lip stuck out even further, and his weasel tongue flicked over it.

Cay counted the cash. "It's fifty short."

"Yeah, well, things are tight this week . . ."

"Grond shit. Where's my money, Sheeny?"

"Are you sure? Count it again. That bump on the head might have made you dizzy – erk!" His words were choked off as she lunged across the barrier and seized him by the throat.

"Don't fuck with me, Sheeny. I'm not in the mood."

He squirmed. She pressed tighter, grimly satisfied to see his eyes bulge in fear. She rooted on the desk and grabbed a couple of notes without looking.

"Hey, that's too much!" He could squeak for his precious credits even through her grip on his windpipe.

"Call it a fine for messing me about." She reached into his breast pocket and extracted a packet of smoke sticks. "I'll take these too." She pushed him back, slamming him into the wooden wall of the booth. "Pleasure doing business with you, Sheeny."

"Pleasure's all yours," he grumbled, massaging his throat. "That was my last packet. Are you in tomorrow?"

"Not until next week." She had tried to get a quicker fight but none were available. The extra money would help tide her over until then.

As she turned away he called after her. "How long are you going to keep this up?"

"Keep what up?"

He snorted. "You're what, thirty? You won't be able to fight forever, even if you think you can. Then what are you going to do?"

She turned back, waving the envelope. "This proves I can still fight."

"For how long, Cay?"

"For as long as it takes."

"As long as it takes for what?"

With a harsh laugh, she let the door slam in his frustrated, swivelled-eyed face. She could still fight, and win. She was still lucky. Luckier than some, anyway.

*

OUTSIDE, SHE LEANED against the corrugated iron wall of the building and lit one of Sheeny's sticks, drawing the smoke deep into her lungs and holding it there until she felt the narcotic buzz through her system. She breathed out, carefully stubbed the smoke out on the wall and stashed the rest of it in her pocket for later. It would keep her jazzed for the two-hour walk home.

The route back to the Delphi, for much of its length, took her down the narrow track between the Grond Metrotube and the chain-link fence that marked the boundary of the space port. Only the Grond were allowed to ride the express transit that bypassed the Delphi. To protect them from having to see the areas humans were restricted to, the whole length of the track was sheathed in a curved hemisphere of slate-grey metal. The outside of the tunnel was decorated along its length with holo-graffiti, layer upon layer of it, tracking the aspirations and frustrations of the generations of humans that had walked this same track. Political slogans against the Grond, overlaid with tributes. Gorf and Natty RIP, in eight-foot high neon letters, festooned with birds and snakes and vines that fluttered and writhed in and out of the shimmering letters. The paint smelled fresh, and she wondered who Gorf and Natty were, and what they had done to earn such a tribute. Had they been dissidents, or creatives? Someone's son, someone's brother, someone's little girl? Either way they were gone now, but their memorial was glorious, love for them emblazoned on a wall to remind the world that they had lived.

Cay trailed her fingers along the smooth metal of the wall. Her cuts and bruises were aching again, and she stopped to light the smoke she had preserved earlier, cupping it in her hand against the wind that whistled across the flat plain of the space port to hammer into the side of the tube. She finished it while she watched the dance of the graffiti, summoning the strength to resume her long walk.

The tributes and the slogans gave way to a section painted with landscapes, trees and sunsets, cities shining in the sky and mythical beasts dancing. She was halfway home now, and she stopped for an instant to admire the wall, as she always did. For a moment she felt sorry for the Grond, speeding through in their metal tube, separated from this flowering of human creativity. They didn't like to admit it existed, to admit there was something mere humans understood that the Grond could never grasp. There was no art in the Grond cities, no more than there was in the Delphi, where people had too much to worry about, and no room to think about art.

Cay could hear the occasional swish as a train rushed by, soft and swift, insulated by the tube. There was no insulation from the spaceport though; the roar of the orbitals ripping their way up through the atmosphere, g-force accelerating into a wet sky the colour of milk. The orbitals carried the Grond off-world and back, and they sometimes carried humans. Not people like Cay, but lizard-lickers, who made their credit selling out their own people to the Grond. They could afford to travel to the stars. Cay had been offered that chance once, but she preferred to make her credit honestly, in the fighting cage. She didn't want to think about the orbitals, the distance they had to cover. She had plenty of distance of her own. She put her head down and kept walking.

The holo-graffiti faded out before she reached the Delphi, as if the light and colour couldn't bear even to approach the habitation. From there, the train tube curved away to the west while the spaceport fence carried straight on. In the space between the two worlds lay the capsule-blocks and industrial units that made up her home environs. The Delphi had been thriving once, like the other human cities. But that was before the Grond arrived, with their orbitals and their hives, and one by one they had shut down the human cities, cut them off from each other, crushing their trade. Now all the Delphi was good for was providing manual labour for the Grond factories, making components for orbitals that no-one who lived there would ever be able to afford to fly in.

Cay quickened her pace, eager to be out of the wind and off the streets. Her usual pharma lay at the bottom of an administrative block that had mostly fallen into disuse, because what was there to administrate here? She passed the little girls in their high tops and short skirts, leaning against the shuttered window, ready to sell themselves for a fix. She had vowed she would never be like them. She had fought over ten years not to fall into that life. Now she was old and tired but the girls were still there, a new generation every year.

She eased open the door, grateful the place was quiet. She didn't know how Ben got by. She suspected he had some kind of back-pocket deal with the Grond, but she liked him, so she wasn't about to ask. It would be a pain to find another pharma who could provide her particular range of needs so cheaply, and with so few questions asked.

Ben had black hair and a face the colour of jaundice. He was leaning with his elbows on the counter, reading a tatty and lurid paperback. She watched his eyes deliberately finish his paragraph before he looked up and nodded to her. "Cay. How did it go today?"

"Female Grond. Scrappy bitch."

He didn't have to ask if she'd won. If she'd lost she wouldn't have the credits to buy pharma. He was already moving towards the shelves at the back of the store, practiced fingers flicking over the boxes and bottles.

"Usual?"

"Please."

The boxes were beginning to stack up on the counter. The red pills and the green ones, the big white tablets to be taken with the foul-smelling milky liquid, the steroids with their little capped needles that made her veins tingle as she looked at them. The hormone blockers and the protein powder.

"The Grond are leaning on me." He tapped the steroids. "These are going up next month."

"Again?"

Ben shrugged. "Sorry."

"Shit." Without the steroids she would struggle. A price hike would scrape off even more of her meagre income. "Couldn't we come to some arrangement?"

"I'm already sticking my neck out for you, Cay. You know that." He indicated the drug stash with a sweep of his hand. "If the Grond found out I had half this stuff I'd be in all sorts of shit. And the pills—" He broke off, twisting his hands. "Don't you think this has gone on for long enough? We don't know the long term damage, and after six years—"

"Is this the preamble to upping the price, Ben?" Cay snapped. "Because we talked about this last year and you damn near doubled the cost. There are other pharma, you know . . ."

"I know. And I like you, Cay. But you could be killing yourself, and . . ." He trailed off with a shrug. "I'd hate it if something bad happened and I was at fault."

"There's nothing I can do about it, can I? Short of going fully illegal? I don't want to do that. I trust you, Ben. At least I know what I'm getting from you is safe, not cut with rat poison or bleach." She relented and drew the packet of smokes from her pocket.

"I'm just looking out for you. Someone has to."

"I appreciate your concern. Smoke?"

"Ta." He took the stick and slipped it into his pocket for later as she counted out the credits on the counter. The haul from the fight looked a lot thinner now.

"You want a bag?"

She nodded, and he slipped the drugs into a plain brown paper carrier, rolled tight at the top. It looked suitably nondescript.

"When are you fighting again?" he asked.

"Next week."

"Well," he hesitated, "don't get killed."

It was his traditional goodbye. If she died in the cage, Ben would know. He would go to her capsule and take care of things for her. They had an unspoken deal.

"I'll try not to." She grinned, but he had already picked up his novel and resumed reading as if her interruption had never happened. If the Grond came in, he would deny seeing her.

Cay left the pharma, clutching the precious bag tight to her chest. Her capsule was over by the space port fence, and she made her way between the towering blocks and through the alleys between the industrial complexes, limping now. Her boots were rubbing and the walk from the arena had given her a blister. She had a little salt. She could soak her wounds in a bucket when she got home, if the water was on.

She turned a corner into a long alley, closed in on either side by sheet metal fencing. Up ahead something clattered, and her stride slowed, instinct prickling. If it was a rat, and not too diseased, that was extra protein. But it sounded too big to be a rat.

There was a tread behind her. She turned around, looking along the blade of the knife to the kid that clutched it. He looked about seventeen, and he had patches of fake Grond-skin tattooed onto his cheeks. When had that become the fashion?

"Don't do it, kid," Cay said. "I don't want to hurt you."

"Give me your money, then!" He had a friend backing him up, younger and sick-looking, and when Cay glanced back over her shoulder there were two older lads behind her. One stuck his tongue through the yawning gap in his teeth and wriggled it obscenely.

"You dumb kid, you should have jumped me before I hit the pharma." She indicated the bag in her hands. "I've got no credits left now, have I?"

"Then we'll take that." The boy with the knife nodded at the bag.

"Over your dead body . . ."

"That's the idea – what?" The hand holding the knife shook. Cay dropped the bag between her feet and rolled her shoulders. She still ached from the fight with the Grond but these were children. She could take them.

She beckoned the leader closer. "How about you and me, kid? Mano a mano."

He peered at her closer. "You're not a man . . ."

Cay's foot lashed out, catching his wrist. She hoped to numb his arms so she could snatch the knife, but his grip was too loose. The blade span high into the air and over the fence that hemmed them in. Her boot swept on to make contact with the kid's chin, throwing his head back with a shattering crunch. She spun around, a fist catching the gap-toothed boy in the gut, sending him staggering. His companion stumbled away as she came for him, and he pointed, gibbering.

"What?"

"Lady, he's taking your bag . . ."

"Fuck it!" She spun around to the fourth mugger. To where the fourth mugger had been. He had her pharma bag and he was accelerating down the alley away from her.

She needed that bag. Her life, her future, lay in those pills and powders. She couldn't afford any more this week. Without the steroids, she would be more likely to lose the next time she fought. And if she lost she might go on losing, her confidence shattered. She had fought for so long, and now everything she had worked for was vanishing down the alley with her assailant.

Adrenaline pumped through her veins as she hurled herself into a final burst of speed, stretching out to grab the back of his shirt with snatching fingers as an orbital roared overhead. She jerked him back. His mouth was working but she couldn't hear his words, and whatever he was trying to say was cut off as she wrapped her arm around his throat and twisted until he stopped kicking.

She let go and he slumped in the dirt at her feet, his neck at an eye-watering angle. Some of the pills had spilled out of the bag when she retrieved it, but it wasn't ripped, and it was easy to roll back up. Cay squeezed it to her chest.

The orbital had passed over but her ears were ringing. She looked down at the boy. His mouth hung open, as if he was trying to finish what he had started to say. The other kids had run or staggered away, and she didn't have the energy to hunt them down. Her hand twitched towards the smokes in her pocket, but stopped – she could trade them. She had smoked one and given one to Ben, but the rest were a source of credits and she wasn't going to turn down any money she could get.

She checked the boy's pockets. A five. A bonus. She closed his eyes and stood over him for a moment, feeling as if she should say something. She wondered if he had parents who would look for him. But the words withered on her tongue and it had taken her too long to get home. Martine would be worrying.

Martine lived in the same capsule block as Cay, a few floors below. The lock on her door was broken, smashed in an almost-forgotten fight. Cay pushed it open and moved through the dusty light towards the kitchen table, where the old lady was asleep. She caught her shoulder and shook her awake.

"Cay? Did you get food?"

"Tomorrow," Cay lied. "I said I was going to go tomorrow. I got your pills."

Martine patted her hand. "You're a good girl, Cay. How was the factory?"

"Same as ever." Cay mixed up the milky liquid in a stained plasteen mug and handed Martine the white pill, broken into two easy-to-swallow halves. Martine knocked it back obediently, making a face at the bitterness.

"I don't see why I need these," she grumbled.

"For your blood, remember? The pharma said."

"For my blood?"

"How's Hari been today?"

Martine beamed, showing blackened stumps of teeth. "Good as gold. She's asleep out back."

Cay glanced over at the corner, at the pile of blankets. "Out back?"

Martine pointed vaguely. "Over there. I don't know why I said out back. We had a back yard, when I was a girl . . ."

"Of course you did." Cay took the pack of smoke sticks out of her pocket and pressed them into Martine's hand. "I got these. You want to buy them?"

The old woman's hands did her seeing for her, running over the smokes in the packet, counting them off. "There's only eight in here," she chided. "You trying to rip me off?"

"There's no fooling you, is there? Will you give me ten for them?"

"For eight smokes?" Martine snorted. "I'll give you three."

"Five?"

"Done." She reached into her pocket and slapped her ancient leather purse down on the table. "There's three notes in there. I counted them, mind."

Cay opened the purse. There were three notes, a five and two ragged tens. She took one of the tens and pushed the purse back into Martine's hands. "Five," she reminded her, helping her light up a smoke. In the sudden flare of light, the older woman's eyes gleamed white and opaque. "And I'll get food tomorrow. I'll even cook."

Martine nodded, yawning, her mouth a black hole. The pills Cay brought her made her tired, but they helped ward off the worst of the dementia that afflicted her. Cay needed Martine sane, but not too sane. Sane enough to take care of Hari while Cay was fighting in the arena, but just daft enough not to realise what Cay was doing to her own daughter.

"I'll take Hari home now, shall I?"

Martine nodded, leaning back, smoke stick hanging from her bottom lip. Cay retrieved it and gently stubbed it out. Let the old lady enjoy it later.

As Cay lifted the blankets aside, Hari stretched out sleepy arms to her. Cay gathered her daughter to her chest, cradling her and kissing the soft crown of her head. She retrieved the bag of pharma and let herself out into the cold evening air, feet ringing on the metal steps as she made her way up to her own capsule.

The single room was cold, and a line of drying nappies hung from the ceiling on a wire cut from a dead power cable. Cay swiftly transferred Hari to her own ragged blankets. She popped out a red pill, and a green one, chewing them between her own teeth until they were soft, before she transferred them to Hari's toothless mouth, making sure she swallowed. It was a familiar routine; they had been doing this most days for the past six years, Cay feeding her daughter the pills that would arrest her development, keep her in a state of infancy.

While Hari drooled and gurgled, Cay transferred the day's profit to the tin she kept under the floorboards, under the blankets. She was getting there. It had taken over seven years so far, and it might take another two, but one day she would have enough money for a one-way ticket on an orbital. Off-world, away from the Grond, from the Delphi, and the fight arena. Just one ticket, but if Hari was small enough to fit in a sling on her chest, she would travel for free. If she had to save for two tickets she would never make it. She would be far too old to fight before that day came. Already her joints were stiffening and her reflexes slowing. One day she would die in the arena, if she didn't get out, and what would happen to Hari then?

She tied off her forearm and tapped her veins until she found one that hadn't collapsed, and shot a steroid into her bloodstream. That would keep her going a little longer. Tomorrow was a food day.

She crawled into the blankets next to Hari. Her daughter smelled of warmth and milk and love, and one day they would be off-world and she could grow. They could both grow. Cay wrapped herself around her daughter and held her tight against her chest. As another orbital roared above their heads, shaking plaster from the ceiling in a gentle snow that drifted down around them, she began to croon a lullaby.

Asenath

Kim Lakin-Smith

T UCKED BETWEEN THE medina to the east and the residential
blocks to the north was the area of Santa Spišské known
as the Crease. A two by fifteen kilometre slice of the city,
the Crease was home to the "Izobani" – Jeridian outcasts who
counted among their number the mentally feeble, physically
weak, sexually deviant and criminal. Jeridia's strict caste system
and increasingly orthodox morality meant many everyday folk
were also forced into the ghetto. Lump houses piled on top
of one another like clothhod droppings. Heat got trapped in
their folds. Abandoned municipal buildings housed families
and freaks in rotting rooms. The air stank of sweat and tannin.

Megumi had worked in the Crease for fifteen years, but she
still felt uneasy on those narrow streets at night. She would have
made the journey by day if there hadn't been the risk of being
followed. Her only hope was darkness as the dark hid those
who would do her harm, so it might keep her out of sight too.

The heat was stifling. Sweat ran down her throat and stained
the underarms of her dress. It wasn't just the temperature
that made her feverish. Never before had she appreciated so
fully that her life was in danger. It felt utterly surreal to be in
the Crease at this hour, fluttering about like a moth that's lost
the light.

At last she arrived at a pair of rusty gates. "Casa Caca' was daubed on a sheet of corrugated iron in neon yellow paint. The sign was propped against the wall of a long building with a curved, tiled roof.

Megumi walked up the path, taking care to avoid any upended tiles or broken stone edging. She tried one of the large double doors at the entrance; it resisted her efforts and she had to force it open with a shoulder. Folding her lace skirt close about her legs, she stepped inside.

The hall was dusty. Paint sloughed off the walls. A dirty white marble staircase led up. Megumi crossed the hall, listening for a rush of feet or the click of a gun being cocked. The heat resonated – an eternal buzzing in her ears.

She started up the stairs, taking pains to make as little noise as possible. Her boots left imprints in the dust. The intensity of the heat and quantity of steps took their toll. She panted slightly as she climbed.

Arriving at the fifth landing, she leant against the wall to catch her breath. The upper reaches of Casa Caca were as hot as a bread oven. She heard the scratchy warble of a gramophone record. Behind locked doors, a baby cried.

Megumi made her way down the corridor. She counted off the graffitied doors. The last was reinforced with wooden batons and corrugated iron – she'd arrived at the right address.

She knocked sharply. The sound echoed across the landing.

A panel slid back. Red-rimmed eyes appeared at the slot. A Pinkie.

"Kaj Želiš?" *What do you want?*

"I want to speak to Asenath."

"Who says Asenath wants to speak to you?"

Megumi reached into her pocket. She held up a roll of notes. The eyes narrowed. "What's the job?"

"Bodyguard one of my patients." She pocketed the roll again and held out a business card. Fingers reached for it and withdrew. "Megumi Midori," the Pinkie read out loud. "General Practitioner. 251, Marlow Avenue, Santa Spišské."

No caste definition, for which Megumi was grateful. Unlike Jeridians, Showmaniese didn't compartmentalise men according to their social status. Instead, her people believed in hard graft and self-made opportunities. It was just a pity about their disregard for human life – a trait that distanced Megumi from her own.

The Pinkie thrust the card at her and shut the panel. Megumi heard the sound of bolts being drawn aside and chains jangling. The door opened. Before she had a chance to complain, the Pinkie's arm reached out and yanked her inside. The man patted her down roughly. When his hands lingered at her breasts, she kicked out. The Pinkie laughed and bolted the door behind them.

"Only weapons this broad's got are two fat titties," the man announced. "Wouldn't mind her firing those on me!"

"Maybe you try your luck later, ya, Ragorne? For now we hear more from our potential employer." A figure got up from a seat at one end of a long table. Megumi blinked; the room was lit by kerosene lamps and it took her eyes a moment to adjust. Her first impression was of a tall, slim male with burnished red skin and hair greased into a mohawk. But the voice was a woman's.

The Pinkie sniffed and backed off, leaving Megumi to study the speaker's face. Hard, high cheekbones, tigerish eyes, full brown lips. A ladder of piercings ran down the woman's throat.

Megumi swallowed. This had to be Asenath – Jeridian warrior and leader of the Tai Mowa, a gang of rebels who refused to be drafted into either the government's Blue Coats or the People's Artillery Army. Megumi understood their logic. Jeridia was tiny; it didn't deserve to be embroiled in political wrangling or bloody civil war. Unfortunately the country's economy was dependent on its giant neighbour, West. Jeridia had also suffered the same lethal fallout from the insecticide – Soul Food – that blighted the rest of Sore Earth.

Steeling herself, Megumi said, "I have a proposition."

"Save the propositions for later." The gang leader smiled with her cats' eyes.

Megumi pressed on. "My name is Megumi Midori. I am a doctor. My practice is behind the Scarlet Cup brothel on Aziel Street."

"There are no doctors on Aziel Street or anywhere near the Crease," said a gruff voice.

Megumi had been doing her best to ignore the other gang members at the back of the room but now she was forced to acknowledge them – three men, Jeridian braves going by their pierced throats and mohawks, and two hard-faced Western women dressed like harlots.

She lifted her chin. "I'm the only one."

"Why would a doc work in the Crease? Not like Izobani have the dollars to pay for your services," said one of the women – a blonde in a tan leather waist cincher, bloomers and a tattered chemise.

"The outcast needs medical care as much as any man. I provide that."

"In exchange for what?" The gruff voice belonged to the largest brave who sat smoking a hookah pipe.

"Good question," said Asenath.

Megumi held the gang leader's stare. "In exchange for favours owed."

"She's a shitting debt collector!" spat the Pinkie, Ragorne, at her back. "Know what that is, Lizzie-Anne, Arlene? Newbies to Santa Spišské like yourselves ain't had cause to encounter scum like debt collectors. They work for a boss, often as not one of the Showmaniese overlords. This bitch treats the poor and, in exchange, they owe her boss a debt which he is free to call in anytime."

"It's the work of grubs feasting on the rotten end of the city," said another of the men. Jackogin bottle in hand. He was wearing the red calico tunic of his warrior caste.

The gang stirred. Hands reached for the handles of scimitars.

"Wait! How dare a bunch of thugs for hire judge *me*? I debt collect because it's the only way to guarantee my personal safety and continue my surgery. Wherever possible I fail to record the debt, but I can only continue treating those in need under these circumstances." Megumi was breathing heavily again. The room was unbelievably oppressive.

"Pour Miss Midori a drink, Arlene," Asenath told the second woman – a redhead with spidery lashes and a scar down one cheek. "Leave off the door, Ragorne. The doctor has stated her case clearly enough."

Motioning to a high backed chair at the opposite end of the table, the gang leader said, "Sit, Doctor. We have business to discuss."

*

JACKOGIN. COLOUR OF worn leather. Like smoke on the tongue. Megumi didn't look the sort to like it. Asenath wondered if the doctor was too bloody-minded to let on. Most Showmaniese had a palette more disposed to tropical flavours and sweetness.

The gang had joined them at the table. Her fellow braves – Ebo, Lisimba and Hondo – plus Hondo's half-brother Ragorne and the newcomers, Lizzie-Anne and Arlene. Asenath had tested each and every one in terms of integrity, combat skills, and worth. Their loyalty was impeccable.

So far, the doctor had told a pretty tale about volunteering in Santa Spišské's darkest crevices. She had alluded to body guarding but the criteria had not been defined. Instead, Lizzie-Anne was torturing the woman with a description of her latest kill – a pimp with a taste for underagers and dealing in Dazzle Dust.

". . . so I tear off his balls and feed them to him . . ."

"What is the exact nature of the job?" Asenath interrupted. The question was an important one and Lizzie-Anne had the sense to shut up.

Megumi knitted her fingers. Asenath noticed the gold wedding band, the neatly filed nails.

"Blood Worms are taking my patients."

Asenath nodded. The others were more vocal.

"Flesh dealing scum!" spat Arlene.

"You can't be surprised, Doctor. Trade in the sick and dying like you do and sooner or later, Blood Worms will come sniffing." Hondo knocked a fist off Ebo's.

"I had never heard of stealing the living and selling them to surgeons before I moved here. The fact that so many of my countrymen engage in the practice is abhorrent." Megumi's soft brown eyes glistened. Black hair fell to her shoulders.

"How do you know Blood Worms are responsible for your patients disappearing?" Asenath asked. "Folk go missing all the time in this city."

"Because the bastards came by to introduce themselves. Said they wanted to thank me for bringing the vulnerable out of the woodwork. Said I was doing the city and the Jeridian race a favour by weeding out the weak."

"Many of my countrymen would agree with that sentiment." Asenath took a smoke stick and a match from a wooden box on the table. She dragged the match across a sulphur strip on the box lid. "I believe folk have the right to life if they do not harm others and they respect Mama Sunstar." She lit the smoke stick, shook out the match, and exhaled. The air misted in front of her.

Megumi's confusion must have registered on her face because Asenath nodded and said, "You are surprised I keep with the old religion, ya? The same one that made me a pariah." She put her elbows on the table and lent through the smoke. "It wasn't Mama Sunstar who wrote down the words in the Black Book, or diluted her teachings with those of West's Saints. Far as I can tell, the castes are man-made, as are the morals on which those castes are built. Only the voodoo endures, and the rule: "Honour those slain by your hand else they haunt your dreams."" Asenath jabbed the smoke stick in the doctor's direction. "Keep the devils off her land also. Although in this regard we are failing because the Blood Worms have come a-knocking."

Megumi lent across the table. Her tongue skimmed her lips.

"I cannot offer much in the way of financial reward but a debt collector can offer promises of their own. I am a doctor. You and your friends may have use of me now or in the future."

"Which reminds me," interrupted Lisimba. He passed the hookah mouth piece to the redhead, Arlene. "If these Blood Worms are picking off your patients, doesn't that affect your employment as a debt collector and, by proxy, your employer? A Showmaniese overlord will have more than enough manpower to deal with the problem."

"The Blood Worms pay my boss a percentage of their earnings." Megumi got up and started to pace. Her shoes clacked – high heeled and tied with thin black ribbons.

"I guess the return is better on the flesh trade than favours owed." Megumi dragged a hand over the top of her head. Her agitation was contagious. Ebo drummed the table with his fingers. Lizzie-Anne got flinty-eyed.

"And who exactly is it you work for?" asked Hondo.

Wisest of her gang, thought Asenath. She nodded slowly. "Ya, some say there are as many Showmaniese overlords in Santa Spišské as there are roo rats in the open sewers."

The doctor stopped pacing. She put her hands on her hips. "His name is Akihiro Jun."

Hatred rippled through Asenath. Akihiro had sent more of her fellow Jeridians to the grave than any other overlord. Among them was her Commodore.

Asenath shook her head. "Of course it is."

"Of course?"

"Only in that Mama Sunstar does nothing accidentally."

"So you have heard of Akihiro Jun?" Megumi looked nervous. Maybe she wanted the transaction between them to go smoothly and Asenath had appeared to reveal a personal vendetta against her employer.

Asenath reeled in her emotions. "He has a reputation. But we are not interested in your employer, only the Blood Worms." *A lie.*

"We're doing it then?" Hondo interrogated her with his stare.

"On two conditions. One, the good doctor here provides us with medical care as and when we need it. As you say, given our line of work your offer has value." Asenath smiled wryly. "Secondly, you have dinner with me, Megumi Midori."

The gang snorted.

Megumi let her arms hang loose. She appeared to consider the offer.

"Okay."

"Lucky bitch," shot Ebo under his breath.

Asenath heard Arlene whisper, "Which one?"

*

THE HOG PEN was heating up when they arrived. Asenath gestured to one of the tables arranged around the fight cage.

"Sit."

The doctor did as she was told. Asenath signalled a waitress.

"Hello handsome." The young woman popped out a hip. She eyed Megumi and lost a little of her sparkle. "What can I get you?"

"Jackogin. Make it a bottle. And for you?"

Megumi faltered. One thing was obvious, Asenath decided – the doctor might work in the Crease but she wasn't used to its darker crevices.

"You want Kislo Mieko?" asked the waitress sourly. *Buttermilk.*

"Rakija," said Megumi.

Asenath raised an eyebrow. The fruit brandy was pricey enough to suit the doctor's breeding, but it was also very much a drinker's drink.

"Shot?"

"Half jug."

The waitress looked to Asenath, who nodded and added, "Shot for yourself." It was enough to send the waitress away to the bar.

"I can pay for my own liquor," said Megumi, apparently aware of her upmarket tastes.

"You can, I am sure of that. But I asked to take you to dinner and that means settling the bill."

"Dinner?" Megumi let her eyes roam over their surroundings. The Hog Pen was a grime bar complete with back room whoring and nightly cage fights. It wasn't somewhere most people would bring a date.

"Despite appearances, they serve the best Ful Medames and baklava in the district. Also, I can earn our supper." Asenath pushed back her chair and stood up.

Megumi was quick to understand. Her eyes went to the fight cage.

"I'd ask if you were serious but I suspect that would insult your warrior heritage, not to mention your profession."

The waitress put their drinks on the table. Megumi poured a generous measure of the fruit brandy.

She glanced up. "What you waiting for? I doubt it's my permission."

Asenath showed her teeth. She strode away.

*

THE HOG PIT's fight cage was one of the few places that Asenath Sekula felt at home. She had been born into one of Jeridia's ruling Brah families, circumstances which delivered her from the abject poverty of the Izobani and the incessant labouring of the Veez majority. Instead, she was presented with four respectable paths in life – priestess, teacher, judge, or warrior. Her brother, Solomon, inherited their father's cerebral nature and studied to be a teacher. Asenath had no such patience. Her skills were maniacally physical: the need to burn up excess energy like a match put to a source of natural gas, a love of victory over weaker opponents, and the desire to master weaponry and fight methods until she was deadly. Her years at the Warrior Akademja in Lazarocruz were inevitable. As was her banishment from the caste on account of another aspect of her nature. Loss of all she had been born to had hardened her. In recent years, Asenath considered herself more machine than muscle.

Time stretched. She paced inside the cage, waiting for her opponent. The game saw

volunteers pit themselves against whatever champion the Hog Pit had in store that evening. Asenath's past conquests included a five tonne Grizzleclaw brought all the way from neighbouring Sirin's fossilised forest. Mostly though, she went up against street fighters.

The crowd pressed against the mesh of the cage, murmuring expectantly. Asenath eased her shoulders up and back. She wondered if Megumi was watching or still seated. Perhaps she was the sort to enjoy the spectacle of the fight and the spill of sweat and blood.

In the centre of the cage, the referee announced, "Today's challenger is Lady Killer!"

A cheer went up from those who recognised Asenath's moniker.

"This is Lady Killer's twelfth bout and she is undefeated – a record which causes our most excellent hosts to groan every time on account of the damage done to their coinage. Tonight though, we at the Hog Pit are excited to introduce a very special champion: Zero!"

Asenath saw the crowd part. A figure strode towards the cage door. Male, judging by the hefty stride. Shorter than Asenath but broad.

The champion stepped inside the ring. Asenath felt a stab of anticipation. The man was a Sirinese gangster with some of the most extensive bodmods she had ever seen. Where the majority of his breed made do with a neck cuff or a brow bolt plate, this brute had concertinaed metal arms and a tool set for fingers.

Both fighters pressed their hands into prayer and bowed. The referee laid out the rules of honourable combat: no biting, no fish-hooking, no eye gauging. Asenath just had a chance to wonder if the gangster was the honourable sort before the referee drew up his hand sharply between them, signalling the start of the bout.

Storming forward, Zero launched a flying kick at Asenath's skull. She sidestepped the manoeuvre and stabbed a heel into Zero's shin. The man hissed and spun around, driving a metal fist at her face. Asenath bent back at a severe angle to avoid the punch. The revolving hand skimmed millimetres from her face.

Flipping 360 degrees, Asenath landed in a crouch and slammed out the heel of her right hand. She connected with the Sirienese's left knee and felt it give. Zero let out a grunt but continued his attack. Asenath heard the whir of deadly, bio-morphed hands, the snick-snick of mechanised knives descending. She was quick, but not quick enough. Pain ripped across her right shoulder.

Asenath bounced off the cage wall and the crowd roared as they got the first-blood they'd been thirsting for. A metal mass launched towards her face again. She dove left and got in two jabs to Zero's ribs. The man gasped. Asenath rocked back onto her heels and, shutting off the pain in her shoulder, launched a series of volleys against the Sirinese.

Her advantage didn't last. She was an infinitely superior fighter but Zero had hardware. He blocked and drove a steel-jointed elbow into her collarbone. The blow cut into her flesh again. Asenath sucked air between her teeth and stumbled back.

Holding his arms out slightly from his sides, Zero separated his fingers; the tools glinted under the spotlight. At the opposite side of the cage, Asenath bared her teeth. The thrill of the fight was more intoxicating than any hit of Dazzle Dust. She focused through the carnage of noise and reminded herself that every opponent had their weakness. The secret was to avoid those deadly rotating hands and concentrate on Zero's flesh parts.

Again, he came for her. This time, Asenath crouched to avoid the blows, drove out a leg and whacked the front of one foot into the reflex spot on the man's left ankle. She somersaulted aside as Zero collapsed to his knees, momentarily floored. Asenath was on him straight away, driving punches into his kidneys.

Content to let her exhaust herself, Zero stayed tucked in. Asenath cursed internally. Her options were to stay and pummel the man to no effect, or back off.

The decision was made for her when the bell sounded and the referee forced them apart. Zero stalked off to the opposite side of the ring, nursing bruised ribs. Asenath shook the sweat from her hair, squatted on her haunches and pressed her hands to her forehead. While the Sirinese was sucking down water and taking a rest from his gum shield, Asenath slowed her breath and focused entirely on one goal – to emerge as victor. In her mind's eye she mapped the vulnerable spots on the Sirinese's body – genitalia, kneecaps, windpipe, nose.

The respite was short lived. The bell rang for the second round. Zero strode back across the ring, neck bunched, jaw tense.

Height, agility, flexibility, and years of training . . . Asenath ticked off her list of advantages. He came at her hard, arms revolving in their greased sockets; she found her moment and launched an uppercut at his chin. As the man staggered, she landed a sidekick, her foot connecting with his groin.

Zero roared in agony. She kept up the assault, driving multiple kicks into his soft belly and chest. He reeled backwards, the metal limbs making him top-heavy.

Asenath locked into the rhythm of her attack, raining down blows until Zero hit the floor. He lashed out, forcing her to arch back and weave to avoid the slicing hands. She might have been battling her shadow.

Her opponent hit home twice. Asenath clenched her jaw, feeling the hot spill of blood at a forearm, the back of a wrist. For a split second, she understood fear again – that emotion she had trained so hard to conquer. Then she saw Megumi's face amongst the sea of strangers outside the cage, and she was struck by a sudden wave of boredom. The fight had satisfied the crowd's need for gore and violence. Time to wrap things up.

Zero staggered to his feet. His bare chest was already blackening with bruises. Asenath suspected that a good few ribs had suffered hairline fractures. One thing was certain – the entertainment was not complete until she put Zero's specialist biomods out of action.

Uporaba človeka moč proti njemu. "Use a man's strength against him." Her Commodore's favourite mantra.

Charging at the cage wall, Asenath leapt up and kicked off the mesh. Momentum carried her into a somersault. Her right foot connected with Zero's skull, her left with his chest. He lost his balance and stumbled back. Asenath landed, feet firmly grounded, reached for the man's shoulders and propelled him hard into the cage wall. The whirring digits ripped into the mesh and knitted with it. Zero bucked again and again in a desperate effort to get free.

The referee stepped up.

"Yield?"

Asenath flexed her fingers and bunched them into fists.

"Yield," said the Sirinese through bloody teeth,

The referee held up Asenath's arm and the crowd erupted.

*

Megumi laid her knife and fork down on the empty plate.

"You were right. The fava beans were excellent."

Asenath soaked up the slops with a piece of pita bread, wolfing it down. Nothing stimulated her appetite like a fight.

"How is your shoulder?"

"It is fine. The waitress bandaged it for me."

She became aware of the other woman watching her and said, "What do you want to know?"

"Excuse me?"

"The way you are staring suggests you have questions." Asenath put her elbows on the table. "What do you want to know?"

Megumi cocked her head. "You are Brah: Warrior caste . . ."

"*Was* Brah." Asenath swigged from her cup of Jackogin. "I was expelled. Now I'm Izobani. Why else would I live in the Crease? Your next question, no doubt, is why was I expelled?"

"Yes."

Asenath shook her head, amused. The doctor wasn't shy about asking personal questions.

"I do not lie with men," she answered just as bluntly.

"You are celibate?"

"No, I do not lie with men."

"Ah." The revelation didn't seem to cause waves. But her ostracism did. "Is it really as simple as that in your culture? And how did they know, those in authority I mean?"

Something about the way Megumi asked her questions – bare-faced and apparently without prejudice – made Asenath more truthful than usual.

"I fell in love with my Commodore." She pictured Commodore Nefer. Skin like a sunrise. Stretched out naked on the bed in her private quarters. "We had a brief relationship. It ended when Nefer decided her religion mattered more." Asenath sounded sour, and she was. Nefer had renounced her act of transgression as a momentary lapse in moral fibre – an admission which won her the right to stay on as Commodore and Brah.

"Mama Sunstar does not condemn. Hers is the old religion though. Too often this country has been influenced by West, never more damagingly than in its adoption of the Saints and their sanitised ways. Commodore Nefer said sorry for her so-called sin and was welcomed back into the fold. I chose to dance on with Mama Sunstar and the creed which teaches all consensual love is sacrosanct. It was a choice which lost me friends, wealth and status."

"And your family?"

Asenath threw back the remainder of her drink. She poured a fresh shot. "My family might be Brah, but they are good people. They live in Zan City now. My father thought it prudent to leave Jeridia – or as he calls it, "the dying plain'."

Megumi nodded. "Every day I wait for news from my family. They promised to send for me once they found a place where the grass still grows. This poverty." She held out her hands to the tumbledown bar. "It's all consuming."

She looked sad suddenly and Asenath held up her cup. "A toast. To beauty in unexpected places."

Megumi smiled as they clinked glasses.

*

CASA CACA WASN'T the kind of place Megumi expected to visit once, let alone twice in the same day. As a medic, she had often visited the bedridden in the Crease. But she hadn't knowingly entered the domain of criminal Izobani before. Now though, Asenath's whiskey-soaked voice and sparring skills had sunk hooks into her. She was not so much invited back to the tenement as dragged by her fascination with the woman.

The Jeridian brave gestured her inside the empty apartment. She closed the door. Megumi was aware of her wedding band. The heat of evening pressed in.

It was Asenath who strode over, grasped the back of Megumi's head and kissed her. Not a loving kiss. A sharpness of teeth and a tongue forced between her lips. The brave's strong hands were already moulding her breasts, the swiftness of it prompting Megumi to gasp and kiss back deeper.

When Asenath pulled away, Megumi felt a wave of disappointment. But the brave was shedding her clothes – the skin-tight vest to reveal a taut stomach and small breasts, the moleskin boots and suede jeans peeled off and discarded.

Moonlight blazed through the large windows. Asenath's legs were long and muscular; they shone like polished redwood. Her hips were narrow and she was shaved where her legs met.

"You like to look?"

Caught out, Megumi redirected her gaze to the Jeridian's face.

"No." Asenath took hold of Megumi's chin. "Look."

Megumi endured the tight grip a few agonising seconds. She pulled away and started to undo her dress.

Asenath smacked her hands aside. "I do it, ya."

The Jeridian leant in and soaked up the heat from Megumi's lips. Megumi felt a fresh burst of desire as Asenath broke free. Strong hands were busy with the buttons of her dress. Megumi stumbled under Asenath's pressure and rested against the edge of the long table.

"Arch," commanded Asenath, dragging Megumi's dress down off her shoulders. Megumi floundered, not understanding the instruction.

"Arch your back." Asenath fed a hand around to the base of her spine. The brave lowered her head and Megumi arched, feeling the spill of breath across her collarbones, the wet heat at her nipples. Asenath's free hand slid down her stomach and in at her underwear. The brave's fingers splayed and quested, and finally dug in. Megumi bucked, her legs automatically rising, her heels gripping the other woman's hips.

Asenath forced her to stay arched, the soft brown mouth feasting at her breasts while a tight bud of fingers took her deeply and relentlessly. Megumi wanted to run her hands over the brave's bandaged shoulder, share in the intimacy of touch. But apparently Asenath had no need for it. As demonstrated by the cage fight, she was built to conquer, Megumi realised, while struggling to brace herself against the table. The knowledge that she was helpless against the warrior terrified and intoxicated her. She wanted to break free. Her arms were cramping while the lace of her underwear cut in at her hips. Yet she couldn't help soaking up the pleasure enforced on her.

Pressing harder against Asenath's flanks, experiencing the confusion of tongue, lips and mouth passing from one breast to another, she reached the tipping point then fell away from it as if her body was teasing her.

"Please." The word escaped her lips before she could even process why. But Asenath understood, switching the thrust into a steady swirling motion. Megumi came in a sugared rush, gulping down air and shivering deliciously. Asenath slowed her hand and finally stepped away. She allowed Megumi a few moments to quiet her heartbeat. The oppressive heat settled in between them again.

Later, when the Jeridian had used her twice more and taken whatever pleasure she wanted in return, Megumi slipped back into her dress and hunted out a cramped bathroom. She scooped up mouthfuls of metallic brown water from the faucet.

Returning to the main room, she found Asenath lounging on a worn couch. The warrior had put her jeans back on but was otherwise naked.

Megumi drummed the fingers of one hand on the table. She felt the woman's gaze on her. "I'd best go." When Asenath didn't reply, she started for the door. "Who are you protecting really?"

The question came out of nowhere. Megumi's breath caught in her throat.

"Excuse me?"

Asenath was on her feet and across the room in seconds. Megumi panicked as the strong hands that had touched her so intimately went to her throat.

"This great concern for your patients, which led you to my door? I do not think it is the whole truth. This neighbourhood is too dangerous for a little rich girl, because that is what you are. Ya, you enjoy the thrill of a backstreet bar, a cage fight, casual sex. But I see your loathing to step out of this room and into the arms of the night. The Crease is not your neighbourhood, even if you do help its poor in daylight. Those silk underthings beneath your pretty dress cost more than any Izobani earns in a month. You say your family are travelling and they will send for you, but something keeps you here, something precious, something the Blood Worms want and you must protect." Asenath brought her face close. Megumi felt her breath on her lips. "Or should I say someone?"

*

THE SUN WAS up by the time Asenath awoke. She rubbed a thumb and forefinger across her eyelids – just as a loud rap sounded on the front door. Had she sensed the visitor's approach?

"Enough noise. I come now!" Asenath peeled herself off the saggy couch. Her scimitar lay on the table; she picked it up and used the tip to slide open the spy panel in the door.

A rheumy eye stared in at her.

"Late night, was it?"

Asenath closed the panel. Laying down her blade, she unbolted the door. Tadinanefer hobbled inside, the colourful robes of her order at odds with her gnarled face. Asenath had no idea how old Tadinanefer was; the priestess looked not so much old as pickled. Her forehead was decorated with a crude depiction of the evil eye, drawn in the traditional paste of crushed Blue Glow beetles and designed to ward off spirits. She walked with a twisted cane and stank of incense.

"Got any brew?" The priestess eyed the table.

"I'll steep some." Asenath went to the kitchenette. Five minutes later, the leaf mulch was brewed. She poured two cups of dank, tannin liquid.

"What's her name?" called the old woman.

"Who?" Asenath put a measure of Jackogin in Tadinanefer's cup, the way the priestess liked it.

"Who? Oh Asenath, you at least got her name? The girl you fumbled a few short hours ago." The priestess thumbed her nose. "I sniffed out the pair of you."

Asenath grinned. "I got bored, ya."

"Bored!" Tadinanefer shook her head. Joints cracking, she settled onto one of the high backed chairs. "Horny more like."

"Maybe." Asenath took a gulp from the steaming cup. The brew wide-eyed her. "Her name is Megumi Midori. She's a doctor. Works out back of a whorehouse on Aziel Street."

"Never heard of her. Then again, I ain't one for conventional medicine." Tadinanefer tapped her stick against the carpetbag beside her; it contained the tools of the old woman's trade: elixirs, herbs, mineral pastes, and a surgeon's toolkit.

"What *have* you heard? I presume Lizzie-Anne asked you to put the word out."

"Yes, the little strumpet came knocking last night. Said you were mindful of Blood Worms. None in sight, I told her. But she says look again and would you know it? There's a gang holed up at Stick Row. Got themselves attached to an abattoir." Tadinanefer sucked her gums. "I'm not imagining the horrors they get up to there."

"Any visiting surgeons in town?" Asenath asked. Blood Worms stole people but it was the surgeons who paid for living flesh and experimented on it.

"There's talk of a surgeon holed up in Zan City. Lots of dollars. Into the unique."

"Unique?"

"Odd skin tone, high intellect, athletes, anomalies and so forth. Surgeons will always pay more for unusual specimens over your common Izobani." The old woman slurped from her brew cup. "Blood Worms pick on us because Jeridians heal faster. Makes us better subjects for the bio-morph implants. Pinkies sell well on the black market too, while a Showmaniese or Siriense anomaly with proven healing ability will attract a mighty price."

"Megumi has employed us as bodyguard to one of her patients. She eventually let on that our charge is a six year old boy. A Twists survivor. Blood Worms have already tried to snatch him twice."

Tadinanefer snorted into her cup. "Ah, it makes sense now. Lots of rumblings among certain parties in the Crease about a hunt for a boy. Talk of bounties, hefty ones too." The rheumy eyes pinched. "Sure you want to get involved, Asenath? You and your friends have a nice little earner in protection, but there's something whiffy about this situation. Has to be more to the kid than this Megumi is letting on. Surgeons don't offer sums like those being bandied around without hoping to acquire something special. Something *unique.*"

Asenath sat down, put her elbows on the table and steepled her fingers. A child was being pursued by Blood Worms and Megumi was doing everything in her power to protect that child. Asenath thought about the soft burn of Megumi's tongue, the strangeness of a woman who treated Izobani and drank Rakija, but who seemed at odds with the Crease.

The truth struck Asenath like a blow to the jaw.

"A mother would go to dangerous extremes to protect her son. The boy is a Twists survivor and Showmaniese, which would make him one of these rare commodities you mentioned. It would certainly explain the bounties on his head."

"The kid is Megumi's son. Why didn't she just say so?"

"I do not know." Asenath lent back in her chair, arms stretching, legs going out under the table. She knitted her hands behind her head. "When will the Blood Worms come for him again?"

"Blood Worms won't wait about," Leaning down, Tadinanefer rooted around in her carpetbag and produced a small black velvet bag. Unfastening the neck, she shook five tiny bones onto the table, spread them about and clucked her tongue. "They will strike tonight. So where is the boy now?" The priestess sniffed. "Is he here?"

"With his mother, I presume." Asenath picked up her scimitar and ran a finger along its shining blade. "Thank you, Tadinanefer. Let's hope I will be in need of your other services before the day is out."

*

251 Marlow Avenue was a featureless block hewn from the grey bedrock on which the city was built. Once upon a time the building's harsh edges would have been softened by fauna and flora. But the same lethal insecticide which had created West's dustbowl had leeched Jeridia's land, and neighbouring Siria. Asenath had no doubt that the residence was exclusive – it was on the right side of town and among other utilitarian but well preserved homes.

She rapped her knuckles against the large front door. At her back, the rest of the Tai Mowa gang assessed their surroundings.

"Ask me, these richies haven't got it much better than us," said Ragorne. "Sure, they've more space and no open sewers, but these buildings look like tombs."

"We came to Jeridia to escape West's dustbowl. Recently it seems we've just exchanged dust for rock," shot Lizzie-Anne while Arlene chipped in, "No wonder Blood Worms are picking us off. We've nowhere to hide in this hell-hole."

The door was opened by Megumi in a black kimono, her dark glossy hair swept back. Behind her was a bright hallway. Marble floor, wide staircase, red papered walls and a monstrous chandelier hanging from the ornate plaster ceiling. The interior was a world away from the stark exterior.

Asenath glanced over a shoulder. "Apparently some of us know how to hide very well." She found Megumi staring at her, almost accusingly.

"Come in." The doctor stepped aside. Asenath and her gang filed into the hall. Megumi closed the door and bolted it.

"You live here?" Hondo tightened his eyes.

"Yes."

"And you chose to work in the Crease?"

A pause.

"Yes."

"Wow! You must have one big heart to go with them big titties." Ragorne knocked elbows with Hondo. The wiser brother shook his head in bemusement. Both appeared uncomfortable when Megumi looked over at one of the doorways off the hall and said, "Come in and meet my friends, Chi."

The boy let go of the door jamb he was hugging and came into the hall. He had a slight limp. The arm which hugged a knitted roo rat was disfigured by the familiar ropey flesh of a Twists' sufferer. Unlike most, he had fought off the disease. He was one of the lucky ones.

"Hey there, little 'un." Ebo squatted down, the sheathed scimitar at his back knocking against the floor.

"Hey." The kid tried a wave. Ebo waved back.

Megumi stroked the boy's hair. She cleared her throat. "I must tell you that Chi is my son. I was afraid you wouldn't come if you thought I was just some rich bitch looking out for her son."

"We know that already." Asenath considered the boy. "What we don't know is why you spun us some yarn about a doctor's surgery out the back of a whorehouse." Her gaze flicked to Megumi, who was biting her bottom lip. "Why'd you think a sob story about your patients being picked off by Blood Worms would appeal more than the truth?"

Megumi shook her vehemently. "The doctor part was true, at least until I got married. Then things changed. Chi became my priority, especially when I realised my husband was not even close to the man I had thought him to be. When Chi became a prize to be fought over, I knew I had to get out of my marriage." She held out her hands. "This was my parents' house. I brought Chi here with his Nana. My patients from the Crease helped me track down your Tai Mowa gang. They said you could be hired to act as our protectors."

Asenath wasn't letting up. "But why lie?"

A housemaid wearing a plain apron and a careworn face appeared at the doorway. Megumi gave her son a hug. "Go with Nana now. She will fix you some yogurt and ruby fruit."

The boy looked pleased. He hobbled back through the door.

Megumi dropped the act. She paced up and down the hall. "I didn't think you would help, not if you knew the extent of my situation. Why would anyone help? It's tantamount to suicide."

Asenath sensed the gang getting edgy.

"What shit is this?" Ragorne slung his rock rifle down off his shoulder. His lips curled back from his teeth. "I'm not liking this situation one iota." Ebo rubbed his chin. Lisimba glared off into the corners of the hallway.

Asenath shut them up with a hiss. "It's not so different from the tale she told yesterday." She eyed the doctor. "These old patients who told you where to find us, you still treat them?"

Megumi nodded.

"You treat all of them?"

"When I can. It hasn't been easy for me to escape unnoticed."

"Of course. The controlling husband. And do you still debt collect for the overlord you mentioned?"

"No."

"So you treat these paupers for free, all the while flouting your husband's rules and doing your old employer out of debt revenue?" Asenath managed a sour smile. She fed a hand behind Megumi's neck and squeezed, offering comfort – or asserting authority. "Our doctor here is not a bad sort. But she does have one vivid imagination." Asenath felt Megumi tense. She tightened her grip. "Friends, I'd like to introduce Megumi Midori, only her real name is Megumi Jun – wife of Akihiro, Showmaniese overlord and cold blooded killer."

"Shit, Asenath. Shit!" Ebo looked like he might rip Megumi's throat out.

"Akihiro's wife? Good Souls almighty." Lizzie-Anne aimed her rock rifle at Megumi's head. "Shall I shoot her now or once she's guaranteed us safe passage outta here?"

"Put the rifle down," said Asenath. "Now!"

Lizzie-Anne did as told, but the gang looked primed to take Megumi apart. Asenath didn't blame them.

"So who are we protecting Chi from really? Blood Worms or his father?"

Tears streaked Megumi's face. She trembled under Asenath's touch.

"I didn't trust Akihiro not to sell Chi to them, to the Blood Worms. Chi is Showmaniese with AB negative blood type. He survived the Twists, which makes him a rare commodity."

In the pause that followed Asenath assessed the situation. She had Akihiro's wife and son – worth a fortune in ransom money alone. But Megumi had paid her dues in the dangerous if close-knit community in the Crease. Plus, Megumi's son had already survived the horrors of the Twists; Asenath was damned if she was going to hand him over to his father or Blood Worms. In her mind's eye, she saw Chi strapped to a mortician's slab, a surgeon teasing out the boy's innards and feeding in steel bones and wires. Asenath had lost too many friends and family members to that bloody trade.

But she was being presented with access to Akihiro and that was invaluable.

"Let them come. We bodyguard the boy. The mother fends for herself. You agree, ya?"

The rest held up their weapons and nodded.

"Thank you . . ."

Megumi would have said more but Asenath held up her hand. "Do not speak. We've had our fill of lies. Just show us the layout of the rooms and let us do our job."

*

No one joined the Tai Mowa gang without expecting to make enemies; Akihiro Jun was one of the most powerful. His business interests spanned narcotics to whoring to extortion via a network of debt collectors. Asenath understood how Megumi as a young, impressionable doctor could have encountered the sharp-suited overlord and fallen for his good guy impersonation. She suspected the doctor had married

Akihiro in ignorance and gone on to bear his child under the same illusion. When had Megumi seen the edge behind Akihiro's charm?

Watching Megumi now, stood before a large, white-washed window in the drawing room, arms folded, Asenath couldn't help feeling slightly sorry for her. She liked the way Megumi operated in the divide between wealth and poverty,

But the bitch had lied – and lied repeatedly. Now the Tai Mowa gang were in danger. Yes, they had chosen to stay, every one wanting a shot at one of the big bad overlords who left stains on their lives. But had they known the truth of the situation ahead of time, they could have offered up peace prayers, chosen their weapons with more care, even opted out if the spirit wasn't willing. There would have been no judgement; each member of the Tai Mowa shared the same philosophy – that every man chose his own path.

But now Megumi had chosen for them and time had run out. Asenath heard the sound of a heavy implement strike the front door. Megumi turned sharply, the softness gone from her eyes. She had sense to stay quiet, even when the Nana came bustling in.

"What now, Miss? Chi is sleeping. Do I bring him downstairs?"

"You go back up and watch over him," Asenath cut in. She looked at Megumi. "You too. Stay with the boy."

Megumi went to leave. Asenath gripped her arm.

"What of your husband?"

Megumi's eyes tightened.

"Kill him."

*

THE DOOR SPLINTERED and swung open to reveal a broad Showmaniese with a smoke stick between his lips and a steel ramrod in hand. The man stepped back. Akihiro strode into the hallway, shouldered by gangsters. Asenath stood at the bottom of the stairs, arms at her sides, scimitar in hand.

"Good evening, Akihiro."

Akihiro smiled. His small black eyes were bright as a bird's.

"I know you. Lady Killer, am I right? You like to brawl in the Hog Pit's fight cage." He glanced at his men. "You recognise her, right? She's good." Undoing his jacket button, he slid his hands into his pants' pockets. "So, what's the score, Lady Killer? Megumi pay you to play bodyguard?"

"That's exactly the score." She gestured to the doorways leading off the hallway. Each was occupied by one of her fellow Jeridian braves. Shoulders broad as rhinohorns. Mohawks spiked with green reed sap. Neck piercings glinting. Asenath held out her scimitar and pointed up. "Got a few nursemaids installed upstairs too."

Akihiro tilted his chin and looked down his nose at her, exposing the black "V" tattooed across his throat. "Is it inconceivable I should want to see my son? Or that I am entitled to object to my wife running away and taking Chi with her? You have met her – it is not out of the question that everything she has told you about me is a lie."

Not remotely out of the question, thought Asenath. Then again, if Akihiro believed he could rewrite his malignant personality in her eyes, he was equally delusional.

"I have been employed to keep Chi safe from Blood Worms, and from you."

"There are no Blood Worms after my son!" Akihiro rocked back on his heels, chuckling. "Megumi has woven a pretty tale no doubt, about how special Chi is – which he is, but I say that as a biased father – and about how I am willing to sacrifice my son for financial gain. I ask you, Lady Killer, do I strike you as that sort of a man?" Akihiro smiled again, revealing nothing except a gold-capped incisor.

Asenath stared at the overlord. "Do you remember Commodore Nefer?" Akihiro looked blank and she continued. "I trained under her command. When I knew her, she was a strong brave. Later she was reduced to poverty when the Twists struck. The disease could not be cured. Instead, Nefer was reduced to debt collecting for a Showmaniese overlord. When she became too sick to work, the overlord ran her through with his sword. This I learnt after the fact." She showed her teeth. "I not only believe, but I *know* you are the kind of man to sell your son to Blood Worms. Throw your wayward wife into the bargain too, ya?"

Akihiro's smile stiffened. "Now that's a shame, Lady Killer. I hoped you had brains as well as brawn. I am not a kindly enemy. Why antagonise me?" He took his hands out of his pockets and folded his arms. "I presume your friends have their own motives for taking against me?"

Each Jeridian knocked the flat of a hand against their throats, a traditional insult and one which stressed revenge.

Akihiro nodded. "Okay then." He glanced to either side. "Karera o korsu!" he told his men.

Asenath didn't speak Showmaniese but she understood the command to kill. She glanced up in praise of Mama Sunstar and requesting the deity's protection. Ebo, Lisamba and Hondo offered their own prayers. Lowering her eyes, she saw them draw their scimitars from back holsters. Asenath gripped the handle of her own.

Akihiro's men split into four units. She made a swift assessment of the slim, suited gangsters with lemony skin, high cheekbones and the traditional "V" tattoo at their throats. Street fighters without code or honour – which meant, in spite of the odds, she and her fellow braves stood a chance.

Her fight instinct kicked in. The five gangsters allocated to her charged at the steps. She drew her scimitar around and up in a blur of silver. Two men produced rock pistols. Three wielded tanto short swords. Akihiro really did believe in the look of his men being as important as their abilities; Asenath hoped to use that to her advantage.

A shot from one of the rock pistols skimmed her ear, burrowing itself into the wood of the stairs. Asenath took the opportunity to dip down alongside the shooter before he could reload. There was no room for maiming in this game; she dragged her blade across his tattooed throat and was already dodging shots from the second shooter before the first hit the ground. Rock ammo was crude, the pistols and rifles prone to violent kickback and miscalibration. Firing at short range increased the accuracy. Fortunately Asenath had three swordfighters between her and the second shooter.

Maintaining her higher ground on the staircase, she wove her blade back and forth in front of her, daring the swordsmen to strike. They took it in turns in wade in. The first used his tanto like a staff, blocking Asenath's slices but unable to get a hit in. He exhausted himself and started to back off when the shooter missed Asenath but made a mess of the swordsman's ear. The man yelped and clutched his bleeding head.

Asenath was distracted by the second swordsman who proved nimble on his feet, matching her for grace as he arched to avoid her blade. The chimes of swordplay came at her from all directions. Her braves were performing their own violent choreography. The air stank of sweat and spark powder.

If the gangster matched Asenath's grace, he couldn't match her relentlessness. The scimitar sliced his shoulder. Blood welled where his suit tore and he backed off quickly, face contorted against the pain.

As the third opponent powered forward, tanto in hand, Asenath felt a rip of pain at her outer thigh – rock shot. She cursed, skidded under the swordsman's arm and dragged her blade across the shooter's chest. The pistol fell from the man's grip; she caught it in her free hand and turned sharply. The third swordsman received a short range blast to the throat. The man slumped to the floor, gagging on his own blood.

The victory was short lived. Asenath heard a roar from one of her own – Ebo. Her gaze whipped over to the doorway he'd been guarding. The brave had fallen to a gangster's blade. He fought on, teeth stained red, the blade's hilt jutting from his ribs.

Asenath threw back her head and sang an eerie, warbling note which cut through the crush of blades and grunts of men. Whirling around, she sliced the throats of the two injured gangsters who'd backed away. She charged to Ebo's side. Too late to save him; he'd been cut too many times.

She tore into the gangsters, severing a carotid artery, a jugular, the ligaments at the back of a third's knees.

"Moj nagradu!" *My prize.* she cried, beheading each. She met Ebo's gaze. He blinked in acknowledgement. His chin rested forward on his chest. Asenath offered up a second war cry.

Turning to the fray, her instinct was to help Lisamba and Hondo. But she saw Akihiro and several gangsters at the top of the stairs.

"Go for Akihiro!" shouted Hondo.

She offered up a prayer for the braves locked behind walls of swords, and slit the throats of two shooters positioned near the front door. Now the battlefield was even, she reasoned, taking the stairs three at a time.

The sound of gunfire told her that Akihiro's men were attempting to clear a path through Ragorne, Lizzie-Anne and Arlene, who fired back. Her people had the advantage, having built a blockade from a wardrobe and a strip of corrugated iron which had covered a wood chute outside. Asenath heard the pings of rock salt bouncing off the sheet metal.

Reaching the top of the stairs, she pulled up sharply and peered around the corner to see figures on the landing, all dressed in sharp suits and cream fedoras. It was impossible to distinguish Akihiro from that angle. No matter. She would work her way through the gangsters until he was the last one standing.

Her thoughts were interrupted by the sound of wood splintering and a scream. Asenath recognised the voice as Lizzie-Anne's. Judging by the strength of the cry, the girl had received a serious wound. The barricade would not survive much longer.

Asenath stepped out onto the landing, the blade of her scimitar bowing out from her side like a claw. She ran forward and sliced the throats of four gangsters as easily as threshing grass. The last managed a strangled cry as he died, alerting the rest to her presence. She saw Akihiro direct a couple of fighters and a shooter her way then give his attention back to having the barricade cleared.

The gunman peeled off a couple of shots. Asenath snaked to avoid the blasts. Her mouth tensed. She hated shooters – no elegant combat, no skill, just point and click. How was she meant to concentrate on swordplay with those stinging rocks careering her way? She charged at the two fighters, dropped to her knees and slid between them, her blade cracking off one man's ribs and then the other's.

She forgot them instantly. Lizzie-Anne, Arlene and Ragorne were engaged in a scuffle at the door to Megumi's bedroom. Lizzie-Anne was tucked behind a low divan, spraying rock shot from a rifle, her face distorted in pain. Ragorne had disarmed Akihiro's shooters with his ranch whip, cracking it off any skull in reach. Arlene had a look of grim determination. She peeled off shots whenever a Showmaniese gangster made a dash at them.

Asenath was running at the gangsters when she spotted a mine cone device in one man's hand. The pin was pulled, the cone turning liquid silver. She pulled up sharply.

"Grenade!" she cried over the noise of gunfire.

The mine cone was thrown clear, the conical design protecting those behind from the sonic pulse which visibly arched out, vibrating off the walls and furnishings, and incapacitating her gang.

Asenath felt a tug of dread in her stomach – she was hopelessly outnumbered. The panic switched to relief as Hondo and Lisimba arrived on the landing beside her.

"Mine cone," she mouthed, registering their disbelief. The weapon was costly technology, usually restricted to government warfare. Akihiro had to have friends in high places, or at least be lining the pockets of a corrupt official.

"Protect the others until they recover and don't let the bastards release another grenade," she told the Jeridian braves while watching a figure break off from the other Showmaniese, try the bedroom door handle then produce a key. "Akihiro," she said under her breath. Leaving Hondo and Lisimba to make their presence known, she sidled up to the bedroom door and slipped noiselessly inside.

Chi lay on the bed. Megumi was brushing his hair back off his face and whispering soothingly. The Nana stood at the foot of the bed, rock pistol held in a quivering hand. Akihiro had paused halfway across the room.

"You stay there, Lady Killer," said Akihiro softly. He knocked the pistol out of the Nana's grip with the flat of his short sword and pointed the tip at the woman's chest. He spoke over a shoulder. "I have the right to appeal to my wife to come back to me. I have the right to say hello to my son."

Asenath wasn't so sure but it wouldn't pay to sacrifice the Nana's life needlessly. She shut the door, dulling the noise of the fight outside.

Akihiro nodded. He gave his attention to Megumi.

"How is a husband meant to fix problems in his marriage if his wife won't talk? Come now. Let's work this out."

Megumi rolled the boy behind her and slashed at Akihiro's outstretched hand with a kitchen knife. Akihiro roared as blood dripped from the wound onto the carpet. He rammed his sword home into the Nana's chest while Chi hid his head in the folds of his mother's kimono. In spite of the Nana's terrible wheezing, the child stayed silent. Perhaps he was accustomed to violence. Or perhaps he sensed that he too would be put to the sword.

"So that is the way of it?" Akihiro stared at his hand.

"Leave us alone, Akihiro." Megumi's eyes crystallised. Her face twitched with fear as she looked past her husband. "Asenath?"

"Lady Killer knows her place when it comes to relations between a husband and a wife, don't you, Lady Killer?"

Asenath heard the sneer in the overlord's voice.

"I fucked your wife," she said simply.

Later, Asenath would question her decision to distract Akihiro and have him spin around to face her. She would wonder if her method had been too crude, if she had made Megumi distrust her bodyguard and take action. With the full knowledge of how it would end, she saw Megumi take her knife and drive it into Akihiro's shoulder. As the overlord's features pulled in and set hard, Asenath raced across the room, arms pumping. Inside she knew it was too late. Akihiro turned and slid his sword between Megumi's ribs. Chi kicked backwards and worked his way up the bed, breath coming fast like a panting desert dog.

Megumi stared past Akihiro's shoulder at Asenath. Her eyes softened and became incredibly sad. "Chi," she mouthed.

Asenath didn't pay attention after that. Akihiro dragged his blade free of his wife's chest in time to block the scimitar's descent. Asenath circled the blade in repeating figures of eight. The Showmaniese blocked her every time, his face slick with sweat. He risked wiping a hand down his face to keep the salt water from his eyes; Asenath saw the opportunity and nipped the tip of her blade across the wrist of his hurt hand.

"Red bitch!" The overlord tore into her. From somewhere Asenath heard Megumi's last rasping breaths. There was no time to reminiscence or regret. As her Commodore had instructed, she needed to focus on the now.

A child was crying. A blur of voices and violence came from beyond the door. Amid the relentless smash and fall of blades, Asenath knew she had to use her opponent's strength against him. Akihiro – Showmaniese overlord, husband, father, collector of paupers' debts . . . Her mind backtracked. *Father.* Whether Megumi had been truthful about Akihiro's intent towards his son or not, Chi was still a precious commodity.

The thought cost her. Akihiro broke through her defences to slice into her collarbone. Asenath hissed, more out of indignation than agony. With no time to process the depth of the wound, she used the glee on Akihiro's face to fuel her reactions. Ducking beneath his arm, she ran up alongside the bed and directed her scimitar towards the crying child.

"No!" Akihiro's hands flew out in front of him.

Her gaze flicking between the two, Asenath saw crushing fear in the young boy's eyes and the oval shape of his father's mouth. Within the second, she called Akihiro's bluff and sent her scimitar flick-flacking through the air. It struck the overlord in the chest – the same lethal wound he had inflicted on Megumi.

Asenath forgot the overlord and looked down at the boy. Chi appeared to have fainted. "Poor child." She laid a hand on his head. The kindest thing would be to end his life too – now while he was unconscious and protected from the reality that, within the space of minutes, he had become an orphan. The moral part of her knew she would not do it. Instead, she waited for him to come to.

As she did so, she homed in on the silence. Had Akihiro's men taken victory? Had her gang destroyed the threat and retired downstairs, knowing better than to interrupt her in one-on-one combat?

"Sleep," she told the boy and crossed the room to Akihiro's body. Putting both hands on the hilt of her blade, she pulled it free and froze. Footsteps sounded out on the landing. She watched the door handle turn. The door opened to reveal five rock pistols trained on her. One shooter might miss. Five guaranteed a strike.

She straightened up as a man strode into the room. Western, tall, and dressed in a government Blues' uniform.

The man put his chin near his shoulder. "Fetch the boy."

Two Showmaniese filed inside. They approached her with caution.

"Don't mind the woman. She knows there are too many guns pointed her way to object." The man's accent had a rough edge; he was a dogsbody as opposed to someone of higher rank. Asenath heard the sound of bedsprings and a grunt of exertion. The men walked back past her. One held Chi in his arms. They disappeared through the door.

Reaching over her shoulder, Asenath slid her scimitar into the sheath at her back. There was no action to be taken. Her fellow gang members were either dead or held at gunpoint. The Akademja had taught her to know when she was outnumbered.

"How much will you make on him, Blood Worm?" she muttered.

The government man lit a smoke stick. He exhaled a stream of smoke. "Enough to risk going up against Akihiro. But you've only gone and saved me the bother, Lady Killer." He knocked the flat of a hand against his brow in mock salute.

Turning his back, the man walked away. The last gunmen shut the door after him, leaving Asenath alone in the room except for the dead.

*

MOONLIGHT STREAMED IN at the large windows. Asenath had extinguished the lamps. The priestess brought her own candles, six wads of brown tallow, each fat as a man's arm. The tools of her trade lay on the table: hacksaw, thread, curved needles, scoops, paring knives, skewers, and similar apparatus. The carpet bag sat open on a chair; every so often Tadinanefer dug around in it for some new herb.

"Had a sticky feeling about that bodyguard job. Gave me cramps just thinking about it. But sometimes it ain't up to an old hag like me to interfere. Sometimes the young have to do what they will, even if it kills them." Tadinanefer paused in her ministrations, holding the severed head by its hair. A sigh escaped her papery lips. "Ebo was a good "un. I didn't care for that Lizzie-Anne much, but it's not like she deserved to get belly-sliced." She scooped out the head as she talked. "And you say Ragorne bore the worst of it too? Bruiser like him'll pull through. I got the knowledge in my bones about that much."

"And what about the kid, Chi? Do you have knowledge in your bones about his whereabouts?" muttered Asenath from the couch. She took a long drag off a smoke stick. Her shoulder and collarbone ached where Tadinanefer had stitched up wounds.

"Yes, I have that too, but what do you need it for, hmm?" Hobbling to the back of the room, the old woman lowered the head into a pot of boiling water on the stove. She didn't bother to rinse her bloody hands, just returned to the table and bent over to retrieve a fresh head from the sack, bones crackling as she moved.

Asenath exhaled heavily. "I failed in my duties as bodyguard. If the boy is still alive, I will make good on the grounds of my employment."

"Employment? Paah! Little need for honour code when your employer is dead, the poor bit." Tadinanefer touched the evil eye symbol at her forehead.

Asenath took a fresh drag and let the smoke sit in her lungs. "I am tired," she said quietly. Smoke bled from her lips.

"Of course you are." Tadinanefer put the head on the table. It was Akihiro. The overlord had died with the expression of hate he wore so well.

"The others have the sense to lay up a while. Ragorne is letting Arlene tend to him." Tadinanefer winked. "There'll be a babe born from that arrangement, mark my words."

Asenath watched the priestess take a scalpel to Akihiro's eyes, plop them out of the sockets like ruby fruit from the pod. "I need to honour the dead before I rest," said the warrior. She nodded towards the head.

"Of course you do! But it's a few hours since the killing. These heads could have gone another day or so."

"No, they couldn't. There's no let up in the heat these nights. No ice to store them either." She ground the nub of the smoke stick into a cup by her feet. "I need to make my peace with these spirits so I can focus on the living – by which I mean, find Chi."

"And what if you find him? Do you play happy families? You killed the boy's father in front of him!" Tadinanefer started to muddle the brains with a skewer poked through an eye socket. "No mama, no papa. Maybe the boy is better off dying on a surgeon's table."

The words were harsh, but Asenath heard the sadness that underpinned them. "I just need to know where to look for him," she murmured. Rising from the couch, she walked over to the table and stood watching the priestess pack the eyelids with seeds. Candles flickered. Shadows played over the walls.

The old woman sighed. "So you won't let it rest, hmm? Well, I can only tell you what I've heard. The boy is being transported to Zan City. Some high and mighty surgeon is willing to pay a hefty price for his creed and blood type." She brushed her hands off one another, scattering seeds over the gored table.

Asenath narrowed her eyes. "My family live in Zan City."

"There you are! Kill two birds with one stone." The priestess chuckled to herself. The laughter trailed off and she stared across the table at Asenath. "That enough for you to go on?"

Asenath nodded stiffly. Zan City was an island of stone in a solar strip. A place to get lost in. It was also three thousand miles away in the vast dry country of West. On one hand, that kind of distance gave her the chance to catch up with the Blood Worms. On the other, there was no single route to the city; her best bet would be to reach Zan City ahead of them.

"Know how I can get there quickly?"

Tadinanefer snorted. "The hell if I know! Jump aboard one of them wagon trains shifting dust. Join a circus!" She threw up her wrinkled hands and hobbled off to the boiling pot. Akihiro's head was set bubbling alongside the others.

Asenath crossed her arms. The Tai Mowa gang were loyal but weakening. It was time to leave her colleagues to their own devices in Santa Spišské and set out on a new adventure.

Tadinanefer rooted around in the sack again. Asenath knew it contained one last head. Megumi's long black hair gave the old woman something to grip onto; it flowed around the bloodstained face like thickened shadows. The doctor's enticing eyes were closed, the finality of death the more acute for her beheading.

"Wait." Asenath put a hand out as if to protect Megumi from the priestess's butchering.

Tadinanefer squinted across the table.

"I did not kill this one. I took the head to keep her safe from Blood Worms and their flesh dealing." Asenath faltered and then added, "She meant something."

It was difficult to sum up what, if anything, she had felt for the doctor in the short time they had known each other. Physical longing, yes, and a sense of liking. Emotion enough for a Jeridian warrior to want to honour a lover in death. What she did know was that she owed Megumi a debt.

She picked up a paring knife. "This one I do. Teach me how."

The Coyote

K R Green

ONCE, SOMEONE HAD tried to kill Kai. She smiled, remembering the attempt.

She'd heard his footsteps from two floors above; the stairwell's gentle echoes the loudest sound in the flat. She'd never taken her hearing for granted; she was trained to pick out individual sounds that others ignored.

But, in this place, the ability could bring on a headache if she let it get to her. Between the roars of laughter, bottles clinking and percussive footsteps, it was impossible *not* to know where people were and what they were doing. The city's sirens wailed in the background, and her captor's dingy flooring creaked underfoot.

She opened her eyes and stretched her back, uncurling her legs from underneath her. Many thought meditation impossible in a loud and cramped space, but she found the rhythms of voices comforting, when she wasn't fighting to tune them out. Most things were manageable if you didn't fight them.

Kai glanced out of the small window, her eyes adjusting to the sunset. A couple of street lamps had begun to glow. Not long now. She would get there in time, and she would find it. They would make it home.

Her room was clearly a holding pen; just an empty chest of drawers and a bed with blankets. The wallpaper was peeling and it stank of mould. How many Circlet members had they held in this place?

A door slammed, cutting off the laughter outside. Heels clacked against the wooden floor, striding closer to her room. She focused her hearing, groping around under the bed for her weapon. She would only get one shot.

"Sire, we have the last one."

"Then your work is done."

"I . . . Yes Sire." The voice faltered, clearly worried. "She was very tricky."

"That is why you were hired. Now be silent."

So it had been the Royalists. Trust the Royal Buddhist Sect to place the environment above the deaths of millions in war. They wanted the flame to save the bees, and would harm anyone who got in the way of that. Brighton held it for healing the sick in the city. If she could find it, the Circlets could re-shape the third world: fix the things humanity had brought to collapse, and heal the millions harmed in the wars over oil and weapons.

Each sect felt justified, and only her past with the Brighton Sect would give her this opportunity to find it. At least they weren't ignoring the needs of their people.

Of course the Royalists were hiring thugs, often using tricksters like the very old or young to deceive their enemy. She hadn't expected the old man at the bus stop to fight her, and yet here she was, locked up in a first floor bedroom.

But she could remedy that.

The click of footsteps grew louder, and the visitor halted by her door as jangling keys scraped the lock. Kai clenched her teeth against the noise, fists curling, willing it away.

The bolt on her door echoed as it moved, and Kai rolled her shoulders, her long sleeves ruffling.

Her visitor was short, only a teen, definitely not a seasoned fighter. The striking thing, beyond the high-pitched voice and heels, was the line of fluffy stubble attempting to grow on his face. His cloak bore an insignia she vaguely recognised but could not place. He looked as imposing as a duckling.

"I hear you've given my people a lot of trouble."

How could a teenager have *people?* "I'm not trying to cause any trouble," Kai said. "You brought me here. Any moves I've made in self-defence have been your own fault. Left alone, I could continue on my way."

"I'm not about to let you leave."

Kai narrowed her eyes. "I have things to do."

"Then it seems we have a conflict of interest."

"People resolve conflicts all the time." Behind her back, Kai tightened her grip on the shiv she'd crafted and tensed her legs.

He looked her up and down. "You are in no position to fight."

Perfect. People underestimated her, because looks were deceptive. That had kept her alive more than once. She made a mental note not to make the same mistake with this boy.

Kai lunged forward, shiv in hand, aiming for the boy's neck. It wasn't much, but it was amazing the damage a scissor blade could do.

He spun around lightly, one hand seizing her wrist, twisting the shiv away from him so it lightly scratched his neck. But he bled. She landed a kick in his stomach as the shiv clattered on the floor. He grunted, but kept his balance, bracing himself against the doorway. She slammed her fist into his face.

She heard feet running, a bottle smashing in a distant room. Using the wall as an anchor, the teen pushed himself at her, grappling her torso and throwing her down. She twisted as she fell, fists flying wide as she crashed onto her hip.

Footsteps. Two men ran in from the adjoining room, one of them clearly drunk. They pulled the boy from the doorway.

"This isn't over." The boy spat as the guards hustled him from the room. Her door slammed, and Kai heard the bolt slide home.

She shoved the boy's keys in her pocket, grabbed the shiv, and pulled her satchel from under the bed.

Taking a deep breath, she rolled the blanket around her arm, pulled a hat down over her forehead, and looked back at the room. She had everything of use, including the remaining scissor blade for a second shiv. It was a good job they no longer carried guns, else she'd have had no chance. But the police had seized many gangs' weapons, and supplies were short. Still, she was tired, and they knew she had a weapon. Now was her best chance to escape.

She wrenched the little set of drawers across the door, and turned to face the setting sun.

She wouldn't look down. It would be simple. People did this all the time.

Kai forced her cushioned fist through the window, wincing at the sound of shattering glass. Not risking second thoughts, she pulled herself over the edge, flattening the blanket over the bottom sill, where sharp glass poked up, and rolled through the gap. Then the bile hit her throat. She swallowed it back, trying to keep her breathing steady as her stomach contemplated injury. *Death is worse than a few bruises.*

Ignoring the pain in her hip as she twisted to get a solid grasp, Kai clung on with both hands until her body lay flat against the brick. Death could bring peace, but a crippled body was the worst possible fate.

She was wheezing now, the sound like a cornered animal crying for its mother. Then the banging on her door began. If she didn't go now, she'd be re-captured, tortured and likely killed.

People had survived much worse. With a prayer to the ancestors, she slammed her mouth shut on an instinctive scream, pulled the blanket down and let herself drop.

*

THE STREETS OF Brighton were notoriously wild, filled with colours and dancing, with gulls as large as foxes, and people of every age and shape. But they were too loud for Kai.

She was sick of running into fights, of joining crews who only wanted to exploit her powers. She just wanted to get home. And without a real home to return to, that gave her only one option. Still, she had the compass, taken from a Royalist's body, and she knew about the flame. She just needed answers, and the blessing of the Gods.

They would be able to track her here, through the cobbled streets and paved alleys. She trod carefully through the forest that draped around the edge of town, heading for the cliffs. Her hip burned as the hill steepened, and she struggled for breath. Despite the intermittent gusts of wind, it was much quieter here, and she took a few moments to meditate as she reached the open field at the summit. Dunnocks chirped, little brown specks flitting in and out of the tall grass. A magpie clacked in a nearby tree. The Royals might track her to the city's edge, but here she had the advantage.

After a brief rest to catch her breath, curled up in the shade at the base of a clump of bushes, Kai continued her journey. She was careful to duck and weave through the trees, and walked a little through a small stream. She was shivering now, but wet feet were a cheap price to pay to keep her safe. She smiled as she heard the bark of foxes echoing up from the distant streets. Hopefully they'd followed her out of the city.

The monastery looked like any of the cottages nestled among these hills, with an idyllic view of the sea, gazing over the remains of the burned down West Pier, sticking out of the sea like discarded scaffolding. The Scottish Buddhists had set up home here, running their sessions in the centre of town, but living away from the city and their origins. From the outside, the two buildings could have belonged to anyone, with pale blue cement for walls, and little windows which were never closed. She knew the lama stayed somewhere out here, near the cliffs at the edge of town.

It took all Kai's strength to turn away, to head down the other side of the hill she had climbed, back into the bustle of the lanes. She could not risk the open country of the South Downs; she would return instead to her tutor in town. The Downs had seemed a sensible direction to head after her escape, but she needed to meet up with Duncan. She could only hope her childhood here would encourage him to help.

Anyone tracking her would be thoroughly lost in the trees behind her, and would likely not search the city now she had made sure she was seen leaving.

Pulling the blanket over her head, she walked past closed store fronts and along the cobbled walkways. She was heading for the seafront, for the quiet kind of darkness offered by the pebble beach; where the final stars were just visible above the pollution.

The lights of the pier were the brightest thing for miles, the city quiet as her watch ticked past five thirty. As morning rose, tinted pink sunlight streaked through grey sky.

The blanket around her swished in time to her footsteps as she passed a man who had slept another night on the pavement. She frowned at his frost-covered coat, the only difference from yesterday.

Sat ready for the six o'clock commuters, he was already organised; huddled on the corner, coughing out the words of his trade into clouds of condensation. Yet as he tried to sell the Big Issue by the bus station, people walked straight past, often without a glance his way.

Kai offered him what she hoped was a reassuring smile, and stepped onto the pebbles. The crunch underfoot took some adjusting to, but it was a pretty sound if she didn't try to block it out. A gull squawked over the waters, sunlight shimmered off the Channel. Nothing spoke to her like the sound of ocean waves. When she concentrated, she swore she could hear the hushed conversations of marine life.

Her breathing slowed, and she let herself enjoy the view as she inhaled the scents of modern city life. Chips served to drunk students at three am littered the beach, and brought the gulls down to land. At this distance, she almost liked the smell.

After a walk through the streets to re-orient herself with the city she'd once known well, she checked her watch. The centre wouldn't officially be open yet, but someone should be there from seven.

Brighton Buddhist Centre lay in the heart of the city; a tall brick terraced building that had been a block of offices a few years before. The door was hidden down one of the cobbled side streets of the Lanes, used only as a short cut to reach shops at the other end of town. That brought a calming sense of safety for someone seeking shelter.

She knocked gently and entered without waiting for a response. Although they would not be expecting her, she knew nearly everyone, and if the building was unlocked someone must be in. She passed the cloakroom, swapping her ripped blanket for a plain coat, and took the steps up to the main community room, following the smell of incense, wincing as her left side creaked. She'd landed badly from her escape, but between her left knee and right hip, she was managing.

Orange and red hangings adorned the ochre walls, decorated with depictions of the Buddha, tigers and a serpent. But she heard nothing. No chanting, no music . . . An uneasy feeling crept up her spine. An ambulance siren screeched outside.

"Hello?"

She stepped into the upper room, the floorboards groaning too loudly. The room was bright, with white walls, and the far wall was covered in a mural of some icon she did not recognise. A few mats rested on the floor. Kai wondered why the incense still burned, and why the door had been unlocked, if the place were truly empty.

She checked the other two rooms; a small study on her right and a little bedroom on the left. Both were deserted. She could only hope the Royals hadn't tracked her here. Gulls squawked outside, shrieking to greet the day and blotting out all other sounds.

When she walked back down to the reception at the front of the building, she saw a figure approaching from the end of the hall.

"Duncan?"

The figure didn't change stride, but as he neared, her shoulders relaxed. Duncan wasn't a true Buddhist, but he was the receptionist and servant of the lama. He was the main contact between her lodgings by the cliffs and the city's hub. Kai had heard rumours, though the lady's arrival had been a quiet one – the only female member of her order believed to have been reborn as enlightened.

"Kai. Good to see you again."

She bowed her head as Duncan approached, stepping to one side so he could enter the building. "Your timing isn't the best."

She followed him back inside. "I'm sorry," she said. "What's going on?"

Duncan sighed, halting. Nearly a foot taller than her, with broad shoulders, he took up most of the space in the corridor. "You come seeking shelter from your troubles. We cannot put the community at risk."

Kai clutched her stomach, trying to hold in the sinking butterfly feelings. She couldn't have come all this way for nothing. She had to gain access to the centre to have any chance at finding it. "I don't know what to offer."

"You will have been followed. If you have not been found already, you soon will be. You are in danger, but you coming here puts us in danger too. I believe the lama will ask much of you."

"But I am a Circlet member."

Duncan scratched under his ginger beard. "You have been chosen, but you must still earn your place. We will not turn you away, but she will expect you to devote yourself to serving the community, just as you did when you were last here."

Kai swallowed. She'd always found comfort in her get-out clause. Circlet girls were chosen as children to follow the path, and they were thought to be blessed by Tara, a female representation of Buddhist enlightenment. She shouldn't need to complete any pilgrimage or temple tasks, or need to explain her circumstances. The last time she'd been caught, in London, she'd hidden in one of the devotees dormitory rooms with no questions asked.

"Why the change in the rules?" she asked. As a child, she'd merely kept her room tidy and attended the ceremonies. They would ask more of her now.

"I do not know. We have a new leader since the last assassination – a lama by the name of Sinead Rinpoche. Since the situation is so particular, I can take you to her."

"Thank you, I think that would be best."

He picked up a backpack, emptying out some rocks, a few bottles of water and some dirt-covered rope, which he substituted with a thicker and cleaner one. He exchanged his raincoat for another; this one a dark green shade, and settled the bag upon his back once more. It was important to keep the lama's location hidden, and Kai glanced down at her jeans, black anorak and skeleton satchel. She wasn't exactly camouflaged, but she preferred to keep her belongings with her.

"Come."

Kai followed Duncan towards the ocean without comment, her stomach somersaulting as she tried to recall what she had heard about the trials the Scottish Buddhists put people through. There was an undisclosed test of faith, often described as facing the fear of one's own mortality. She shivered as she remembered all the times she'd thought she might die. At least she was no stranger to the contemplation of her end.

The heavy cloud cover kept the day from brightening too much, and few people were out at this hour. And the fewer people, the less noise. They walked past the Pavilion, heading through the gardens to reach the hill which would lead up towards the monastery.

She tried to shrink herself, uncertain how safe it was to be travelling in the open. But Duncan had known her as a child – if he felt it was safe to move, she trusted him. Still, her instincts were difficult to ignore.

In the distance, to the north, she could make out the protrusions from the Duke's Picture House; the stripe-covered legs extended into the sky; giving the impression that someone had fallen through the roof. Apart from making Brighton the quirky place it was, the Picture House was a good landmark for keeping her oriented,

The grass was damp, and Kai found her pace slowing, lagging behind Duncan, taking care not to slip as they climbed the hill. Eventually, they were only a few metres from the edge of the cliffs. One mis-step and she could tumble right into the sea.

It was quieter here, and the smell was markedly better, although the water and wind brought their own voices to the air around her.

"You are well, though?" Duncan's voice was distant. Having heightened hearing didn't help her pick his voice out over the wind.

She resisted the urge to shout her response. "I am. Are you?"

"Indeed."

He had never been a big talker, but she'd not known him before he enrolled, which she understood often altered people's language. Someone seeking enlightenment would be aware of the impact of their words upon those around them.

He led her closer to the edge, where the air was tainted with the salt ocean spray. She had forgotten how easy it was to walk from city to national park. She tensed as they reached the overhang, eyes scanning the horizon for any sign of followers.

Gulls chattered away and she spied a guillemot bobbing about on the waves as they crashed against the rock-face. *Don't focus on the sounds.* She'd be overwhelmed if she tried to single out any sound, so she kept her attention fixed on her other senses. Her nose wrinkled at the strength of smells, seaweed and droppings colliding with fresh scent of the sea.

"Here we go." Duncan knelt beside the edge of a worn crevice, and attached his rope to a hook drilled into the rock. He tossed the rope over the edge, and stood back expectantly.

Kai froze.

"Would you like to go first, or second?"

Kai clamped her mouth shut before her answer could escape her. *Neither.* "I . . . I don't understand."

Duncan showed no loss of patience or frustration. But she felt the weight of his stare.

"I didn't realise. I . . ." *Oh stop stuttering Kai.* "I'm sorry. I'd like to go second, please."

He nodded, and with a surprising amount of grace for such a large man, he lowered himself over the precipice in a single motion, vanishing from view. Kai had never rock-climbed in her life, and the idea of grappling down a cliff-face didn't sound like fun to her.

A first storey window in an attempt to avoid death was a much different situation to willingly clambering onto a rope over a cliff.

She knelt beside the rope, telling herself not to look down. She let herself breathe heavily for a few moments, to release the panic in her chest. Then a shout from below snapped her out of it. She had to go now, before she lost her nerve completely. This had to be part of the test.

Slowly, she crawled around to face the field, eyes locking on the crest of the hill. Then she stepped backwards, careful to tense her arms and grip the rope carefully. She whispered to herself, though she could barely hear her own voice over the roaring wind. "It's just like back home, stepping back onto the ladder from the attic. Come on, Kai."

But when her feet scrabbled and failed to find a foothold, the panic surged once more. She was going to fall and die. Or worse, she'd survive, but be a vegetable. Her hip twinged, as if warning her against the possibility. If this was just the journey to speak with the lama, what would the test be?

But as she panicked, her body began to respond to her aching arms and she slowly descended the rope. She'd taken on many missions and always come out okay. Her movements were stiff and her wrists throbbed, but she was getting nearer.

She remembered Duncan packing the rope, coil after coil – just how long was it? How far down would she need to descend?

By the time she gathered the nerve to look down, she was only a few metres from a rocky lip. She let herself drop the last couple of feet, sighing deeply.

"Duncan?" The man was gone.

There was a small crevice cut into the rock, but she could see no light or movement within. She would need to crawl, if this was the only opening.

"Kai?" His voice came from below her.

You have got to be kidding.

She glanced over the edge, and saw him, another forty feet below her. This time, she moved before the fear could manifest. She grasped the rope again, and swung herself over the edge, slithering down as fast as her hands could shift.

He put an arm out to steady her as she landed, the rest of the rope pooling at her feet. "Here we are. Remember to be respectful."

They were on a small rocky beach. Kai resisted the urge to bend over, hands on knees, and pant away the terror. She had to act like a Circlet member. She was a dignified and blessed being, after all.

She glanced back towards the city, hidden from where she stood by the curve of the cliffs. She could still see the remains of the pier, jutting out into the sea, and that brought her comfort. Although the ocean birds drowned out the city's noises, she wasn't too far away.

When they stepped inside the cave, her skin prickled at the temperature change, and she was able to see light glowing at the end of a long tunnel. A few hangings decorated the walls, and candles rested in metal holders, spaced at regular intervals. At the far end of the tunnel, a shadow against the light, a figure sat in the lotus position. She wore orange robes, and she was young and pale, her blonde hair tied in a bun. Scottish travellers had taken the Buddhist teachings and made their own sect on the edge of Brighton's bohemian lifestyle. This woman was a modern, Brighton-style Rinpoche, complete with eyebrow piercing and an aqua streak through one side of her hair.

Kai swallowed, and approached, lagging slightly behind Duncan. It was so strange to come from the bustle of buzzing community into a quiet, dark cave. She'd been brought up in Brighton, and had learned many teachings from them, but in theory, Circlet girls were separate from all the different factions. She could only hope they would lend her aid. The lama met her eyes and smiled benignly. One of the knots in Kai's stomach dissolved.

"You seek shelter?" Her voice was pleasant, without cruelty. Perhaps she could see reason.

"Yes." Kai bowed her head, cursing herself for not remembering the proper address. Her training had been thorough, but a decade of fending for herself had eroded many of the customs she'd been taught as a child. "I request the hospitality of the monastery, and of the Brighton Buddhist Centre. I am a devotee of the Circlet, and I am in danger."

Sinead Rinpoche continued to smile. "Living is dangerous, for us all."

Kai scrambled through Duncan's words, seeking something to offer the lama. "I wish to share my teachings."

"And to learn, no?"

Kai hesitated, looking around. On one side, the tunnel opened out into a small side room with a table; separated from the main tunnel by a carved archway. "Yes. To learn of your teachings, your dharma."

The smile didn't change. "You will remain with us for a while, even once the threat has passed. We will clothe and shelter you, help you to prepare meals. And in return you shall teach us combat."

Kai felt her cheeks burn. "Combat, Your Holiness?"

"We do not fight yet."

"Fighting is not a noble cause. I had hoped to avoid it here."

The lama's eyes closed. "The Royalists force our hand, and we fear the wars in Asia and Russia will soon find us."

Kai bit her lip. What could she say to that?

Footsteps sounded behind them, and Kai followed Duncan as he stepped to one side. The lama's expression did not change.

Something familiar about the boy set off Kai's internal alarms.

She looked at Duncan, and then at the lama; neither had moved. The two servants behind the lama's chair stood with neutral expressions. This was the sanctuary of an important order member. If her memory served her, visitors were very rare. Yet the boy seemed to know the way, and Duncan did not question him. He walked up to the lama, bowed, and extended one hand, holding the other in his cloak.

Kai weighed up her options in a moment of hesitation. Was he naïve, or did he harbour a weapon?

He bowed his head a second time, holding eye contact with the Rinpoche. That was not a mistake. He shifted slightly, and Kai sensed the tightening of his muscles. She tensed in return, holding her legs steady and keeping her breath slow. Three, two, one . . .

Kai pounced, twisting her body between them. The boy's blade struck hers, the thrum of metal echoing in her mind until she felt dizzy and they both leapt back. The boy's face remained neutral. That was not a good sign.

Duncan spoke, but did not move. After all, he was no fighter. "Times are tough, Kai. Fighters follow you, and we are not prepared."

Kai recognised the insignia on the boy's wrist from her captor's cape. The feud between two sets of supposed pacifists had grown out of control. Why would they send a child here, to do such a task? It didn't make sense. She cast her senses over him, but could find nothing useful behind his composure. He was a young boy who had intended to see the lama, and he had brought a knife.

Sinead Rinpoche spoke behind her, the lama's voice no different from before. "Combat can be important, and fighting is sometimes needed to bring peace." Had she planned this fight just to prove her point?

Kai shook her head, meeting the boy's gaze. "Be careful. If you're not trained in the blade, you're just as likely to cut yourself as your opponent."

The boy narrowed his eyes, lunging to one side. "I am Sol. I have been trained to defend, and to kill."

His eyes flickered the instant before he attacked, and she dodged to block him once more. Her shiv strained against his dagger; the scissor point pulling away from the tape with the tension.

She growled through gritted teeth. "Stop this."

The child's voice was full of venom. "She persecutes us. She must die."

Kai nearly laughed. "She will only be reborn. Don't waste your life for this."

The child hissed, swiping at Kai's arm with his dagger. "It is already gone."

Many thought of Buddhists as peaceful people, ignoring those who showed their dedication using fire. Self-immolation was not often seen in Britain, but the Royalists had been "invaded' by their Scottish beliefs, and they would fight despite claiming to take vows of pacifism. The flame of the Circlets, the one she sought, was an artefact everyone appeared to deem worthy of violence. Especially to those who lived here. It had, after all, been discovered in Brighton's land.

The blade tore a strip from her ruffled sleeve, lightly scoring her flesh. Sol hadn't lied: he wasn't new to fighting. "You wish to learn of combat? Loose clothing is a hindrance in many aspects of battle, but your opponent cannot accurately place your body for arrows or hits."

Kai swiped forward, slicing the boy's shoulder pad; careful not to break his skin. He couldn't be older than ten. She'd never harmed a child this young.

The boy's anger reddened his face, and his breathing became laboured. He may have had some training in the techniques, but his stamina was lacking.

Rinpoche Sinead bowed her head. "Thank you, Sol. You have shown Kai our request. You may rest now."

Kai saw the confusion in his eyes. Had this been a set up? The boy was straining, still poised to attack. He thought himself proficient enough to kill, yet he wavered at a single comment. As long as she wasn't cocky, Kai might be able to undermine him just by sharing her knowledge.

Then Duncan was between them, cutting off any more conversation. "You will cease fighting by your own control, or be forced into submission. Either way, you shall not continue to fight. Which will it be, child?"

"I'm not a child, I'm eleven! And you will pay for your actions." Sol lunged for Duncan, but the man merely grabbed the boy's wrist, and picked him up with a sweeping arm around his waist. The dagger dropped to the floor.

The Royalists had brought this child up to hate, so early on in his life. Fury passed through Kai, and the desire for vengeance. She held it in check. She was leaving that behind; leaving all of this politics behind once she found it. For now, she was in front of her new teacher, and she needed her support.

Sinead Rinpoche spoke. "Let him pass."

Kai stepped back, and Duncan replaced Sol on the ground. Now the boy's face paled, and his hand began to shake. His gaze darted around the room, although his body remained still. Sinead Rinpoche remained seated. "Do you wish to learn of our ways? You are welcome to stay and eat with us."

"So you can poison me?"

"So we can learn about each other. I wish to understand your hurt. Kai here can teach you to defend yourself, if you treat us with respect. But you are not going to harm me."

Kai watched him carefully. His face paled further, and his left hand trembled a little. "I . . . I need to check with . . ."

"You will stay for lunch. You would be most welcome. After all, you cannot leave."

Then Duncan stood behind him, blocking the way out. The child nodded, a whimper escaping his lips as another robed figure came into the cave and nodded at the Rinpoche. She led Sol to a side room in the cavern, where a table lay ready for a meal. It must be strange to walk in to kill and be calmly invited to lunch.

The Royalists clearly hadn't trained him too well. That meant something greater was to come. He would only be a messenger; one they didn't expect to get back. Kai shook her head. She needed to focus on her role, which was not to protect this clan from the Royals. She was just here for the box.

The lama turned her head to face Kai.

"You have passed the test of faith," she said. "You overcame fear and anger while in this room, and defended us as you saw fit. I request that you take a robe and return to the centre. Meditate for a day and a night. Duncan will accompany you and will see that you are not traced by the Royals. While here, you are under our protection."

Kai swallowed. "I thank you, Holiness." The term did not seem to anger the lama. Perhaps she remembered more than she'd thought. She stepped towards the other room, but was stopped by the same robed figure at the arched separation. The visual block stirred questions in her mind, and she fought the urge to ask them aloud.

Sinead continued to speak. "You will train us in combat, and in lieu of a pilgrimage or service, you will ascertain this boy's beliefs and train him to support us. He is . . . important."

Kai could hear the child sobbing in the other room. Did everything have to be a riddle? "With all due respect, Holiness, I cannot train an enemy."

"He is a child, led only by his peers and his guardians. Now, we are his guardians. He wants answers, and we can help him find them."

Kai swallowed a sigh. She wouldn't be here long enough to worry about the boy. But his presence did spark her curiosity. "What do they want, sending children to fight us?"

"To unnerve us, and to persuade us to give them the flame."

Kai fought to keep her expression in check. Everyone wanted the sacred flame. That was why the Circlets had been chosen and trained to fight.

Kai hesitated an instant, knowing it was rude to ask. "He was not an actor for my test?"

"He was, but I knew he agreed because it presented a true opportunity."

Duncan stepped forward. "The Royalists have been sending children to give us messages, assuming we will not harm those who pose so little threat. We give them a chance to hear our answers to their questions, and try to answer theirs, so they may learn of the true way."

"And if they maintain the Royalist viewpoint?"

Duncan looked at the floor, and while Sinead met her gaze, Kai looked away from the lama's eyes. "I see," she said.

The other robed woman held out a folded set of robes to Kai. She took them, twisting to see around the servant into the next room. The boy's face was hunched over a table, staring through tears at a slice of dry bread. His whimpering had died down. With a quick glance around the room, she bowed to the lama and retreated back up the tunnel to the beach with Duncan in tow. She would find no more answers here.

*

MEDITATION CAME EASILY at first, following the thrum of music at a nearby club, and the chatter of people at bus stops, but within an hour, her thoughts began to chatter again. Wearing robes over her jeans offered some comfort from the hard floor of the Buddhist centre. She was ruminating on the day, reviewing every detail. This was how she had learned to fight, learned how to survive without the monastery's protection. Reliving the moments of her fights, she noticed things she had been too busy to see at the time. The dining area had marked the end of the cavern: one long tunnel to an open chamber, where the Rinpoche sat, and then a curve to the left into a small side room with the table. And that was it. So where did they keep everything? There had been a wooden chest on one side of the cavern room, and more wall hangings.

She had to locate it. Did they really keep it here in the centre?

She ran through the surrounding area in her head, careful not to discard any of the information of her senses. There was a little hut behind the centre, and another room on the ground floor. Either could hold the shrine.

She had been in every room in the building, and nothing stood out as the artefact's resting place, which left only a few options.

She could sense Duncan bumbling around the centre, getting ready to sleep. After another hour, she heard him settle. She had to be swift. Standing up, Kai moved her muscles slightly, testing the creak of each floorboard before placing her weight down. She made it to the door, which remained open enough for her to squeeze through. She kept her attention on her hearing, listening for both a sign of Duncan stirring, and her own movements.

She shivered as she reached the hallway, content that he hadn't woken from his sleep or meditation. She just needed to see it, to know it was here. Then she could act.

The door squeaked a little as she opened it, but the garden behind the centre was inviting in the darkness, and a large shed at the edge of the grass looked promising.

The noise outside rose quickly, and she had to dive back indoors, covering her ears. A club like the Pav Tav must be serving last orders, turning up the music for their encore. There were negatives to having a religious space within a city. She squinted, pushing through the immediate headache to make out lyrics. Slipknot; their classic ending track for a Tuesday night. Some things never changed.

She remained by the door for a few minutes, controlling her breathing and bringing herself back to the present moment. It would pass soon, and then her ears would forget the beats that were trampling her to death.

It was a long five minutes, but as the music fell away, chattering people were a welcome substitute, barely a nuisance in comparison. She scanned the nearby rooms for Duncan, but found nothing to worry about.

Once more venturing into the garden, she crept up the path towards the shed. It looked more like a temple, with deep orange walls and a statue of the Buddha by the back door. Rather than risk the noise of entering, she hunkered down by the window to listen. A woodlouse crawled across the sill, but nothing larger than ants stirred inside.

She crawled through the window, careful to slide quietly across the table on the other side, avoiding the chair in case it creaked. The shed was larger than it had first appeared, with two or three rooms. She crept through to the main room, the corridor's burnt umber walls reminding her of all the bloodshed this mission had required. The main room was lighter, with candles illuminating the corners, bringing a sunflower hue to the walls.

A figure in a deep red robe and sandals rested in a chair across from the mantelpiece. But she could see it, resting above the dusty fireplace. Nothing else mattered.

The box was slightly bigger than her palm. The lid was up, and the flame swayed in its little pool of wax. She couldn't risk it. Kai crept up to the sleeping monk, and pulled a bandana from her robe pocket, folding it to cover the man's eyes and mouth. She pulled it tightly around his head. The monk struggled for a moment, but the powder worked swiftly, and he would not wake for a couple of hours. His body slumped in the chair, but she had already turned back to the flame.

Much like the holy relics of fantasy, the owner could change everything with this one item. The legend had started small, and even the Circlets were not sure what power it possessed. But they had been charged as its keepers.

And she'd found it. Now she could complete her work; taking it home to study its use. She lifted the wooden box down, careful not to let the flame flicker too much. It was intricately designed; with swirls and leaves carved into the golden lid and sides. The design had been perfected over centuries, the air-holes in the lid allowing the monks to carry fire with them wherever they went. It would allow the candle to remain burning even when it was shut in her bag. And now it was in her hands. She had really done it. She could finally return home.

She closed the lid carefully, pushing against the stiffness of the hinge, and taking stock of the other supplies around the room. A few circles of charcoal, a vial of sacred oil, and a discarded head scarf hanging on the corner of the mantle. She could always use more supplies.

Then she zipped up her bag and left the shed, heading back towards the city. Mission complete; time to go home.

A lone seagull squawked in the night, when most birds were already roosting. The constant light of lampposts and sound of club music was not a problem for them. But amidst the bird's chatter, she could hear the clinking of glasses and slurred laughter as the city wound down for the morning.

Duncan stood at the bottom of the path, his eyes narrowed. Her heart skipped a beat or two, and she clasped her hands together to keep them from shaking. Kai shuffled her weight to secure the straps of her backpack over her shoulders, and waited for him to move.

"You know you are not to enter the temple."

Kai did not reply.

"It is a good thing that the other members arrived this evening. With this indiscretion, it appears now they must oversee your sentence." He pulled out a bell, ringing it softly in the night air. It was much like the ones used in her training as a child. "You have broken your vow. You will be taken to the quarry until you understand the impact of your actions."

Kai's heart hammered. Mairi had survived the quarry. There had always been risk in this mission, but she had not anticipated Duncan involving the other Circlet girls. This would be interesting.

She cast out her senses, glowering at Duncan as she sensed his anger. "You've called them here?" She could hear the swish of a coat, the distant thrum of an engine. Then the air fell quiet, and movement became her main focus.

His eyes narrowed. "You should have known better. You're not the only one with the discipline to learn how our senses work. I didn't realise you were so foolish."

Kai didn't respond. Two figures were approaching through the side gate.

Aileen held a bow over her shoulder, a quiver of arrows hanging from the other, and Mairi flashed Kai a smile as they approached. Two other Circlets, girls pledged like herself, stood behind the servant of the lama; dressed in jeans and black hoodies.

Duncan spoke again, more for the new arrivals' benefit than for Kai's. "I declare you a prisoner of our faith, for your broken promise and the desecration of our temple."

Aileen stepped forward, readying an arrow.

Mairi remained behind her. "What do you say to this charge, Kai?" Her Scottish accent muffled the words, but Kai could work out what she'd meant. They'd been friends, a few years back.

"I have it. Let me go."

Duncan glanced at the girls, startled. "Have what?"

Kai stepped forward, pulling the box from her pack. The others wouldn't believe her unless she showed them anyway, so she may as well reveal it now. Besides, the look on Duncan's face would be priceless.

The man's eyes widened, and then the wind hit him. His eyes remained open as he hit the ground, Aileen's arrow through his throat.

He wouldn't be the last one to die for this mission.

Aileen stepped forward. "It is done."

The girls huddled up to Kai, shielding the box from the wind as she tilted the lid up on its hinge.

Mairi let out a deep breath. "You did it."

"*We* did it." Aileen corrected her. "Just think of all we can achieve."

Kai nodded, returning the box to her pack. It would be light in a few hours. If they took the train now, they'd make it back tomorrow. "Time to head home and get to work."

Kai put her bag down and lifted her robes over her head; folding them up and placing them by the door. Now they were all camouflaged: each wearing the official uniform of jeans and hoodies.

As Kai slid her backpack on again, Mairi followed her gaze out to the North. "What will they do when we return?"

Kai flashed her teeth and followed them back to the gate. Their return to the Highlands had been willed for years, but none of their cult leaders would expect them so soon. They had been like the coyote, stealing fire from under the noses of its master. Linking arms on the street outside the centre, she led them across the grass towards the station.

"They shall call us heroes: the three Circlets who achieved the impossible. They shall finally take notice of the girls who stole fire from the Gods."

The Quality of Light

KT Davies

*B*ATTLES SHOULDN'T BE *fought on days like this,* Alyda thought as the sun broke clean across an ice bright sky. It reminded her of another spring morning, long ago and far removed from today, in every way save for the quality of the light.

They had reached the beach in time to watch the faint shadows of night lift, leaving a band of bright gold around the blued rim of the world. The pearling glory of the sunrise hurt her eyes, printed a haloed image on her vision. Her grandfather was walking up the beach, head down, threading a path between the beams of light that glanced off the salt glazed rocks, off the gleaming helmets . . .

"We're fucking fucked." Sergeant Latham propped his halberd against the crossed pike doorway of the tent and threw his helm onto a straw pallet.

Alyda was watching a column of warriors marching over the brow of the hill, sunlight flashing across their helmets and flaring off the blades of their weapons. "In what particular way are we fucked today, Will?"

The sergeant's pock-marked face was scarlet, his grey hair plastered to his forehead, steam rose off his gambeson. "They've shoved us back over the bridge. Fucking archers have their heads up their arses as usual, and we can't take the horses down that bank. Fucked! Anyway, Captain's ordered the Company t'form up at the bottom of the hill." He blew his nose into his hand and wiped it on his leg.

"We're going in on foot?" Alarm tainted Loridan's question.

Alyda turned to her fellow knight. He was the colour of curdled milk. "So it would seem," she said. And so it began.

It felt like she was sinking into a snowdrift. The tension in her muscles —built up over the course of a week of hard riding— released as the first flush of ice water ran through her limbs. Her fingers tingled, anticipation fluttered in her gut. It was almost unpleasant; to shiver so softly, so constantly. She felt light, as though she was made of air. They spoke of "the heat of battle', but for her, when that moment of certainty came, it was always cold.

She pulled on her gauntlets, worked her fingers deep into the gloves while her page fastened the buckle of her bevor. Her arming cap was close fitting, tightly quilted; it muffled sound, but she could still hear the din of battle rising out of the valley beyond the hill. It was a hard, brutal noise, laden with the promise of pain. A fickle wind gusted from the north bringing with it the rank stench of slaughter.

Latham downed a flagon of murky beer, picked up his helm, and limped through the camp to where the company was massing at the bottom of the hill. Alyda shrugged her shoulders, flexed her arms, checked that every lace was tight and every buckle fastened. "Come on Lori, it's time to go."

Loridan didn't get up. He was sitting on a straw bale, turning his helmet in his hands. "They hung that deserter from the 12th Lancers," he said, staring hard at the ground. "This morning, before dawn. Stripped him of his armour and hung him in the orchard by that village."

"They hung him for stealing; desertion would have earned him a flogging. He knew the penalty for theft."

"He just took the horse to get away."

"It wasn't his horse to take. Now come on."

At twenty, Loridan was almost three years older than Alyda. He was a passionless man, often pensive, always dour; the kind of person who would remember if a single drop of rain fell on an otherwise cloudless day. "I can't do it. I've tried, but I can't."

"Yes you can. Come on."

He slammed his helmet into the dirt; put his head in his hands. "You don't understand, nothing bothers you, you're always so . . ."

"Cold?"

"Aye."

She shook her head. "Not in the way you think. You just have to find a way through the fear."

"I don't . . . What do you mean?"

"Asha's paps, this isn't your first fight. How did you get through the others? Mallon's Reach? Kasmire?"

"I don't know . . . I just did."

"Then do it again."

"How do you do it? How do you find a way through the fear?"

"How did you do that, Grandfather?"

"Do what?"

"How did you walk through the light?"

He laughed and brushed sand from her face. "The trick is, never look at anything square on. You have to be like a horse, keep the light in the corner of your eye and just keep going forward, and then you'll find your way through."

"Is it magic?"

"Aye, perhaps it is."

"They say you're supposed to face your fear," she said. "My advice is, don't. Keep it in mind, but it'll scare you less if you don't look at it square on. Now get up."

They made their way through the camp in silence. Three hundred knights and soldiers of the king's army were gathered here, ready to push north to the borders and send the marauding Tamalak warbands back where they came from. What had been pasture a week before had been churned to a mire by the soldiers ploughing back and forth between the camp and the bridge which lay beyond the hill to the north.

The weary faces of those returned from the fray told the tale of an ugly, scrappy fight. Both sides were bogged down, the bridge between them like a hare caught in the jaws of two hounds, neither willing to give up the prize.

Loridan fell behind and had to run to catch up with her. Wisps of yellow hair had escaped his helmet and glinted in the sunlight. "Wait," he gasped. "I can hardly breathe."

"Me neither," she said, as they joined their company and waited for their turn to climb the hill.

"You don't mean that."

"Just remember what I said."

"I can't do it, not again."

"You don't have a choice."

Light drew her eye to the warriors coming down the hill as it danced across their blood-stained armour, casting them as shadows beneath a filigreed sheen. Alyda blinked away the ghostly images imprinted on her vision, and fixed her gaze on the ridge where a brisk wind agitated their unsullied standard. The measured thunder of war drums echoed across the valley beyond the hill — a rhythmic counterpoint to the rough descant of clashing steel and dying screams.

Loridan clutched his sword to his chest. Neither helm nor mail seemed to fit him; he looked awkward, out of place. "Are you scared?" he asked her. The blustery wind snatched the words from his mouth, thinning the tone to a reedy whisper. Alyda looked at her companion, at the fear shining in his eyes, at the way the breeze spun the errant strands of his hair into a wiry halo.

"I suppose I must be." She couldn't begin to explain that she felt hollow, without substance, as though at any moment she might fly apart; sundered by her dissonant heart.

Her grandfather outpaced her, and vanished in the golden brume that boiled off the sea. Shackled by the ringing surf she watched him appear again, as he cut between the bars of light reflecting off the beach, off the pikes and halberds . . .

The ringing chant of harness marked the brisk pace of their march to the brow of the hill, where Alyda unslung her shield and drew her sword. The hill was just as steep on the other side; half of a sharp v, joined by a river and spanned by a wooden bridge, now thronged with knights in heavy armour and painted Tamalak warriors.

Light raced across the scrubby defile, pierced the cloud-borne shade and ribboned across the valley. Silver and gold flashed from the churning water, gilded helms and blades, casting an undeserved glamour over the carnage. The unarmoured Tamalak warriors held the bridge; their mounting dead a bulwark, their burnished spears a deadly thicket. But inch by inch, the press was moving across the splintering planks. Men and women swarmed both banks, scarred the ground with their blood, and marred the quiet earth with their fury.

"I can't do it, Ali. I can't." Loridan started to back through the rank coming up behind them.

She grabbed his arm and dragged him over the brow. Stones skittered under his reluctant step. "You can't go back," she said. "Lock your shield against mine."

Stumbling and numbed by fear, Loridan did as he was bid. Alyda slammed down her visor. They closed ranks, files compressed, the pace quickened. She was carried along on the roaring tide with Loridan beside her, their cries lost in the tumult.

The first, shuddering impact was when they hit the rank in front. The second, when the rank behind hit them. Driven forward, the lightness vanished. She was part of the wall now, part of the rolling mass of steel. She dropped her weight through her body and dug in. To lose her footing here, to fall amid the press, meant certain death.

The world narrowed to the slit in her visor, the sky became a flickering wing of blue, glimpsed through the fanning bones of polearms being brought to bear. She used her shield as a lever against the back of her comrade, opened the slightest breathing space, and gulped a mouthful of fetid air. A spear thrust between the two knights in front of her. She thrust her sword along the shaft, cut flesh. The knight in front fell against her. Thinking he'd lost his footing, she tried to shore him up using her shield as a brace. He half turned and grasped her shoulder for support. His lifeblood was pumping from his neck in a pulsing flow. He coughed in her face, sprayed blood across her visor as death stole his final breath. Half blind, the taste of sweet iron in her mouth, she stumbled sideways, felt the handrail of the bridge against her hip. The press heaved, the rail cracked and splintered before failing completely.

She closed her mouth against the breathtaking gasp summoned by the hard drop into the icy river. Water surged into her helm, hissed in her ears. All around her she could feel the heavy thumps of bodies hitting the water. She pulled her arm free of her shield strap. Let her sword go and clawed at her helm. The light dwindled to a faint smear of green as she sank into the darkness.

"Keep up, Ali," Her grandfather called. The hiss of sea spray washed the richness from his voice. He sounded distant, far beyond the faint green light. "Come on, Ali . . ."

She stopped panicking, pulled off her gauntlets and drew her dagger. Starting with the bevor, she hacked the buckle from the strap, when it fell away she cut the chin strap on her helm. She would have cut more, but the precious breath she'd hoarded was done and her lungs were burning. She swam towards a shaft of light which speared through the water, a luminous guide to light and air.

The sea roared in her ears, sunlight burned the crests of the waves. She ran to her grandfather, dragging her legs through the foaming darts that rushed upon the shore . . .

The first breath she drew seared her throat. She was under the bridge, swathed in shadow and surrounded by others as desperate as she was to get out of the freezing river. She struck out for the bank. Silt clouded the water's edge, she clawed at the soft earth; it crumbled, dissolved, and flowed away. She fell back, swallowed a mouthful of water, spat it out, and coughed.

The current was strong here and she knew that if she went under again, she would die.

Faced with that certainty, she kicked out, dug the toes of her sabatons into the soft mud of the bank. Upstream, not five feet away, a Tamalak warrior broke the surface of the river, gasping for air. They looked at each other. It was a fleeting acknowledgement, but enough to spur Alyda on. Pain burned through her thigh as the muscles tore under the strain of trying to drive her out of the fast flowing river. The Tamalak grabbed a stunted shrub and began to pull himself onto the bank. Unencumbered by armour he got out before her. She yelled her fury at the bank, at herself, at the Tamalak. It sounded like everyone was yelling, invoking stone-hearted gods, cursing capricious demons, or crying out for their lovers, mothers, fathers. Every voice, hers among them, was lifted in the fervent prayer to whoever would listen: *Let me live now; let me survive this moment.* The Tamalak retrieved a broken spear from the bank and staggered towards her; his sodden woollen tunic slowed him down, but not enough for her to get out of the river. She looked up as he steadied himself above her; indigo paint running down his face. He took a two-handed grip on the spear, and raised it above his head.

With the last of her strength, she drove her mud covered dagger through his foot. He screamed, mistimed the thrust. The spear skidded off her cuirass, winding her. He crashed into the water, tearing her dagger from her hand and almost taking her with him as he tried to save himself. She caught a glimpse of his face just before he sank beneath the murky waters; saw the horror dawn in his eyes a moment before the current dragged him under.

All allegiances were forgotten now, all factions and loyalties put aside. Her battle was with a muddy slope and the river that was trying to draw her into it's the treacherous depths. Hand over bloodied hand; she pulled herself up the bank.

The sand was rough; she rubbed her toes together, felt the rasp of a thousand tiny grains. She was curled up in the cart, a bucket of clams beside her. She looked at her hands, at the way her water wrinkled skin sparkled in the slanting light that ran between the budding trees. She yawned; fell asleep listening to the rhythmic creak of the wheels turning . . .

The ground was rough against her cheek. She opened her eyes, rolled onto her back. The sky was violet, striated with red and gold. She was lying in the cold shadow of the bridge. It was quiet, save for the creaking wheels of a handcart being dragged along the opposite bank, loaded with dead Tamalaks. Somewhere, out of her line of sight, the sun was setting.

Silent Running

Sophie E Tallis

N MY DREAMS, I am dying . . . then I wake and wish my dreams were real.

*

THE CAPSULE HURTLED through space, spinning uncontrollably as it shot through the temporal rift, sparks flaring from its dented sides.

Life support was in critical failure, and the air grew increasingly toxic. The inertial dampers, damaged in the blast, were offline, leaving the occupants at the mercy of the pod's violent forces. Only their body straps saved them from being flung around like rag dolls. Adii was barely conscious. She struggled to keep her eyes open, aware of the pod's increasing velocity, but unable to stabilise it. The three humans were out cold, their pale clammy skin luminescent, death-like in the gloom.

A proximity warning sounded. An object was approaching fast from beneath them.

"Draelloth!" she murmured, groping for her pulsar. A shipping freighter came up beside them – a massive Talkin transport, originally a mining frigate from the outer colonies. Its superstructure dwarfed the tiny capsule.

141

"Draelloth . . ." she whispered again as the ship loomed over them.

Moments later, a huge mechanical arm was drawing the pod into an enormous storage bay.

Adii forced her eyes open, gasping for air. Her lungs felt ready to explode. She could hardly hear the humans breathing now. The co-pilot, Michael Shannon, a great bear of a man, looked half dead. He had succumbed to the pod's forces first, crumpling like a deflated balloon. His dark haired friend, the one they called Caulfield, swiftly followed. But Daniel McKendrick had stayed conscious for nearly as long as Adii had, his bloodshot eyes fixed on her in an expression of hatred.

She managed to unstrap herself and fell to the floor. Whatever ship they were in, it had a gravity drive.

The pod lay on its side, plunged in darkness. Through the slits of the viewing windows, Adii could see a faint greenish light emanating from outside. She fumbled her way over the others and found the hatch door. She forced it open and fell out onto the cargo deck. She struggled for a few moments, the rush of oxygen expelling the contents of her stomach. Her bleary eyes caught a shadow moving towards her. She tried reaching for her weapon . . . then nothing.

*

"How are you?" came a familiar voice. She knew those gravelled tones.

The engines hummed in her ears, telling her she was alive and awake.

Adii slowly opened her eyes. She was in a shabby medical facility, hooked up to some antiquated monitors.

An old man smiled down at her. "Welcome back, Commander Nakiri. We were lucky to pick you up when we did."

"Lithir? Where am I?"

"Safe. Not back on Kaelin, but on our way," Lithir replied.

She forced herself up.

Lithir helped her. "Easy. Your body has been starved of oxygen. You also have two broken ribs, concussion and a nasty gash on your head."

"Just another day . . ." she cracked a half smile and held her head for a moment, her fingers instinctively searching for the sticky mass. The pulsar blast had skimmed her head. If her assailant had been a better shot, she'd be dead.

She sighed. Everything ached.

"You all right?" Lithir asked.

Adii nodded, tasting the metallic tinge of blood in her mouth.

"Well," Lithir continued, "this rusty hulk may not look much, but her Captain is a good friend of mine, someone we can trust. I mean it though. We were lucky to pick you up when we did. None of you would have survived another hour."

"The humans?"

"They're recovering in the med unit down the hall. A rather precious cargo you've been carrying."

Adii shrugged. "A lot of trouble you mean. You may not thank me for rescuing them. Watch out for the tall one with the light hair, the one called Daniel. He asks incessant questions. He could be a problem." She scowled.

Lithir looked at her seriously. "How are *you* . . . really?"

"I've been better."

Lithir pulled himself up on the bed beside her. "I hope you don't object, but I took the liberty of viewing Koia's last flight log and your journal. I'm glad they were downloaded into the escape pod's memory banks, though naturally we will have to erase any trace of them from the records." He smiled. "Who would have thought it, three humans from Earth? I don't know why, but I expected them to look more primitive."

Adii winced, feeling the broken ribs now. "Koia . . . I had no choice but to self-destruct . . . we were attacked; I couldn't let them have the humans."

He placed a hand on her shoulder. "My dear, you did well. As great a ship as Koia was, she was expendable – you are not, and neither are your passengers!"

"We lost one. The captain, his name was Matthews, Stephen Matthews. He was a good man, I think, perhaps the best of them. I fucked up and he got shot. It was my fault. His wounds . . ." She shook her head. "He wouldn't have survived. He sacrificed himself to give us a chance to escape."

"I know. Brave man, staying behind like that. According to the log you were ambushed on Retris Station, trying to find parts for the ship after the Thral attacked you? And then you were attacked again? Is that right?"

She nodded. "Yes . . . we were almost back at the ship, when a sniper started shooting. There was a battle and Matthews got shot. He was bleeding out. The alarms went and suddenly the place was crawling with Thral."

Lithir shook his head. "Retris is a death trap these days. The time of it being a neutral haven for travellers is long gone. Retris attracts the less salubrious element: raiders, mercenaries, criminals; but now the Thral have a stranglehold on it. War is coming, Adii. At this point I think it's inevitable." He sighed. "I am sorry for Captain Matthews, but I find it miraculous that *any* of you survived. Although I've grown accustomed to expecting the miraculous from you! Unfortunately, the pod's visual recordings are unclear. Do you remember anything else about the final attack?"

Adii checked the door; they were alone. "Lithir, it wasn't a Thral ship that attacked us, it was their masters! A Draelloth ship. A *Draelloth ship!*" She swallowed. "The Draelloth haven't been seen in this quadrant—"

"For over a millennium," Lithir interrupted, his face grim. "As I feared, the Draelloth are on the move again. May the gods help us all!"

Adii shifted her weight, her head swimming. She felt a wave of nausea return, then everything went dark.

*

HER MIND RACED — transports on fire off the Miralis nebula, swarms of black ships emerging from a temporal rift, gas giants ringed by ice and rock and a blue pearl shining in an ocean of black. Earth — ancestor to all humanity, mythical mother to the Kaelinian race, hidden from view, from danger, by an anomaly in the fabric of time and space, an envelope of dark matter obscuring the precious system within. For millennia, only the Dekiyol Order had stood between Earth's discovery and destruction by Kaelin's enemies, enemies sworn to destroy every colony, protectorate, every vestige of humanity in the galaxy. Only a select few Dekiyol fighters knew for certain of Earth's existence, and they protected that secret with their lives. Only Adii, Kolya and Lithir knew its exact location, deep within the Gorein sector.

For the last four years, since the bitter end of the Thral War and their joint resignation from the military, Adii and Kolya had patrolled the edges of the Gorein sector, scanning and destroying the frequent anomalies, wormholes, temporal rifts and "corridors' that periodically opened up between normal space and the Gorein interior, stopping any from entering. It was through one of these collapsing rifts, twenty-three days before, that a fragile human craft had emerged, its damaged systems in failure as the four astronauts inside slowly suffocated.

Commander Nakiri had made a decision that day, one that would change their lives forever.

*

ADII WOKE UP in a monitoring tube surrounded by flashing lights and medi drips. It was hardly the clinical med labs you'd get on frigate ships or on home-world. This place looked like an abandoned slaughterhouse. Adii hated med labs. She'd much rather die on the battlefield than on a butcher's slab. She tried to move, feeling her body ache. Another war wound, another scar to add to the collection. Her body was riddled with them: the scars of combat. She'd been put together more times than she cared to remember, spent too long stuck in rehabilitation units, quietly going mad, along with the rest of the inmates.

Unhooking the various tubes and needles, she slid open the glass and managed to sit up. It all flooded back . . . finding Kolya's ship drifting through space, the Thral ambush, Retris, the attack after, watching her ship light up the skies like a dying star. She closed her eyes.

Why did everyone she loved die?

Too much, all of it, too much. She should have died years ago; the gods knew she deserved it.

"You're awake, and obviously feeling better." Lithir stared at her, looking worried. "You passed out again. You were vomiting blood. Your head wound has been seen to, but your lungs are not in great shape. You'll need to be looked at when we get back to Kaelin."

Adii motioned for some water.

"Small sips . . ." He passed her a flask.

"Don't mother me, Lithir. I'm not a child and I'm not dying."

"You're a mess."

She shrugged. "Been worse, been better, who cares . . . ?" She tried to steady her voice. "Tell me . . . It *was* Kolya's ship, wasn't it?"

The old man sighed. He knew that mercurial expression well, the volatile nature that suffered no fools and no fabrications. There was nothing to do other than tell the truth; Adii had an uncanny talent for sniffing out lies and liars.

"Yes, it was. I'm so sorry."

She shook her head, feeling her chest tighten. "Go on."

"I received a coded sub-space message, a distress signal cast out to one of our long range sensors. It was partially decayed, but . . . it was him. He was ambushed. It was a trap. He was investigating an anomaly when they attacked."

"Thral?"

Lithir nodded. "Five ships, maybe six. Kolya said there was increased activity along his section of the Gorein border. He thought they were searching for a nexus, a corridor. He thought they knew something, that they were there for a reason."

"I want to see it."

"You will, but—"

"Now!"

Lithir stood up. "Adii, we have to deal with the humans first. Kolya was killed protecting their very existence. That secret is worth any sacrifice; *that* was the oath you both made."

"Don't lecture me about duty! When have I ever broken an oath?" Her anger blotted out the pain as she jumped down and kicked his chair across the room. "You of all people dare to lecture me on sacrifice? My entire fucking life is nothing but sacrifice!"

Lithir stepped back. "I'm sorry, I truly am. But the issue of the humans must be dealt with first. If we dock at home-world without a cover story for them, we risk exposing their true identities and undoing a millennium of work. Then all those lives, including Kolya's, would have been lost for nothing. Whatever your feelings about these humans, or Earth, they are innocent children. With their level of development, their lack of technology, if the location of Earth is discovered, their home-world would be strip mined and billions killed or enslaved in the blink of an eye. You *know* this!"

"What d'you want me to say?" She rallied. "You want the truth? When I found their ship I had two choices – blast them into oblivion or take them on board. Clearly, I made the wrong fucking decision!"

The room lock chimed. A short, dark haired man stood tentatively in the doorway.

"Apologies, but your passengers are waking up. Do you want them to stay in stasis or be roused?"

Lithir stared at Adii. She looked deflated, her energies spent.

"Don't ask me."

Lithir turned. "Let them wake up. Can you arrange for food and water to be in their quarters?"

The man nodded and left.

Adii threw some clothes on. Why should she give a damn what happened to them? They were ungrateful strangers. Instead of thanking her for saving their miserable hides, rescuing them from a critically damaged craft, all they did was gripe on about their families and home world, asking a thousand questions she couldn't answer. They didn't matter, nothing did. Her ship was destroyed and Kolya was dead . . . Kolya was dead.

*

SHE SAT IN front of the flickering screen. The picture had failed but she could still hear the sound recording, albeit in a deteriorated state. She strained to hear what Kolya was saying through the background noise. The ship's self-destruct sequence could be heard, then the message ended. Again she played the message, and again, fists clenched, knuckles white. Adii wanted to rage and rant. She wanted blood.

The next few days were a blur as they travelled through Kaelinian space. Lithir, ever the adroit negotiator, managed to change the flight plan without too many questions, to include a docking at an outlying spaceport where their passengers could quietly disembark onto a waiting Dekiyol transport.

Commander Nakiri kept herself to herself. She avoided Lithir and the astronauts, especially Daniel, whose own grief at losing his best friend seemed to fuel his rage towards her. She didn't care. She was beyond caring. She ignored each poisonous glare and refused to discuss what had happened.

*

THE VESSEL APPROACHED the shipping port, a small but busy spaceport for commercial freighters and long-haul transports.

Adii stood alone in one of the cargo decks, staring out of a narrow viewing window. Daniel burst into the room.

"Hey! Commander!" He walked up to her, bristling with anger. "You're not fucking human, are you? I mean that's probably a compliment to you, right?"

Adii kept her back to him. "What do you want, Lieutenant?"

"Stephen . . . Captain Stephen Cory Matthews, husband and father to four young children. You just let him die!"

She sighed. "He was dying anyway."

"You don't know that!"

Adii turned to him, her face devoid of expression. She could tell he was itching to hit her. "Yes I did. And so did he."

"So, what, you were *helping* him? You left him to die. You didn't even try-!"

"He made a choice, Lieutenant." She kept her voice deliberately flat. "He made a choice: his life for ours."

"It's so easy for you, isn't it? What are we to you? Just a fucking inconvenience? It must have been a tough call for you, deciding whether to pick us up or let us burn!"

"Are you finished?"

"Oh, I'm sorry." He moved closer, spittle gathering in the corners of his mouth. "I forgot you lost something important too. Not your best friend for twenty years, the nearest thing to a brother . . . but yeah . . . you lost your precious ship. What a fucking loss!"

Adii kept calm which seemed to enrage him more, but her eyes were deadly serious.

"You think you know me?"

Daniel's face was inches from her own, his eyes black. "I think you're dead inside, that's what I think."

"Is that right?" she said, coldly.

He grabbed at her arm. In an instant she punched his windpipe, seized his neck, kicking his legs out from under him, and threw his full weight to the floor. She stood over him as he clutched his throat, fighting for air, and waited.

He stared at her, his face reddening, his eyes wild.

"Maybe," her voice was no more than a whisper, "I should have left you all. Or blasted you out of an air-lock while you slept."

She waited as his gasps became rasping, desperate, and his legs began to spasm. She watched the tiny blood vessels in his eyes strain. Then, she bent over him.

"You know *nothing* about me, Lieutenant. You'd best remember that!"

She pulled his hands away from his throat as he struggled against her, then with a crack she hit his windpipe again, and walked off. Daniel sprawled on the floor, gasping.

*

"She's right. You do not know her," said a voice nearby.

Daniel looked up to see Lithir, offering him a hand. He shoved it aside and staggered to his feet.

"Jesus! You fucking people!" he coughed, his voice hoarse. "She's a psycho! You people are supposed to be what . . . defenders, protectors of Earth, you and your band of merry fucking men? Jes'!" His larynx felt like shattered glass.

Lithir stood impassively, a disappointed expression on his face. "You're very wrong about her. She's risked her life countless times for our people, and yours."

"*Really?*" Daniel spat blood onto the floor. "You know, I think I understand her pretty well. If we've got people like her protecting Earth, then we really are fucked!"

Lithir wandered past him and over to the window, staring at the stream of traffic outside, then turned. "That destroyed ship you came across, the Lokai, do you know who it belonged to?"

Daniel looked blank. "It was just junk."

"I don't suppose she told you, why should she? His name was Captain Kolya Takri. He was her, how do you say, life partner? When she found his ship, destroyed, she knew he'd been killed. That has been confirmed, I'm afraid. He left her a message which she has now seen." He turned to face Daniel again. "She said nothing, did she?"

"Only that she knew the ship." Daniel muttered.

"She had a younger brother, Ensha. I'm sure you didn't know that either. She loved him very much. He died six years ago at the beginning of the Thral War." Lithir looked at him plainly. "She tried to save him, but failed. She is haunted by that. He died in her arms, horribly. She has nightmares, night terrors actually, almost every night. She relives those dreadful events and it makes her sick. If she doesn't remember to turn in her sleep, she'll choke on her own bile."

Daniel gasped, and for a moment he forgot the pain in his own throat.

"We all live with our pain, Lieutenant, and Commander Nakiri has more than most. Her burdens may not show, but she carries them all the same." He paused. "You should know this. According to the ship's log and the time of Kolya's message, if she hadn't rescued you she could have reached Kolya and saved him instead." He placed a hand on Daniel's shoulder. "I am truly sorry about Stephen. He sounded like a courageous man and a good friend. I *am* sorry for your loss."

Daniel felt the weight of Lithir's hand slip slowly from his shoulder and with it his anger seemed to melt away. He turned to ask something, but the old man was gone.

The drone of docking ships continued outside.

"Jesus," he whispered, "Way to go, Danny boy!"

*

ADII LEANT OVER the basin and rinsed her mouth. She wiped the mirror and stared at her reflection. Dark shadows circled her eyes, red from crying. She hated any sign of weakness.

The hum of the engines changed in tone as the Dekiyol transport gathered speed. They had left the docking port and were on their way again, heading for a safe haven for the humans.

She felt the bile rising in her throat again and choked it back. Despite her contempt for the astronauts, especially Lt. McKendrick, she had a job to do. No time for anger or self-indulgent destruction, though it had taken all her self-will not to kill the little fucker! Because of them, she hadn't been there to help Kolya. In this whole rotten universe, she'd failed the one person that meant the most to her. He had died alone and outnumbered.

A knock at the door brought her senses back.

"What is it?" she snarled.

Lithir appeared in the doorway. "We need to de-brief the astronauts. You should be there."

"Fine."

"What are their names again?"

"Don't play mind games with me, Lithir. The data was on the ship's log. Knowing their names won't magically endear them to me."

The old man held her gaze until she complied.

"Fine," she sighed. "The short dark haired one is Lt. Peter Caulfield, the co-pilot is Michael Shannon, they call him "Mike'. You know about the dead one, and the other one is Daniel McKendrick. Are you happy?"

Lithir looked satisfied. "Are you coming?"

*

THE ASTRONAUTS PACED their quarters like caged animals, except for Daniel who slumped on one of the bunks, staring at the door. Lithir had shuffled them on board quickly and kept them away from the rest of the crew.

Peter looked weary, as they all did, but Daniel sensed his mounting frustration. "Are they going to tell us anything? Where the hell are we going? When can we go home?"

Michael dug his hands into his pockets. "I'm not sure that is an option anymore."

"What?" Peter looked shocked.

"You really think they're going to send us on our way? In what? The Explorer is gone. I'd say the likelihood of seeing our families again is zero."

Daniel remained silent, but he knew Michael was right. None of them would be seeing Earth again.

The door opened and Lithir stepped inside with Commander Nakiri. Daniel sat up, his eyes fixed on Adii. She hung back, arms crossed, a detached expression on her face.

"We're flying to a Dekiyol planetoid for full de-briefing. It's a short flight, you'll be safe there." Lithir leaned against the door so he could watch the corridor outside. He lowered his voice. "We have a mixed crew on board here, some trusted Dekiyol rangers and some commercial pilots. For now, I ask you to keep your identities a secret. I know you look a little different from most Kaelinians, a little shorter, due to your planet's gravity, so if anyone asks, you're miners from the ice colony at O'Tarris. That will explain your paler skin, too."

"You really think that's necessary?" Peter asked.

"What happens to us when we get to wherever we're going?" Michael asked, studying them both closely. "We all want to know -what are the possibilities of us getting home, getting to Earth? We have families. Stephen had a family."

Lithir cast a glance at Adii, who remained expressionless.

"In truth," he replied, "we have no answers for you at this point. I'm sorry. I'm sure that's not what you want to hear, but this is as unprecedented for the Commander and myself as it is for you."

"We're just grateful to be alive," answered Daniel, still watching Adii.

*

SHE KEPT HER gaze resolutely fixed on the floor. Kolya was worth ten thousand of these humans. She should have let them die.

All of a sudden the alarms blared and the transport lurched violently to one side.

"What's happening?" called Lithir, steadying himself against the increasing gradient.

"Quiet!" Adii snapped. She felt the ship straining, its juddering engines reeling under the pressure. Something was very wrong. She threw a pulsar gun to Lithir. "Stay here," she shouted. "Lock the door and shoot the locks from the inside if anyone tries to get in!"

Lithir fumbled with the gun. "What's happening?"

"We're under attack! Don't open this door for anyone except me. Lock it *now!*" She ran into the corridor outside, pulsar drawn and ready.

A massive blast ripped through the ship, and the transport lost its gravity drive. Adii felt her internal organs lift along with the rest of her, a clever move for any attacker. Without a gravity drive, every floating occupant became an easy target. Strangely enough the human astronauts, in their primitive craft, would be best equipped to cope with this suspended chaos.

Another explosion rocked the ship and confirmed Adii's suspicions. She knew the difference between a cannon blast and sabotage . . . that explosion came from a detonation within the ship, not from an outside assailant. The Dekiyol transport groaned and lurched once more, then all the screaming engines fell silent and Adii was plunged in darkness.

She waited for the emergency lighting to come online, but nothing, all systems were down. She sensed the air vents closing. Life support was offline. In a ship this size and with a skeleton crew, they probably had a day of breathable air before the atmosphere turned toxic. This was a co-ordinated attack.

She quieted her breathing. A twenty year military career had taught her battle techniques, but the Thral War had taught her guerrilla tactics, and turned her into a killing machine, driven by grief and rage. Despite her enforced "convalescence' and the "healing programs' she had been made to attend after the war, she had never lost her edge, or her rage.

She sheathed the pulsar gun and took out her killing blade. It was time to hunt.

Removing her shoes and any articles of clothing that could make a noise, she waited for her eyes to adjust to the dark. She had trained herself in this too. Her night vision was excellent.

Allowing her body to find its equilibrium, she used what had been the ceiling to swim along the corridor. She sensed no movement, no sign of life. She moved swiftly, following the only muffled sounds to be heard, the faintest echoes from deep in the belly of the ship. Her eyes found the shapes of dead crewmen floating lifelessly in the gloom. Blood drifted in the darkness, globules bouncing against her skin, bursting open in her hair.

Her senses alerted to a slow moving shadow coming down the corridor. Three shadows. They were walking, not floating. Magnetic boots. Adii floated above their heads, they hadn't seen her. They headed for the astronaut's quarters.

She felt a twinge of regret. This would be over too soon and she wanted it to last.

She pushed off from the ceiling and headed for the last of the figures. The continued sounds of fighting from deep below told her these weren't the only traitors on-board.

She glided down, blade twitching in her hand, wanting its target.

It found it.

In one deft movement, she landed on the shoulders of the last man like a black spider, and grabbed the back of his head. She pulled it back before he could react, and plunged the knife through his eyeball and into his brain. She felt the hilt scrape against the bone of his eye socket. Sure it had gone in far enough, she slid it out, wiping the jelly on his cheek as she let his limp body drift to the floor, his boots anchoring him like a piece of waving sea kelp.

Onto the second.

She saw the next man freeze and turn. Had he heard anything? Too late. Before he had a chance to call his accomplice, her blade drove deep into his skull. This time, and to Adii's surprise, a gargled sound escaped his lips. The first figure turned.

"Quiet!" he hissed, then cursed as he saw the glint of steel in the dark.

Adii had to move quickly. She saw the gun being raised. She threw the killing blade with deadly accuracy and saw the hand go limp and the gun float away. It was almost comical, even in this gloom, seeing these slumped, swaying figures. Adii drifted over to the last attacker and pressed her foot down on his head, pulling the knife from his skull with an awful sucking sound.

Three down, but how many more were there?

She checked them all and stripped them of their weapons. No tags, pilot cards, nothing to identify them other than the universal translator units hidden under their clothes and fixed above each one's voice box, to disguise their accents.

She checked the corridor again. Silence. Placing one of the units against her ear, she fiddled with the reverse button.

"Who are they?" she whispered, and heard the unit repeat the words in a distinctive Oskillian accent. Adii smiled. "Got you!"

Oskillus was one of Kaelin's outer colonies, and a sector that many Thral ships had been seen travelling through. Adii had long suspected it of colluding with the enemy. Here was the proof.

The sounds of battle echoed through the darkness. She longed to join the fight, but clearly the attackers knew about the passengers. She'd killed three, but more would follow. She had to move the humans first.

She floated back to their quarters.

"Oskillian traitors!" she whispered.

"Adii?" She heard Lithir's worried voice from the other side of the door.

"They're Oskillian traitors," she repeated. "Open the door, we need to move!"

Lithir hesitated. "How do I know it's you?"

Damn Lithir and his protocols, but he was right. With a universal translator you could emulate anyone's voice.

"Ask me a question then, but hurry the fuck up!"

The door opened, and a floating Lithir greeted her, hand trembling. "I knew that was you!"

Adii checked the corridor again. No sound, no movement.

"They know you're here. We're moving," she whispered. "Take anything off that will make a noise and take these!" She threw the attacker's weapons to each of the humans. "Arm yourselves. I've deactivated the safety. It's like any gun so just point and squeeze, preferably not at me!"

Checking once more, they issued out of the room and into the corridor beyond. Adii deactivated the magnetic boots on each of the dead attackers and pulled their floating corpses into the cabin before jamming the door shut.

"Right, let's go," she said.

Grabbing onto each other, Commander Nakiri led them towards the rear of the transport. The humans were surprisingly good in the zero gravity atmosphere, floating almost in formation behind her. They might just make it to the cargo deck before being overtaken. Lithir, on the other hand, was conspicuous by his flailing.

"Where are we going?" Peter whispered.

"Cargo holds," she replied, "away from the fighting."

Her frustration at hearing the battle raging below was palpable.

They turned several corners and found themselves in a cavernous space. One of the ship's main stair shafts, seven decks in all. Explosions echoed through the ship. The glow of fire and pulsar blasts illuminated the stairwell. The cargo holds were down two levels, nearer to the fighting.

The emergency lighting spluttered into life.

She preferred the dark. They were an easier target like this, but it was a good sign that the ship was coming under control again. The question was . . . *who* was in control? Daniel and the other astronauts stared at her; she was covered in blood.

More sounds could be heard, coming from behind them, more magnetic boots. Adii hesitated. It was too open here, they needed shelter. She floated across to a store room and over-riding the door mechanism, prised the door and bundled them all in.

"Move!" she hissed, grabbing Daniel and Michael and pushing them inside.

The attackers were almost at the human's cabin now. They would discover the bodies of their fellow traitors any moment.

She tried to close and lock the door again, but it wouldn't budge.

"Damn it! Stay here," she whispered. "Shoot anything that comes around that corner that isn't me!"

Adii pulled out her blood covered knife. She caught the look of horror on Daniel's face, and it almost made her smile.

She floated back across the stairwell and down the corridor, reaching the first corner as a hail of pulsar fire blasted into the human's quarters.

Hunting time again.

Slipping around the corner she braced herself against the ceiling, just the other side of a large bulkhead. Wedging herself against the structure and ensuring she kept her legs out of sight, she waited.

Five sets of magnetic boots ran down the corridor towards her. How she wished the lights were still out! She could surprise one, maybe two in the dark, but not five. She unclicked the holster of her gun, feeling it float in its sheath.

"*Find them!*" snarled one of the assassins, "They've gained the bridge again. We're losing the ship, we've got to find them!"

She waited as they passed below her.

Dropping down on the head of the last attacker, she slit his throat in one swipe. He gargled something. The fourth man turned and she plunged the knife into his heart. As she held the blade in place, she pushed off from the wall and kicked the third assailant in the face, sending him hurtling sideways as she drew her gun and shot the other two – one in the head, one squarely in the chest. They fell like scattered leaves, their boots still anchoring them to the floor as if they were sheaves of corn ready to be harvested. Recovering, the third attacker fired back at her. The blast went wide but caught her in the shoulder, throwing her back. With her hand still wrapped around the blade embedded in the fourth man's heart, she withdrew it and threw it at the third figure, catching him in the throat. He dropped his gun and clasped his gushing neck.

Adii floated over to him.

"How many more?" she asked. "Tell me truthfully, and I'll kill you quickly. Tell me a lie and I'll gut you like a fish and go after everyone you love, your wife, your children, mother, father, brothers, sisters, everyone . . . so, what's it going to be?"

She hovered in front of him, barely aware of the bleeding hole in her shoulder.

The attacker gurgled.

Adii bent closer. "Sorry, your lungs are filling with blood. I didn't quite catch that. How many are there?"

"T . . . wenty, twenty," he choked.

"In total?"

He nodded.

Eight down, only another twelve to deal with.

"I was forced . . . I . . ."

"I'm not interested in excuses. You're a traitor to your own people. I don't care if the Thral have your family hostage, you *never* betray your own people." She slid the knife from his neck and plunged it, hilt deep, into his stomach, cutting upwards.

He screamed as the air turned red.

Let this be an example to the others. Betrayal will get you butchered.

A noise behind her made her turn, just as a pulsar blast fired. A sixth man collapsed. Adii looked up to see Daniel floating there, gun in hand, a startled expression on his face. She straightened up, a horrifying figure with wild eyes, utterly drenched in blood.

"I told you to stay," she said.

"I thought you might need help . . ." he muttered.

The gravity drive engaged. Everything crashed to the floor. The corridor resembled an abattoir.

The com system crackled into life. "We have regained the ship, we have regained the ship!"

Adii recognised the voice as D'nor, the vessel's navigator. He was trustworthy. "The Thral agents have been neutralised. We're sweeping the ship for any others. All other personnel, report to the bridge immediately!"

Adii sighed. She'd seen situations like this spin out of control, whole ships overrun or even destroyed. Pirates and raiders were mostly to blame, attacking transports to steal cargo or assassins infiltrating a crew to complete a contract, usually on the captain. But Thral spies amongst a trusted Dekiyol crew? She'd never heard of anything like that. How the hell did they know about the humans? That meant at least one conspirator on the bridge, inside the control deck, neutralising the pilots and auxiliary crew and gaining full access to the ship's records, including its passenger manifests.

"Traitors!" she spat.

Daniel stood quietly, his back against the frame of a door.

"You look shocked," Adii commented.

He blinked. "I suppose I am. I suppose . . . I just, I've never seen someone killed before."

"And?"

"You appear to get pleasure from it, from killing." Daniel sounded accusatory, whether he had meant to or not.

Adii stared at him. "I *suppose* I do," she replied bluntly, deliberately using his wording, "I suppose that makes me a monster in your eyes, probably in most people's eyes." She sighed and relaxed a little. "Lithir says I have rage issues. He's right. I've had a belly full of traitors in my time, who betray their own people for what? For money, for power?" She shook her head. "Traitors who slaughter thousands. They're a cancer. Those "people' -they deserve my rage. So yes, I enjoy killing them, not just because they deserve it, but because it's one less traitor who can slaughter someone else."

It was an ugly truth which when laid out for all the world to see, made perfect sense. Whether it was Vichy France, Ukrainian troops betraying their own country for a slice of mother Russia, or the traitors in the Mars conflicts, selling out their neighbours and union allies for a pot of money, war was always brutal.

Adii was just a blade, used to cut out the cancer of treachery, and an effective blade at that.

She watched the sour expression on his face with some delight. Conflict, death, *was* distasteful and ugly.

For all his bravado, this human man was an innocent, as Lithir had said. After everything she had been through, everything she had seen and done . . . there was something beautiful in that.

Unnatural History

Danie Ware

T HE THING WAS huge. It filled the pale stone of the old hall from floor to broken roof. It was a monstrous ripple of texture and colour, glinting and seething, pulsing with hunger. It had consumed everything, accepted the building's long history as fuel for its size and might, and now it rose before us, looking down at our foolishness with a wide and mineral grin.

There you are, it seemed to say, *come to Me at last.*

Huddled behind me, the group from the old train weren't fighters. They'd heard the bike engine and spilled out from the abandoned station at South Ken – they'd greeted me like some street-hero of old, patting my arm and babbling horrors. They'd pointed at the rifle over my back and then vaguely, helplessly northwards. They'd known it was there, known it would come for them, known it would roll forward over the overgrown ground, and leave that wide swathe? of desolation behind it . . .

They'd known they could do nothing to stop it.

Now, they cowered in front of it like acolytes. I was their Priestess, their scarred Goddess of Dirt and Boots. The doorway and the long steps down to the derelict street were behind us, but nothing lay that way, only the endless creeper, and the corpses of long-forgotten cars.

In front of us . . . by the Rotting Gods, this monster wasn't the first of these things I'd seen, but it was easily the biggest. It blocked the mighty hall like a lump in its throat. It bulged across the floor and obscured the stairways. Ash-grey light fell from the ruined roof and glinted upon its shoulders.

"Katja! Katja! *Kate!*" The train group's leader was calling me. He was an older man, savvy enough to survive, to watch – I could feel he was gesturing, but didn't dare turn and look. My eyes were on the monster. On the history of the world held within its body.

You, I told it silently, *are as dead as this bastard city.*

I cocked my father's old bolt-action, that satisfying "ker-chank, ker-chank' that I'd learned as a teenager. The thing rippled again, stretched as high as the roof, the light dancing, the movement smooth and fluid. There was bone in there, sucked in and held in suspension – it was dark with age, huge pieces of it now broken into filthy shards. Some of it was still pierced though with twisted, rusted steel. There were bits of animal and crystal, stone from the walls and floor, metal from the bannisters, old wood from the last of the furniture. The broken glass of the shattered windows made its eyes, and they glittered with the remnants of the patterns within.

When it moved, it rumbled like a building coming down.

But I didn't care. Rotting thing. With tight focus, I put the old rifle's butt against my shoulder, sighted, took one glass eye clean out of its head. It rocked back, keening, then its face inverted and opened again like some blossoming of urban debris. And the eye was replaced, winking at me.

Shit.

Somewhere behind it, the weed-grown staircases joined at a single white statue – the head of an old man who watched the scene in silence, his judgment withheld. Whoever he was, he was unimpressed by my shooting.

The train people were crying out now, instructions and fear. Their leader shouted at them to stay quiet, his voice firm. I cocked the rifle again and took a second shot, this time at the monster's grinning mouth. It swallowed the round whole, spitting tiny fragments as if it would belch in satisfaction.

Shit, shit, shit.

Not wasting more ammo, I slung the rifle and ducked to pick up my old shield. I'd made this when my father died, from a dustbin lid and an old road-sign – made it the day I'd held to my promise and gone to find other survivors. I'd been nineteen, and my father had been my everything – parent, trainer, insight, courage. Gods and Rot, he would've known how to deal with this bastard thing. But he'd been dead twenty years – more. This was my world, now, the world I'd made my own.

The beast shuddered with textures, they ran over its surface like water. It lowered itself to a bulbous fatness, and eyed me with its vast head cocked to one side. Cold grey light flashed from its movements, made me blink so I almost missed it – the bulge that was one flank exploding into a huge, uncurling tentacle. It threw it out at me, scattering pieces: hard edges of bone, fragments of the little stone creatures that had once clung to the walls. I blocked it with a crack that skidded me backwards, slashed down at it with my heavy old Bowie knife, the blow brutal. Crippled, the tentacle crashed to the stone floor, twitching, but a slurp of the beast's underside simply sucked it back up again.

Rotting *hell.*

I'd no idea how long this thing had been in here, seeping through doors and levels, swelling as it absorbed every artefact and memory—

It shuddered, making the old walls shake. Pieces of the roof fell to shatter before it, and it rolled forwards, picking up the bits as it came. A second tentacle, this one with a claw-tip, like some huge and scrabbling insect. It clacked shut just short of my blade-hand, withdrew, but not fast enough. A flashing over-and-backhand with the knife and the end clattered, severed, to the floor. I kicked it away before the beast could roll forwards again. But this wasn't good enough, just wasn't taking enough of its body mass. The little ones exploded from a well-aimed round of .303, or they fell to pieces if you hacked hard enough – but not this thing, it had to be ten times the size of anything else I'd seen. I felt a tremor that might've been panic, dismissed it. And as it rippled again, I could see now – there were bodies in there too. Pieces of human life that may once have lived or visited here, or taken refuge in this great hall when the end of the world had come.

*

I WAS TEN when it happened, alone in the flat with my father. My mother and brothers never came home. I remember little: chaos screaming in the streets below, the violence that roared from block to block, gunshots and shouting from the Morrison's at the end of the road. Sirens, but not for long.

Other memories are jumbled, all mixed up with my father's severe expression, the determination that sat across his shoulders. The chugging queues of vehicles, later abandoned. The lights going out; the final flicker as the flatscreens all went dead. My father with his old radio, seeking answers, anything – and then, grimly, the day he turned it off.

We had sandbags that lined the flat's doors, a water butt, and enough tins to make us sick of beans for good. He reactivated his old Lee Enfield, hand-loaded the rounds for the magazine, dug his survivalist stuff out the back room. And he had a treasured bike with a sidecar that I ride still – now fuelled by wood gas. An old milk can, some steel pipe and a bit of angle iron make a solidly decent genny. But that was later.

When it first happened, he wouldn't let me leave the building, even leave the flat. As the eaters shambled and ate and tore outside, and as the war against them raged, we simply closed the curtains. At times, people found us and begged us for help, but we never let them in – even when I was old enough to feel guilty, and I shouted and cried and blocked my ears as I heard them dying outside.

Once, a group of teens tried to break our door down, but my father shot their leader through the head.

And I remember the day the silence came, the day the eaters finally stopped – starved or slain. I was older by then, old enough to learn to cock and shoot the rifle myself, old enough to watch the empty streets below, and to report on what I saw.

"How'd it happen?" I'd asked him once, wondering what the story really was. There was a roadway down there, a vastly complicated system of lines and queuing vehicles, all of them rusted now, their purpose long-lost. The central isle was overgrown, crawling plant-life reclaiming the forgotten world. It had sent out its winding tendrils and now grew up the outsides of all the blocks like ours, its flowers opening to the dead grey sky. There was one just outside the window, its deep red colour brighter than anything I'd seen.

"Doesn't matter now," he'd told me, shrugging. "Tribalism. Greed. Righteousness. Too many flags, and all of them fuelled by hate. When the end came, I think we deserved it. Now, Katie-kat, we survive."

*

THE THING IN the great hall didn't care about the end of the world. It wheezed at me through its mineral teeth, their crystal colours gleaming cold. I'd taken others like this with crude flamethrowers or basic explosives, but this one looked about as combustible as the stone around it.

Shit.

It was moving faster now, closing on the doorway where the train people were huddled. I snapped a look back at the dark-skinned, grey haired man that led them, "Keep its attention." When I got a nod in return, I ducked past the beast's bulging flank, scanning its bulk as I went. Maybe, if I could find a hollow, a weakness . . .

But it was sharp, had no intention of losing track of me. As I moved, its grin spread and separated, its head split clean down the middle and two new eyes turned to follow where I was going. The face moved within the body, tracking me like a searchlight. A flickering bulge of textures ran after it. I knew more attacks were coming and I tensed, muscles tight and wary, heart pounding, shield raised. This damned monster was going down, one way or another.

But there was no huge tentacle, no single clacking of claw. This time, the surface of the thing boiled and the fronds that came forth uncurled like the tendrils of the creeper outside, like a myriad spider-legs. They were everywhere, all round me, five and six and seven of them, perhaps more. They were cold, angled, made from rusting steel wire, jointed and creaking, with jagged edges like teeth. And they came at me in a flurry, whipping and spiking at my face and shoulders. Behind them, I saw a darkness – a maw in the thing's side, another mouth, ready and waiting. From it, came the spitting surge of the monster, need and hunger. Shuddering, I punched the shield edge-on, caught two of them with the screech of metal-on-metal. I pulled it back and struck again with the flat, making more of them recoil; the blade caught another and cut it, sent it twitching, it to the floor. The maw puckered at me, grotesque in its eagerness, and I slammed a boot down on a tentacle that was winding close to my booted ankle, skidding as the metal rasped over the stone. Then there was nothing left between myself and it.

Right, you rotting beast.

I could see its flank clearly now; the open maw, the buds of new tentacles. And I could see where it was layering up defences, a thickening of metal and stone to protect itself against me. But the spidery tentacles came again; more of them emerging from the outermost sides of the maw. An eye opened above it, the raw facets of some long-forgotten crystal. And then, I had an idea.

*

ONE DAY, MY father returned with food – with roaches, and with rats the length of his forearm. As both silence and confidence grew, he ranged further, and he took me with him. He told tales of the old world, of the broken glass towers that rose over us, reflecting the clouds in their shattered facets. Tales of the silent streets, and of the tessellated buildings, metal and brick and stone. Tales of the shining-huge curves of the river, and of the myriad bridges that crossed it, all now derelict and swamped in creeper. We went down to the waterside, and found treasures on the stony beach – rusting metal, discarded coins that made him chuckle. He made the genny to the fuel the bike, and we could go anywhere.

He was invincible, unstoppable, ever-confident. And when he died, it wasn't by eater or madman – we'd seen no life other than our own in years – he was killed by a rat-bite that poisoned his blood, an infection that ate him from the inside out. He had strength enough to get home, and there, he made me promise that I would find others, and not remain alone.

And I cried. And then, I made my shield. And out I went, bike and rifle with me, into the rotting and empty city.

*

I KNEW IT from experience: these beasts had a critical mass. Enough damage, enough bulk lost, and their conscience dissipated. They fell back to a pile of debris. The theory was sound. This one – rotting hell – this one was just that much bigger than the rest. I had to try something else. From somewhere, the train people were shouting. I could hear their leader, telling them to be ready, be *ready* – and I guessed that the thing was attacking them too. So much the better.

Gods and Rot, this might even work.

I shouted at them, "Attack it, throw things at it, everything you have!"

And, as their noise increased, I went in against its flank, kicking, shield-bashing, hacking at the flailing tentacles – they were clumsier when I was close. And slowly, slowly, it massed up a wall of heavy defence against the continuing assault.

*

THE CITY, MY father had told me, was over two thousand years old. It sprawled to one and half thousand square klicks – though once, you could have walked across its centre in less than an hour. Its outermost limit was demarcated by a massive and looping roadway, now a crumbling graveyard of rusting vehicles. And it had once been home to more than eight million people – eight *million*. The number was beyond me. I'd seen no face, other than my father's, for nearly fifteen years . . . eight million. What had happened to them all? Had they all become eaters? Or eaten?

The flat was safe enough, in a tower at the Elephant, and I knew my way north to the river, to the broken bridges reflected in its surface. From there, I began my exploration, the sound of the bike raw and shocking in the silence. Its invasion made the swarming creeper shiver. But nothing around me cared. Only the rodents and roaches, only the shadows scudding as the clouds crossed the dead-grey sky. As time passed, I found myself talking to the rats, with their glittering piss-yellow eyes, or crying at the nothing when another hope turned out to be ashes, drifting cold on the empty wind.

On the river, I found a great ship, a huge metal monster listing in the water – but the eaters had long since gutted it, and the creaking of its shell scared me. The Tower, too, the ravens long dead, their bony corpses tiny in the surrounding swathe of green. And I found tunnels, endless winding mazes of tunnels, some of them flooded, some of them laden with swag for the taking, some of them still with their metal rails and trains. But there was no-one down there, only the layered ghosts of the millions that had died. It was dark, and it was far, far too easy to get lost. And it was there that I found the first of the monsters.

*

BEHIND ME, I heard them attack. I heard them rage defiance. I heard the scrabble of feet, the clatter of their simple weapons – barbed and rusted treasures from the tunnels at South Ken. I heard them give everything they had and I hoped that the same effect was massing for them too – a bulking up of the thing's heavyweight materials . . .

But they had neither the strength, nor the experience.

As the open maw and crystal eye were obscured by a thickness of pale stone, as my shoulders hurt from the effort and my throat grew raw from the shouting, the hope rose in me that this would be enough . . .

I heard their defiance rise into fear, and their fear into death. And I wondered what I had done.

*

I HEARD IT moving – too big to be a rat. And even as my heart pounded with hope and fear, even as I struck and threw the flare, I knew there was something wrong – that this wasn't human, some lonely figure left behind by the end of the world. In the sudden hiss of light, it was human-sized, but its skin was brick and rust and splinter, its colours garish in the brilliance. Its shadow flickered over me, huge in the curve of the wall. I unslung the rifle, but hesitated. Maybe, maybe – please the Rotting Gods! – *maybe* this thing could be a friend, an ally against the empty and overgrown nothing.

But no, the sense of wrong was overwhelming – the tunnel was empty of rats. They'd not attacked me, or fled, squeaking, from the light . . .

It took me a moment to realise that the tunnel was also empty of everything else.

Reacting to the glare, the thing came forwards. Its shadow swelled as it moved. Skin crawling, I backed away, waited. I felt almost sick. I cocked the rifle but still watched it, some hope still lit like the flare, but dying, even now, with the fading of its light. It was only when it came closer that I understood completely . . .

It was an amalgam, made of old brickwork, pieces of benches, and signs. It had edges of bright plastics, colours from posters and graffiti. It was somehow made of the debris that the world had left down here.

The flare was dying. In a moment, the tunnel would be pitch-dark.

Still, I didn't fire.

It came closer still. Its shadow swelled and juddered. It looked at me – looked *back* at me. There was a bright thread of awareness to it, a gleam of something sentient. And it had *flesh* in there, and bone, and skull, and socket. It was not just the forgotten pieces of a lost culture; it was the people who had hidden down here, the rats I could not find. I swallowed bile. Blinked water. I shot it, point-blank, half in defiance and half in sheer terror. When it recoiled, shrieking like tortured metal, bits of it flying loose, I re-cocked my weapon and shot it again, and again. I emptied the magazine into the thing, five rounds that boomed down the tunnel, that shattered it into flying pieces and left me shaking, panicked and sweating.

The flare guttered, almost dead now.

But it wasn't over. Replacing the magazine with a full one, I crept forwards, slowly, keeping the scattered debris covered. Part of me felt slightly stupid – surely I was just going mad with the loneliness – but I closed without lowering my guard. And then I kicked at the bits, kicked and kicked and *kicked* at them. I slung the rifle, found my father's old magnesium-flare lighter, and I set the wooden bits aflame. They gave me enough light to leave the tunnel, backwards, watching them all the way.

But the thing didn't move again.

OVER ME, NOW raging with its victory, it towered up towards the shattered remnant of the roof. I could see its eyes, high in the grey light, its teeth made of thousand crystal colours. I saw its bulk bulge and rise, saw it grin as it looked down at me and I realised that I'd made a mistake.

It fell forwards. I had time for a scrabble of panic, to reach for the rifle – almost out of reflex – and then everything went dark.

*

THAT SMALL BEAST was the first one, perhaps its own equivalent of a child, I had no way of knowing. After it, there came others – creatures of urban sentience, distilled from the death about them. They seemed to live where people had been – as I ranged wider, and I found more of them, and larger. And inevitably, one day, they led me to the city's other survivors, to those tiny huddles of humanity, as battered and dirty as I was, and every bit as able to survive. And, at last, they led me to the station at South Ken, and to the great halls that still stood there, history and future both now lost to the monster that dwelt within.

*

THE DARKNESS RECEDED.

When I opened my eyes, the hall's broken roof arced silent over me, and the sky skulked a dark grey with the swelling evening. I felt strange, my head swimming. Instinctively, I groped for blade and rifle, but the floor was empty. The beast had gone.

The huge space was quiet, the overgrowth still. Debris from the creature had scattered, dispersed as the driving sentience had left it. I had won.

Had I?

With a peculiar, detached unease, I wondered where it had gone. Without looking, I knew that there was no-one in the doorway. If there were survivors, they had left – returned to their line of rusted carriages, perhaps, to the living they'd scraped from the homes and tunnels around them. But something was very wrong, something . . .

As I went to stand up, my vision blurred, and I stumbled back to my knees, hurting. My skin was prickling and I held out a hand, struggling to focus on my callused fingers, my scarred and wind-worn skin. It all looked wrong, hazy, and I couldn't understand why. I found myself shivering, my stomach turning over with a tension I couldn't name.

A voice said, "Stay where you are."

In the doorway, the leader of the train people stood alone. His dark, lined face was severe and he was pointing my Lee Enfield at me, cocked and ready. He was sharp, grey-haired and wily. His grip was shaky – but Gods and Rot, he couldn't miss from that distance. I tried to speak – what, why? – but even my voice was wrong. It came out like a rasp, a wordless noise that scraped the ruined walls. I tried to cough, failed, lurched to my feet and took a step, holding my hand out – plea or request, I didn't know. I wanted my rifle back. "It's my life', I wanted to tell him. "My security'.

"I said, "Stay where you are'."

The roiling in my belly grew worse. I took another step and I thought that my hands were moving, that there were things under my skin, like parasites. Something I had caught from the monster, maybe, some infestation . . .

It was only as my forearm split open that I understood. Only as the splinters of the debris I had lain upon came roiling out of my skin, only as the dizziness in my head was obscured by a sudden sharp awareness not my own, only as I tried to laugh with a sound like the walls coming down . . .

The grey-haired old man raised my own Lee Enfield and applied pressure to the trigger.

And I understood the one thing I'd never known – where the sentience of the monsters had come from, why they'd always dwelt so close to the city's last pockets of humanity.

I felt myself expand, felt the debris ripple under my skin. I felt the walls of the old hall, the blank white stare of the statue, the crumbling of the roof and the life of the red-flowered creeper. I felt the ruination that was still scattered, still there to be consumed. I felt the life of the human as he shot at me, and missed. His life was mine: more feast, more fuel.

And that last pocket of humanity, cowering there at South Ken – it was just enough to make me live again.

Vocho's Night Out

Julia Knight

VOCHO SURVEYED THE carnage before him, and put up his sword without ever having laid a stroke. "Do you have to do that, every time? Couldn't you leave one for me?"

His sister, Kacha, looked up from where she was wiping her hands on a random tunic. "I can't wait for you, or I'd be here until next year. Maybe," and here she speared him with a look he knew well, "maybe you should pay attention. We're supposed to be protecting this shipment, after all. Not poncing about in front of a mirror pretending to perfect our technique."

Vocho looked at the incredibly boring boxes that they had been paid, through the duelling guild, a small fortune to protect. The prospect of a rumoured heist by the newly notorious thief, Slippery Simno, weighed heavily on their employer's mind. Then he looked at the surfeit of unconscious, and occasionally bloody, bodies now surrounding said boxes, none of which he could lay claim to. This wasn't going to do much for his reputation.

"That seems a lot of thieves for what is supposed to be herbs," he said. "I mean I know there's herbs and there's *herbs*, but even so."

"Not exactly well prepared either, were they? Slippery Simno they are not."

Vocho picked up what could, for want of a better word, be called a sword – if only because of its shape. It sagged in the middle and the hilt turned his hand black. "I've seen better cutlery." Which cheered him up a bit, because defending against a bunch of idiots with swords made out of what might generously be called metal wasn't going to add to his reputation anyway.

Kass frowned at the 'sword' and wiped a slick of sweat out of one eye. "This smells a bit off, doesn't it?"

"We are quite close to the docks."

"Not that sort of smell, you plank. Look, Sustro hired us, best duellists in the guild, right?"

Vocho puffed himself up and struck a pose. "Bloody right."

Kass's eyes crossed. "And he told everyone he was doing it. It even says so on the sign outside – 'Under Guild Protection'. So why would half a dozen dock rats with crap swords even try? They can't have been that stupid. You don't live even to their tender age by being stupid, on the docks."

The pile of thieves were a pathetic sight – half starved, all knees and elbows and sharp cheeks. Most of them looked about twelve, and while it wasn't impossible to be a damned good fighter at twelve – Vocho, naturally, had been merely brilliant – it wasn't likely that any dock rat that age would have any experience with swords, crap or otherwise. Knives, yes. Knuckledusters, blackjacks, coshes, garrottes and that old favourite, a sharpened screwdriver, of course. They'd have had much experience with all of those things, even at twelve. But swords? He doubted they knew anyone who could afford one, even one that bent in the middle.

"The swords don't make any sense," he said. "They'd have been better off sticking to what they knew. They'd still have lost, but it might not have been quite so one sided."

"Ah, but if their swords were any good, or they were, I'd not have gone easy on them and they would be dead." Kass frowned, deep in thought – he could tell because the rest of her was still. There was always some part of her in motion and if it wasn't her hands, it was her brain. "Don't suppose any of them could read the sign, either."

"So it could be just them getting the wrong house?"

"Voch, they're likely illiterate, but not stupid. They didn't need to read the sign to know whose house this is. And Sustro's been telling *everyone* who he's hired to guard his things. And everyone knows we're not cheap. Looks to me they might have thought that whatever it is we're guarding would be worth a shot at trying us on. Or, because I still don't think they were as stupid as to think six of them armed like that could beat even one of us, they were set up."

Vocho paced around the unconscious heap, considering. "I say we open the boxes."

"Voch!" It wasn't often he could shock his sister, but he always felt a twang of satisfaction when he managed it. Guild rules meant no digging into whatever they'd been paid to protect, except on the explicit instructions of their employer. Anything else was 'conduct unbecoming a duellist', which meant a one way trip out of the guild and into ignominy and disgrace. Considering the time and effort he'd spent working up his reputation as Vocho the Great, he wouldn't throw it away lightly. Still, there were always ways around the rules.

"I bet you any money you like that what's in those boxes will tell us what these dock rats are doing crumpled on the floor, besides the fact they met you. No one will know, will they? Our employer is off gallivanting up at the palace with the prelate, and all his workers are tucked up in their innocent beds. The only other people here are unconscious, and I don't suppose they'd tell anyway. Go on, I dare you. Besides," he said slyly, playing his trump card, "it could be for the good of Reyes as well, couldn't it? The right thing, to find out who wanted these boys dead, and why."

It wouldn't fail – it never did. They'd sworn, when they'd taken their master's oath and joined the guild properly, to protect the city-state of Reyes with their lives, and to do the good thing. There had been interminable lessons before that on how to decide what was the good thing, though Vocho had used them for napping. Kass took it all far too seriously to his way of thinking. Besides, a mystery was one thing she couldn't stand. If it was knowable, then she had to know it. Which meant getting her to open the boxes was easy.

"Fine," she said now, with a scowl for him. "You take that end."

Between the two of them, they levered open the first crate. Vocho peered in – straw, and dust. He rummaged a bit, carefully, because who knew?

"You got anything your end?" Kass asked.

"Nothing but mouse droppings. You?"

"Same."

She frowned into the empty box, and tried another with the same result. By the time the chimes of the clocks all across the city were tolling eleven, all in a ragged row that echoed down the streets, they had every box open with nothing to find.

"Well, that's just stupid," Kass said at last. "Why pay us a small fortune to guard some perfectly good, but utterly worthless boxes?"

"A decoy? Our employer, bless his wallet, has used us as a distraction from where his real cargo is. He's been shouting about it all around the city. These poor sods believed the hype. What was it supposed to be, anyway?"

"Hmm? Oh, herbs like you said. Medicinal ones. Only you know what it's like, they never tell you the truth about what's in the box in case we want to steal it, guild honour or not."

He was just considering that when Cospel, their ever present servant cum conspirator, shot in the door and slammed it behind him, waggling his eyebrows in an intricate code that Vocho had never quite managed to decipher.

"It might have got complicated," he said by way of translation. "Bunch of prelate's guards coming this way. Not happy. Very not happy. Very *vocal* about not being happy."

"So?" Kass and Vocho said together. They were on official guild business, paid for and notarised. The prelate's guards shouldn't have anything to do with it.

"So, well, you got half a dozen crumpled people at your feet for a start. And what looks like a load of empty boxes what were supposed to have some very valuable stuff in, but currently don't. You *had* to open the boxes, didn't you?"

"Well—" Vocho began, but Cospel carried on before he could make his excuses.

"Looks like that Slippery Simno has been a bit of a devil up at the palace, or someone has anyway. Nicked the key to the Clockwork God right out from under the prelate's nose. They's searching everywhere."

"I bet they are." Kass was at the door before Vocho had even started moving, peering out into the street beyond. "A bloody decoy," she said. "Else we'd have been up at the palace, wouldn't we? And we wouldn't have thought much of it either, if we hadn't opened the boxes. Cospel, you hear anything about Sustro?"

"Of course, miss." He looked affronted that she should ask. "Though not much. New to the city, see. Seems respectable enough, pays his workers a decent wage, and pays them on time. Deals in this and that, whatever's handy, nothing illegal that I could find out about. Not clockwork though. Never deals in clockwork. Mind, he's Ikaran so what can you expect?"

"What indeed. Looks like we know who our Slippery Simno is. Now we just need to find him."

They watched the prelate's men go past, checking every building. A quick word with Kass, that the two of them were protecting the building and no, they hadn't seen anyone untoward, and the guards went on their way, intent and angry.

"This bastard's got one over on us, and I for one am not happy about it. We'll be a laughing stock if anyone finds out. What we need is proof," she said when they'd gone. "And for that we need to find him"

*

TEN MINUTES LATER found them outside the palace. It was lit up like a defiance of darkness, lamps in every one of a hundred windows. The light glinted on the giant orrery that clanked its way through its motions in what had once been a formal garden but was now a devotional to the clockwork universe the prelate said ruled everyone.

"How do you propose we find him?" Vocho asked. "If he's even still there, that is. Are you going to knock on the door and ask?"

"I'm not, Cospel is. We know what he looks like, right? The prelate is probably unaware that his new friend is also Simno, just as we were until a few minutes ago. If he's undiscovered, why run? Especially when guards are scouring the streets? Even more especially if he's stashed the key somewhere in case he's searched, so he can come back for it later. He's not a hothead like you, Voch. This guy is a planner. Off you go, Cospel."

Cospel went, muttering under his breath.

"We could tell the guards . . ." Vocho said.

"What, and lose all the glory we'll get from catching him? Are you feeling quite well?"

"You have a very good point."

"I always do. Look, anyone finds out he outsmarted us, your precious reputation is in tatters. They'll be giggling from here down to Ikaras. Unless we can present the city with the thief that's been plaguing them for the last few months *and* has just stolen the key to the Clockwork God. We do that, we can gloss over how we came to be guarding a warehouse full of nothing."

Cospel was back in double quick time. "He ain't left yet. Prelate's having a shitfit, naturally, and no one's been allowed out until they's been searched."

"Excellent," Kacha said. "How brazen are you feeling, Voch?"

"Me? I'm always brazen, and shameless with it. Let's go."

The gate was out – the guards and the guild were not exactly bosom friends at the best of times, and if they had a hint that Vocho and Kacha knew who had stirred the palace up like an ant's nest, they'd be wanting all that glory for themselves. Instead, a boost from Cospel saw them over the wall in a quiet corner near the stables. Vocho helped Cospel over afterwards, and they stood in the shadows to consider, while watching people run about the reception room on the first floor. They scattered like panicky chickens, grouped together, scattered again with frowning guards working their way along, emptying pockets and peering into purses. Fans fluttered, swords rattled in scabbards, handkerchiefs wafted under noses, and one woman strategically fainted after a guard found something untoward in her pretty silk purse. At the far wall, tall double doors led out into the rest of the palace, but a phalanx of guards now barred the way.

"If he's still in there, he's got cogs of steel," Kass said. "But we have an advantage."

"We do?"

"He thinks no one knows who he is, he thinks he can just hide the key and wait it out. We know different. If one of us were to walk in and see him, it might shake him up. If we were to point him out as the likely thief, he might panic. If he does, then we've got him."

"If he doesn't?"

"Then it might get tricky, especially if we're wrong. But I don't think we're wrong. There's not many places he can run after he gets through those doors, not many places he'd want to run to in the palace anyway. He'll try to get *out*, as soon as he can. Voch, you go around the back, in case he runs. The door that leads to the orrery. Cospel, you take the front, the doors leading onto the courtyard. I shall walk in and try to scare the bugger."

Vocho was about to disagree – he had a very good swagger and he wanted to use it – when he considered that if the bugger ran, and he would, then he, Vocho, would be best placed to grab every last bit of glory. He went.

He watched from the clanking haven of the orrery, one eye on the door, the other watching people moving in the reception room. He could tell when Kass walked in. A guilds master turning up, especially one so renowned, had a singular effect on all the posh nobs likely to be at a reception held by the prelate. There was a telltale hush, a pause in all the twitterings and scatterings before they started up again, worse than before. The Prelate, gracious as ever, moved towards Kass with a frazzled and quizzical smile.

They didn't get any further than that. Simno, Sustro, whatever his bloody name was, didn't bother with doors. He didn't bother about opening the window either but dove straight through, bold as brass, scattering shards of glass onto the orrery, leaving a wake of gasps behind him. He was pretty good, too, landing like a duellist, rolling with it and up on his feet in a flash.

Vocho just had time for a smug grin up at his furious looking sister as she ran to the broken window before he was off, following the shadow of the man who'd stolen the key to the Clockwork God, the key to the heart of Reyes. Kass was too far behind and Cospel was on the other side of the palace. The glory was going to be his, all his.

*

VOCHO CLAMBERED OUT of a window and from there it was a short jump to a lower rooftop, after Simno as he scampered like a monkey above the streets of Reyes. Vocho followed, though he felt rather less monkey-like, not to mention he felt naked without Kass on his flank, making sure his back was covered as he did the same for her.

Bells rang the third quarter, starting with the Great Clock in the square outside the Shrive, the clock they said ran all the clockwork of the city. Its great booming toll was imperfectly echoed all across the city so that peals of bells chased each other down winding streets, the clocks haphazardly informing everyone that heard them that it was fifteen minutes until the change o' the clock. Time to batten down the hatches and douse the torches before the city changed its configuration in one giant clockwork movement, but it looked like Vocho wouldn't have the luxury of any of that.

Ahead, Simno swung from a drainpipe to land in the dark of some alley that radiated a foetid smell even to the rooftops. Vocho held his breath and followed.

The bastard was fit, Vocho had to give him that, and quick too. He came to the end of the alley and paused for breath. The alley led out into a tortuous street that, on this change, led to the Clockwork God outside the duelling guild, and home. Fifteen minutes from now, after all the clockwork had run its course, it would lead to Bescan Square and the night market. Vocho heaved air into his lungs and looked for movement among the shadows.

Difficult when half the street's buildings were artificers and clockers, all drenching their forges ready for the change. Smoke billowed out of almost every doorway, obscuring the street and anyone on it. He took a chance and went left, towards the God, for now anyway.

He came out of the smoke and steam on the other side, scarf up over his nose to stop him from choking, and came to where the street opened out to encompass a green space. There, there was the bastard, half way across the grass, dodging between the shadows of stunted trees that were blackened with soot. Vocho put on an extra spurt of speed and closed on him.

One last extra push, a reach with his sword to snag the man's breeches, and he was on the floor, Vocho following hard. Oh he was well named, Slippery Simno; he wriggled out of Vocho's grip and to his feet, Vocho half a second behind, his overhand slash stopping Simno from running again. For now.

Footsteps to one side, and Cospel appeared, armed with nothing that would get him arrested again – a dented pewter tankard that in its way was as good a weapon as any. Up on the wall of a clocker's factory, with a clank of mechanisms doing what they should, a dial showed three minutes to midnight.

"Too late to run now," Vocho said, moving a step closer. "No running in the change, if you want to keep your feet."

"Never too late," the man snarled, and a sword flashed in the dim moonlight that sliced through gaps in the curling smoke.

Vocho grinned to himself. A chance to gain a sterling bit of glory, and all to himself too because the perfect Kass was nowhere to be seen. Excellent.

He started as he always did, using Ruffelo's duelling rules for gentlefolk. A sporting chance for the opponent. A thrust, a parry, a riposte that he knocked off line. Ruffelo lasted right up until Simno raked his blade a scant inch in front of Vocho's face.

"You fight like a girl," Simno said with a wheezing laugh.

Vocho dodged the overhand blow, threw the blade off centre with a swirl of his cloak and returned the favour, lunging at a delicate area the gentle Ruffelo would never have approved of. "Actually, I've been fighting like a gentleman. But I can fight like the girls I know, if you like."

With that he lowered his blade a touch, leaving a clear opening that the fool went for. Vocho grabbed the front of Simno's tunic with his off hand and planted his forehead squarely on the git's nose, forever changing its shape. Simno staggered back, his nose gurgling, and Vocho pressed the advantage – a vicious cut to the sword arm that bit deep and had Simno drop his blade, swiftly followed by a boot to the stomach and then, when the poor sap bent forward with a whoosh of expelled breath, a knee to further ruin the nose.

The man sagged slowly, but not quietly, to the ground.

"See now," Vocho said to his unresponsive back, "all the girls that *I* know think Ruffelo's rules are for idiots, and that a good nose shot works wonders. I have to say I tend to agree, though I personally draw the line before we get to the stiletto to the heart, because it makes such a mess and you have to explain yourself afterwards. However, I have blood on my breeches now and I'm holding you personally responsible."

A pained gurgle was his only answer.

"He's a bit of a mess, Voch." Kass appeared from out of nowhere, cat like and disapproving all at once.

"Only because he was impugning your fighting skills. I felt called upon to defend your honour, and give him a demonstration."

That got him a snort of a laugh. "I'm sure you did, Voch, I'm sure you did. But if you were really going for my style, you missed a bit. Right in the cogs. If you catch them by surprise, it works a treat."

Vocho pulled himself into a pose that he imagined made him look haughty and put upon, but which only caused Cospel to choke on his own laughter. "Well, unlike some, I have standards. And a reputation for panache and dashing élan to keep up. And look what I did. Where's the style in that? I fought like, well, like a brute, *and* got blood all over my breeches. For you, Kass."

Kass yanked Slippery Simno to his feet, and held him there while he dripped blood all over the grass. "Tell you what, Voch, you can tell the prelate all about it, and you can add all those twiddly bits to the story that I know you love so much. This time tomorrow, all they'll be talking about is your panache. Now let's get somewhere safe before the clocks go off."

Suitably mollified, Vocho gave her a hand with the dead weight of Simno, while Cospel brought up the sniggering rear. "Fight like a girl. He wishes. More like fight like a pillock."

Vocho thought he was very magnanimous to ignore that.

The Cold Wind Oozes

Kelda Crich

THE COLD WIND oozed over the camp; seeping through the yellow canvas of the commanders' tents, blowing over the common soldiers huddled for warmth around scant campfire or sleeping under makeshift shelters. The cold wind stirred the tentacle horns of the impaled Viking heads arranged in rows along the perimeter. The cold wind carried the smell of that deep sea blood, ripe and rotted, onwards to the East, beyond Yellow England. The cold wind touched everything in camp. The cold wind knows no boundaries.

Within an unmarked tent – no need to alert the Vikings' brass periscopes to her presence – sat Mother Commander Clyfaed. She watched Brandon of Cragacre, sprawled naked and sleeping on the bed. Brandon, favoured son of one of Yellow England's five great families, looked entirely human. The Cragacres took pride in an unadulterated bloodline. They acknowledged no Fladdermus traits in their lineage. But Brandon was young. Some traits revealed themselves later in life. In middle age it was not unknown for a Cragacre to retire to some secluded monastery. Brandon was young, so young, a virgin to the battlefield, if not to the bed. His skin was unblemished, marred by neither Viking sucker, nor scar from a Crab Man's claw.

So young.

A letter of introduction from Duke Archibald Cragacre lay on the side table. In it, Brandon's uncle begged Mother Commander to pay special attention to his nephew. The Duke suggested Brandon may one day make a fine leader of soldiers. The letter, written in tiny script on vellum, lay curled next to a small statue covered in near-translucent weevil silk.

The wind blew against the tent, stirring the Stranglers' Monastery tapestries on the wall. Novices had given their eyesight and sometimes their minds to stitch these tapestries in weevil silk. They told of the coming of the High King from the celestial spheres, and the emergence of the Fladdermus from their sinkholes in the forest. To a lesser extent the tapestries told of the awakening of the others: the Viking Fish God and the Abominable Crab of the South. But above all, the tapestries told of the glorious and unrelenting breath of the High King's mind, blowing over the Yellow Kingdom, over the constant battles with the Viking fish raiders to the East and West, and the Crab Men scuttling on the great fungal plains.

Mother Commander stretched her long fingers, flexing her age-mottled hand membrane. Brandon slept on, blissfully unaware of her scrutiny.

A whisper of cold wind entered the tent and stirred the tapestries. His breath stirred the tapestries. The cold wind knows all secrets.

Mother Commander will still be watching Brandon when he wakes. She will ask him, "Do you think I'm beautiful, Brandon?"

This simple question will make Brandon's eyes bulge with panic. Potential leader of soldiers he may be, but he's not overburdened with wit.

The Mother Commander is known for her appreciation of truth. But there is also the undoubted truth that no woman likes to be unbeautiful to her lover. But how could Brandon say that this old woman was beautiful? Age is not beautiful. A body honed to hardness through years of battle, skin turned cold through years prostrate before the altar stone, eyes turned opaque reading old scrolls: all these things are not beautiful.

Brandon of Cragacre will gape at the Mother Commander, rendered speechless by the lie demanded of him.
And Mother Commander will say . . .
And the wind dies.

*

A RAP ON the tent post outside interrupted Mother Commander's visions of the future. This was her gift, given to her alone by the High King. The High King who turned the celestial spheres of the All-worlds, who blew through voids of future and past, whispered his visions through Mother Commander's needle mind. Such a gift should not be used for amusement. Such a gift should not be used to ask what Brandon of Cragacre will say to Mother Commander when he wakes.

Brother-Adjunct Gwain entered the tent, showing not a flicker of interest in the naked man sleeping in the bed. Gwain was the most ascetic person Mother Commander had ever encountered, only taking lovers on the required Festival days. Aesthetic, clean, efficient. Fladdermus blood ran weak in Gwain, although that was by chance rather than design. His family were serfs, like Mother Commander's own family. In Yellow England the common folk had married freely with the bat-like Fladdermus. Still, Gwain's only physical peculiarity was his eyes; one blue and one green.

"Gwain, why are you here? I told you to remain at the castle. With the Queen ailing, the five families need to be watched."

"I'm sorry, Mother Commander. The Queen commanded me to come here. Apparently, you've been ignoring her messages. She says she is dying and commands you into her presence."

"Then she's dying at an inconvenient time. Tomorrow's battle might push back the Vikings beyond Wing Valley."

Gwain helped himself to an apple from a box of sand. "The lines between the Vikings and Yellow England are a meandering stream, changing constantly over the years. We push, they pull." He wiped the sand from the apple and bit into the flesh.

Mother Commander glanced at the tapestries. A small panel showed a battle two centuries ago, where she'd first wet her blade on Viking blood. On that day Yellow England had shrunk. Mother Commander meant to push the Vikings back beyond Wing Valley and reclaim the land. She'd been looking forward to tasting battle again, but it did not do to tell Gwain everything. Of all Yellow Kingdom's men and women, Gwain was the one whose future she could not read on the High King's breath. "This battle is important, Gwain," she said.

"Did the High King tell you that?"

Mother Commander ignored the question. "Queen Ethelreld is old. She's been a long time dying. What do her leeches say?"

"They say she stands at the High King's gates. But there's more. The Queen commands me to tell you that she's been touched by the High King's breath."

"Does she indeed? And you believe her?"

"It's known that the High King sometimes touches the dying," said Gwain. "And they, like you, see where the wind blows."

"It is known," agreed the Mother Commander. "Although it is also known that dying people are subject to dreams. This could be nothing more than a dangerous delusion."

"She says if you do not come she will tell Duke Archibald about the vision."

"Does she, indeed? She has chosen a troublesome time to become a politician. But she has made a good mark. If it's something important, then I'll want to know before the Duke. Neither do I want the Duke to turn a Queen's vision to his advantage. And she wouldn't tell the nature of the vision?"

"No, Mother Commander."

"I see. Then I'll consider the Queen's command. But it would be a nuisance if I were to travel all the way back to the castle only to find her dead." Mother Commander turned the cloisonné ring on her middle finger, a gift from the Queen.

A whisper of cold caressed Mother Commander's hands. His breath touched her skin. The cold wind knows all secrets.

Dressed in yellow silk, Mother Commander will wait impatiently outside the Queen's room. She will enter the chambers and see the Queen Ethelred, lying close to death in the bed.

"You've come at last," the Queen will say.

"At your command, my Queen."

With a gesture the Queen will dismiss the servants and the leeches.

Mother Commander looks around the room. It feels cold, despite the fire burning in the massive hearth. On the mantle the candles burn red. It is Sevenday. The leech thinks to say something but seeing Mother Commander's face he thinks better of it. He hurries outside, closing the door softly behind him.

"Come closer," the Queen will say. "I have much to tell you."

And the wind dies.

Mother Commander sighed. "She will at least be alive on Sevenday."

"That's three days from now," said Gwain. "Time enough to reach Titchmus."

Mother Commander nodded. But travelling to Titchmus meant missing the Battle of Wing Valley.

*

OUTSIDE THE TENT, a soldier stood on guard, a veteran with Viking tentacles braided into a necklace. A common man, his Fladdermus blood showing in the coarse brown fur that covered his neck and served in place of hair.

"What's your name, soldier?"

"Tarn from Gypsumvale, Mother Commander. Artir is my mother. She told me to remember her to you, if I had the chance."

Mother Commander nodded. She did not remember Artir. In her time, she'd known many soldiers. She reached out and touched Tarn's arm.

A whisper of cold caressed Tarn, played with his dead tentacle necklace. His breath touched this Yellow England soldier. The cold wind knows all secrets.

Tarn of Gypsumvale will walk along the Wing Shore, mud weighing down his shoes. He will swing his two swords in the air. He will be surrounded by the others in his company, men and women dressed in yellow tunics over boiled leather. All good kingdom folk with the look of their Fladdermus heritage. Soldiers strengthened by the touch of the older race, in their snouts and long ears, in their webbed arms and hands, in the lightness of their step. Good Yellow England soldiers, blended of earth and sky.

"Hoi!" Tarn shouts, when he spots the first Viking men emerging from the River Wing, their gills fluttering, their tentacles thrashing wildly from side to side. "For the High King of Yellow England!" Tarn leads the soldiers forwards.

Tarn slashes through the throat of a Viking, before it has a chance to strike. At his side, a soldier screams. His nickname is Squealer, and his voice is high and unnatural. The Vikings moan, raising their hands to their heads, to stop the ingress of this mad-making noise. Tarn grins; most Fish Men cannot abide Squealer's song, although it does not bother the English soldiers. Some Vikings drop their weapons. Tarn's friends move for the kill, drenching the field in unclean blood that stinks of the ocean and rotted things. Unfortunately not all Fish Men are affected by Squealer. A Viking swings a double-headed axe at Tarn. Tarn parries the blow with his sword. With his other hand Tarn smashes his sword hilt into the Viking's face. The Viking thing falls backwards into Squealer. Another Viking is upon Tarn. They exchange savage blows. In his side view, Tarn sees Squealer and the Viking rolling in the mud. The Viking's tentacles quiver and manage to slide down Squealer's throat. When the squealing stops, the Vikings let out a croaking cheer. The Yellow Kingdom's advantage is lost. More Vikings emerge from the roiling water of River Wing.

Tarn parries his opponent's blow, and slides six inches of steel through the Viking's armour, pushing upwards, spilling ropes of rank guts. And still more Vikings emerge from the river. Another Viking is quickly upon

Tarn, screaming, too close for the touch of steel. Tarn's forehead slams into the Viking's nose, a lightning strike, but the Viking's head tentacles lash out. Tarn screams. Instinctively he pulls the tentacle, tearing off half his cheek. Tarn falls, but manages to plunge his sword at an impossible angle into his opponent's groin. The Viking falls, croaking, clutching his bleeding crotch.

In fever pain, Tarn will roll in the mud, seeding his face with infection, while around him the battle ranges. Yet while he endures, the Viking Men fall, until a low horn sounds retreat. And Tarn's company will leave him behind as they surge across the River Wing to claim the land and the valley.

And the wind dies.

*

"THANK YOU, SOLDIER," said Mother Commander. She'd already forgotten his name.

Back in the tent, Brandon was still sleeping.

"The battle will be ours." Mother Commander shook her head to clear the vision.

"Can you see further?"

"No. The High King's breath offers only glimpses."

"A very useful gift," said Gwain.

"When you are Father Commander you'd better not rely on them, Gwain. For weeks they come not at all. Yet today I've been gifted three times."

"The High King is changeable," said Gwain, quoting a popular folk saying. "Does this mean that you go to the Queen?"

"I will," said Mother Commander. "But say nothing of my vision to anyone. Knowledge of the future has a way of changing it."

"I'd have thought that knowledge of the victory would aid our soldiers."

"Then you'd have thought wrong. The High King moves through changing futures. Perhaps if the soldiers knew my vision, they'd become over-confident and the battle would be lost."

Gwain nodded. He walked over to the sleeping Brandon and looked down at him. "Whatever you did to him, you wearied him."

"Wake him," said Mother Commander. "He'll accompany us." She pulled the silk from the statue on the side table. It was an old thing, a Fladdermus thing, carved from ancient glass never found above ground. She passed her hands over the statue, and when she turned back to Gwain her face was a little younger, and the face of the waking Brandon was marked with a few years. And if he noticed the changes, Gwain said nothing.

*

MOTHER COMMANDER, GWAIN and Brandon travelled in a company of ten soldiers, who were glad, no doubt, to have escaped the battle of Wing Valley.

Brandon had attempted to be amusing, until Mother Commander sent him to ride with the common soldiers. Mother Commander and Gwain passed the time discussing court politics. Mother Commander was naturally interested in the Queen's vision. "And she would not even hint about the revelation?"

"No, except it distressed her deeply."

Mother shook her head. "It irritates me that she pulls me away from battle. When you're advisor to the throne, Gwain, you must be more careful than me."

Gwain smiled. "There are none more careful than you, Mother Commander."

That was so. That was why she had retained the position of Mother Commander these two centuries, and with the aid of the Fladdermus statue, secured in a leather pouch around her neck, there was no reason she couldn't reign for decades more. But she'd been foolish. Her sentimentality about Wing Valley had led her away from court at a dangerous time of transition. And there was Gwain to consider. Was he still loyal? Or was the Queen's vision a subterfuge?

"Why is it that I can never read your future, Gwain? Does the wind not blow around you?"

"The breath of the High King touches everyone, Mother Commander. I don't know why you can't see my future."

*

ON THE SECOND day they rode though Stranglers' Wood. Mother Commander had been raised in this forest. When she'd been a child the woods had been oak. But the coming of the High King had brought many new things into the kingdom: animals and plants of a type never described in scrolls, or in the memory of the common kingdom folk.

The travellers wore veils around their faces as the air was cloudy with seed spores. Afterwards they'd need to wash carefully, for it was not unknown for the seeds to root in the eyes, ears, mouths or other moist places. The tenacious spores also germinated in the cracks and crevices of the oak trees, and grew smothering branches that overwhelmed their hosts. The roots of the stifling trees hung in the air, twitching, seeking small animals and the limbs of unwary travellers. Within the trees flitted long-limbed, flying creatures, a cross between a bat and a beetle, a creature only found in Stranglers' Wood. They watched the travellers from behind glossy green leaves.

At the Wish Tree, Mother Commander halted the party. This was the greatest and oldest tree in Stranglers' Wood, a monstrous tree covering several hectares. From its high branches jangled bones, victims of the tree's questing roots and sacrifices to the tree from the common folk. Newly emerged leaf buds were encased in scales, patterned like snake skin and textured like leather. The traveller's feet crunched the discarded scales to powder.

"In the High King's realm the trees are thus," said Mother Commander.

"Then we're fortunate to have this glimpse while here on Earth." Gwain made the half circle sign across his chest.

With great solemnity, the soldiers held a rabbit up as offering to the Wish Tree. The roots snatched the struggling animal and drew it high into the branches, to dangle amidst the wooden gibbets.

"There may come a time when there's only one tree." said Brandon. "Yggdrasil, the World Tree."

Mother Commander frowned. "Speak not of Viking stories to me. Is that what your uncle teaches you?"

"No," said Brandon. "I'm sorry, Mother Commander. I only thought . . ."

"Don't think. It's not your strong point."

"We are close to Stranglers' Monastery." Gwain pointed to the sandstone spires that split the forest vista. "Shall we pay our respects? We have time, I think."

"What do you think, Brandon?" asked Mother Commander

"Me?"

"If you're to be a commander of soldiers as your uncle wishes, you must make decisions. Shall we delay our journey to visit the monastery?"

Brandon looked into the sky for help with such a monumental decision. His brow creased, his mouth moved without words as he pondered the question. Mother Commander waited, marvelling at his stupidity. It was quite wonderful that a man could be so stupid and still function. Brandon would never be a great military leader. But he had other qualities, she recalled. Finally, she could bear it no longer. "I think we should go to the monastery. Don't you agree, Brandon?"

"Yes, Mother Commander, that's exactly what I was thinking."

"Your father's sister is in command there, isn't she? Cécile of Cragacre. I hear that your aunt examines my judgements and finds them wanting. Have you heard that, Brandon?"

Brandon shook his head furiously. "No. Not at all. I haven't seen her for many years, but I'm sure she is a loyal subject. For who would put themselves above the will of the High King?"

Built on a sandstone outcrop over honeycomb caves, Stranglers' Monastery was renowned. From those caves the Fladdermus had first emerged, crawling from their ancient hidey-holes to greet the coming of the High King. It will be politic to visit; the nuns grew fractious under the leadership of Cécile of Cragacre.

The wind stirred the bones in the Wish Tree. His breath stirred the skeletons. The cold wind knows all secrets.

Mother Commander will lead the party to the monastery. Cécile of Cragacre will open the gates herself and will welcome them.

Cécile and Mother Commander greet each other warmly and talk pleasantly of inconsequential things. Cécile will invite the travellers to prayer in the High Chapel. With smiles she'll lead them to the ornate sandstone room, lit with sunlight pouring through the famed chapel window showing the High King emerging from hidden celestial spheres. Cécile of Cragacre bows to the travellers and leaves them to their contemplation, closing the chapel door behind her. Mother Commander hears the twist of a key turning in the lock. Something is wrong.

Underneath the chapel the party hear the sound of movement, the sound of many feet. Fladdermus? The party draw their weapons. Gwain bangs against the locked chapel door, demanding release, while Mother Commander scans the chapel for an escape route. There is none. The minor windows are high and narrow. The large altar window is made of ancient glass, unbreakable. The door is iron-solid strangler wood.

At the north wall, two doors lead from the chapel crypts and the underground caves. "Guard the doors," shouts Mother Commander.

The soldiers divide and run to the two doors as the enemy emerges. It is not Fladdermus, nor Viking Fish Men. The Crab Men come, chitin feet clacking on the polished floor.

"Abominations!" shouts Gwain.

The Crab Men swarm forward, a dozen at each door, pushing back the soldiers, while Mother Commander and Gwain beat furiously at the chapel main door, demanding exit from this killing room. The soldiers attempt to contain the Crab Men at the doors to the crypt, but their efforts are futile. Mother Commander sees a soldier snipped clean in half by a massive claw. Mother Commander, Gwain and Brandon alone are left to battle. Mother Commander will have her fight, after all.

Two dozen Crab Men clatter into the chapel, their heads flickering light in the language of their kind. Her sword unsheathed, Mother Commander steps to the right, in front of Gwain. Screaming she throws herself into the battle, her long sword slicing through the hard skin of the nearest Crab Man, severing its arm. There is no blood. Crab Men are not flesh.

As she fights, Mother Commander's mind is racing. Crab Men in the heart of Yellow England! It is unheard of! Cécile of Cragacre has made an audacious pact. But the High King is entrenched in this kingdom. It is a foolish ploy. Are the Cragacres seeking to convert Yellow England to a bastion of the Crab? Was this the Queen's vision? The triumph of the Crab Men, the Mi-Go from the stars.

Brandon is fighting hard. Gwain's poison blade flashes silver. But this poison does not kill the spongey fungal flesh of the Crab Men. Mother Commander severs the cauliflower head of her opponent and turns to face the next Crab Man, but as she twists she feels the crushing weight of a claw around her leg. Beheaded but not dead, the fallen Crab Man still moves. Mother Commander stabs downwards, her sword seeking another brain. She wishes desperately for a flamethrower. She would burn Stranglers' Monastery to the ground, if she had the chance. The crushing pain in her leg intensifies to white burning fire. The Crab Man is still not dead. Mother Commander glances up at the stained glass of the chapel, at the High King surrounded by stars, as he blows though the void and claims Yellow England as his dominion.

The soldiers are dead. Brandon is dead.

"Save yourself, Gwain," shouts Mother Commander, although she does not know how that can be done, there are too many enemies.

Mother Commander falls. The beheaded Crab Man's claws leave her foot and close over her wrists, severing her hands. She never knew there could be so much blood. With her last sight Mother Commander will see a Crab Man looming over her, a metal canister held in its claw. In these canisters the Mi-Go take the living brains of their prey to their distant worlds. There are worse things than death.

And the wind dies.

"I've reconsidered," said Mother Commander. "Brandon, you will take my respects to Cécile of Cragacre, and tell her that the Queen commands me to make no delay."

"As you wish." Brandon looked pleased to be tasked with such responsibility.

Good. There was no need to alert Cécile to the fact that Mother Commander knew of the treachery. Once she reached Titchmus, Mother Commander would send a hundred soldiers to clear out the nest of Crab Men and to retrieve Cécile of Cragacre for interrogation.

*

MOTHER COMMANDER SET a wild pace leaving Stranglers' Wood. Once beyond the trees, they continued fast on the road, not stopping for sleep. The party arrived at Titchmus Castle as dawn broke on Sevenday.

From there it was quick work for Mother Commander to send a hundred soldiers to Stranglers' Monastery. Then she washed and dressed in yellow silk, and made her way to the Queen's chamber.

Mother Commander tapped her foot on the stone floor as she waited impatiently outside the Queen's room. When she entered the chambers she saw Queen Ethelreld, lying listless on the bed.

"You've come at last," said Ethelreld.

"At your command."

With a gesture, the Queen dismissed the servants and the leeches.

Mother Commander looked around the room. It felt cold, despite the fire burning in the massive hearth. On the mantle the Sevenday candles burnt red.

The servants left the room. The leech thought to say something, but seeing Mother Commander's face he thought better of it; he hurried outside and closed the door softly behind him.

"Come closer," the Queen said. "I have much to tell you."

Mother Commander took the chair beside the bed. She leant close to the Queen. "What was your vision?"

"I'm dying and I'm consumed by regrets, Mother Commander."

"You've been a good queen. You've been a good servant of the High King." That much was true. Ethelreld had established garrisons on the borders, repaired the castle walls of Titchmus and converted it into a fortress that would not be taken easily. "When Lethreld of Davidbrethren was abducted by the Viking men and murdered, you avenged that death in full. You've formed alliance with the Seven Cities and bought the Viking Hauntminster into the kingdom. The common folk of Yellow England love you and pledge their loyalty to you. You've been a good Queen, and now you stand at the High King's gate." The yellow silk of Mother Commander's veil clung to her face, as if her very skin was made of yellow fabric.

"I have done what was expected," said Ethelreld. "But as I stand at death's gate, I've been touched by horror."

"Which is?"

"Everything is a lie," whispered the Queen. Her hand clutched convulsively at the bedclothes. "The first Queen, Laeigratha, came to me in vision, all dressed in yellow tatters. She spoke to me of the after world. It is no place of ease, Mother Commander. It is a strange place of enduring agonies, where the dead dance in pain to the High King's pleasure."

"What else did she tell you?

"Isn't that enough? The High King's realm is not joy, but an abyss. You must make this known to the people, Mother Commander. We worship malice."

"This is the bargain we have made," said Mother Commander. "When the Fish God rose in the Northern lands, the Viking men threatened to drown England. And from the stars came the repugnant Crab Men, seeding the South with spreading fungus. I was young then, but ambitious. I made my way to the castle scriptorium and found old scrolls, written in the Fladdermus tongue, and a priest who could still read the words. I said the High King's words and pledged this land to Him. Then the Fladdermus emerged from their caves and strengthened us. And the High King rode the winds over this Yellow England, and we were pledged to enter his Kingdom. It was the only way, when enemies encroached from all sides."

"No!" said Queen Ethelfeld. "We must rid ourselves of the High King."

"And then what would happen?" asked Mother Commander. "We cannot fight our enemies without him. The gods are risen, the Fish of the Viking North, the Mi-Go Crabs of the South. They do not look to the welfare of our people. Would you see the people of Yellow England subjugated to the Fish Men, or to the Crabs? Would that be better?"

"The price is too high," said the Queen.

"This life is but a pleasant interlude before the eternal," said Mother Commander.

"This cannot be. Everything is a lie."

"It can be and it is, and it will be forever."

"I will make this known," said the Queen, struggling to rise from her bed. She coughed, staining the sheets with a splatter of blood. "This *cannot* remain a secret."

"There are no secrets from the cold wind," said Mother Commander. "Or from me." She took a pillow from the bed and held it over Ethelred's face. A matter of minutes only before the frail Queen was dead. She was not the first sovereign that Mother Commander had murdered. They waited for her in the High King's realm.

Mother Commander sat watching the dead Queen, considering politics. A new ruler must be selected from the five families. The Cragacres had moved against the Kingdom. How should they be controlled? Mother Commander reached for a vision of the future, but it did not come. The cold wind knew all, but it did not always share its secrets.

She would discuss the matter with Gwain.

She considered the options, but sitting in the room with the dead Queen, Mother Commander's thoughts turned inexorably to the time she would enter the High King's realm. Thousands would be waiting for her. They would tear off her silks, and she would scream for a thousand years. This the cold wind knows, and it has shown her many times.

Yet, in those long years of after death in the High King's realm, she will from time to time be sustained by hope. The cold wind does not know all. There is Gwain, who the cold wind cannot touch. In the cold aeons of the High Kingdom, Mother Commander will think of Gwain, and she will know that all things pass, and that some things are not touched by His breath.

And that even to the cold wind, there are secrets.

Sword-Dancer of Azmai

Roz Clarke

I. The Whale

HUNKER INTO MYSELF as I edge through the crowd, into the cavernous circus tent. It's futile: I stand head and shoulders above most of the people of Amitsa. Glances shoot my way; all miss their mark. I keep my gaze inward. She is near, or has been. Like a hound reading the past and the present in scent, I smell magic. Skylla's trace is unmistakeable – freshly turned earth, coppery blood, and the tang of bonemarrow.

It's too warm in the tent. There must be six hundred people here. They've come from all over Amitsa: from Craego, Ygodaygh . . . none from Azmai, but that's no surprise. I was the only one coming down that mountain pass, and along the road I met no-one making the journey from the dragon-god's realm onto the plains. No-one going the other way, either. Trade that once was lively and lucrative has dried almost to nothing.

I take a seat as the lights come up. Plumes of smoke jet from around the edge of the arena. My hand goes to the amulet at my throat. The crowd falls silent.

The show is a re-enactment of the Empire's conquest of the plains, once called *Lim Ren Azmai o Zental'a*, then the Southern Amitsan Plains, and now simply Amitsa,, as if those nomads had never existed and the Empire never reached beyond, from here in the dry south to the Drana'p'an, the isles of the ice-witches that float at the top of the world.

I have to wait almost until the interval before she appears. Flickering corpse-lights dance above the heads of the crowd. Dancers appear between the tiers of benches and fling themselves into the arena. With white feathers in their headdresses and bells around their ankles, they caper obscenely. The crowd whoops with laughter.

What have we become? I wonder. Once we made ships that carried our warriors and traders wherever they wished to go, no matter which way the wind blew. Now, our glory is an empty spectacle.

I was a sea-singer in those days, a living embodiment of Mystececia. I can still hear vir voice in my dreams, but can no longer answer. Amitsa-that-is sits landlocked between the volcanic ridge of Azmai, claimed by the Hostis but yet denied to them, and the black marshlands of the Wettite tribe.

A figure descends from the dark heights, arms and legs entwined in red ribbons. She flicks and twists, and suddenly she's free. It's her: few have such absolute grace, such muscular poise. She stands perfectly still. In the air above her head appear five glowing swords. The mob attacks. She draws two short-swords, and, with seven blades at her command, fights. Skylla is magnificent, but I have no interest in this pantomime.

When the crowd rushes to the bar for interval drinks, I make my way to the conjoined tent where the circus performers prepare. Nobody challenges me. I eventually find Skylla outside, where the full moon hangs heavy and the air is sweet with the scent of trisk shit.

Close up, she looks tired. "The spangles don't suit you, Skylla." Her eyes widen. "And your grandmother would never've shown so much leg."

"Whale." She grinds her cigarillo out beneath her heel. "What are you doing here? And don't—" she looks around, on edge. "Don't use that name. That's not who I am, here."

"You're going by Madame De La Morta, Mistress of the Blades – even on your smoke breaks?"

"Of course not. That's just for the posters."

She leans against the rail around the mounts' enclosure. Her face is impassive, but her hands tighten around the wood, knuckles pale through dark skin.

"I need to talk to you."

"I won't go with you, old vellaw. Nothing has changed. I won't go to war."

I laugh. Her eyes flash with anger.

"Get out of here, *maiyar* deathmonger!" she yells. "Go on!"

"Deathmonger," I repeat. "You always had such a temper."

Her raised voice draws the attention of a knot of performers at the entrance to the tents. One of them lopes over. His face is painted into a grinning skull, but his mouth scowls.

Skylla turns her anger on him. "Why the frown, Kodju? You should be covered in smiles. Here's my mother's guardian, come to lead me to my destiny. Just as you prayed for, to every Laoram who would listen, and every one who would not!"

The young man's face contorts. Stung by Skylla's sarcasm, but strangely hopeful.

"We'll ride to Azmai?" he asks, in an unmistakable accent.

Skylla wrenches around to face the grazing trisk. "You go if you want. Go home, I won't cry for you. I will never fight for this fat sea-monster, or for that little puppet who calls herself Empress."

She turns back and fixes me with a glare. "I am *not* my grandmother."

"Will you stamp your foot, preshka? You wear Osalma's life for this ridiculous show, but you're mad at *me*? Oh, my Skylla. Sometimes I do wonder what the world has come to."

They go back inside for the second half. I stay outside with the trisk and the ripe yellow moon.

II. Osalma

OUR POINT RIDER *tore down a loose-floored arroyo, trisk bellowing, huge feet skidding, its feathered mane erect, as if the treacherous mountain slope could be intimidated by a fan of iridescent eyes.*

Beyond the rider, red streaks from the volcano glowed fiercely against the mid-morning sky. A fearsome shape coalesced out of the glare and arrowed towards us. Azmai. The trembling of the Amitsan warriors was one with the trembling of the mountain.

"On!" cried the Empress. "Can savages and their lizard-lord frighten the Swords of the Eternal Empire?"

We readied ourselves and rode on. When we crested the arroyo and emerged onto the plateau we saw an army of Azmai Hostis before us. Above, the dragon-god flew like a red-gold pennant hung upon the heavens.

I wasn't afraid. I was a Sword-arm of the Empress. A blood-mage, like my grandmothers before me. I'd come across the marshes, and before that the awful sea and the northern plains beyond.

Beside me rode the Whale. Our eyes met. "This is your battlefield, Osalma. Mysticecia can help us little here. I will fight at your back. Courage and victory!"

"Courage and victory!" I yelled. "Let there be a sea of blood, monk-fish, so wide that your Loaram may find us yet!" Then the runners were around us and instinct took over. I gripped my swords in each hand, and the claws of my gauntlets pierced my palms. I raised my arms above my head and the spikes on the inside of my pauldrons drove into the muscles of my shoulders. Enough blood spilled to release my power, I forced the runners forward. They scattered to either side, to press the enemy's flanks.

Trusting my trisk to run straight, I focussed inwards, summoning the Swords of Light. They shimmered into the air, come over from Ap'da: the world-beside. The armies faded and blurred. The Whale beside me grew massive, reeking of seaweed and emanating drowning.

Across the plateau, Loaram Azmai's wings spread wide. The volcano's glow looked like a city, sacked and burning. A reminder of who we were. I clenched my teeth and my fists, driving the spikes in further. I would slaughter our enemies and bind the lizard-god down against the stones.

III. Kodju

WE RIDE THE next day for the capital. The big grey vellaw had a word with Bralue, and he came back and said the troupe could decide: come to Craego and perform for the Empress, or stay here and work on a new show. I guess money changed hands, because Bralue stopped whining about how the troupe would eat for the next month. He is a deceitful old suck pump. We've been selling out for months, but nobody *I* know has been eating duck in wine.

They decided to come, so we ride at the front of a caravan. This feels normal, except for the big vellaw who never takes his eyes off Sally, and the churning in my guts that's never stopping. I reach for Sally at night, but she turns her shoulder-blade to me and I lie awake with my hands pressed to my belly. It's worse than being alone.

I can tell we're close to Craego when, over the shrubs bordering the wide road, we see long, rolling rows of purple flowers. The Whale rides alongside me and says: "We are lucky to be here in spring. The crocuses are at their most spectacular."

"You like flowers?" I ask, trying to sound cheerful.

"It's the closest thing to a view of the sea anywhere in the Southern Plains."

"Why use that name?"

"There are still northern plains, my boy, they just don't kneel to the Fallen Empress any more. Why would they? There's a clue in that name, too."

"Do you call her that to her face?" I mutter. I think ve hears, but ve says nothing.

We reach Craego and pitch our tents in the gardens of the palace as dusk gathers. The Whale takes Sally to be presented to the Empress. When they return, they go into Bralue's tent, and moments later Bralue comes out looking worried, more than usual. He spots me and calls out: "Tell everyone we're doing *Song of the Stars.*"

"But we can't just—" He waves away my objections.

Everyone's yelling about how it can't be done, when Bralue and the Whale come into the tent.

"Simmer down," says Bralue. The mob gets louder.

The Whale makes a strange, mournful, not-human noise. Hush falls. "*Thank* you," ve says. "A performance of *Homeland Heroes* would cause distress to the Hostis delegation. Delicate talks are in progress. Her Majesty begs your understanding."

Sickness roils in my belly. We are to bend over backwards not to offend these murderous savages, so we can negotiate some mealy-mouthed compromise? I want to object, but my voice has fled in disgust.

It's a rough performance. Sally gives it everything she's got and afterwards, pale and exhausted, falls into my arms. I carry her to our tent and help her out of her costume. I salve her wounds. I kiss her hands. She shakes her head when I make to speak.

The Empress comes to congratulate her. "Oh, it was marvellous!" Her eyes shine. What nine-year-old would not enjoy a circus? "I especially enjoyed *your* parts. The Swords of Light!" Sally bobs her head. She doesn't mention the fact that these Swords are mere illusions. When I think about this, my love for her becomes a burden. I'm ashamed for both of us.

While the Whale attends the negotiations, we explore Craego. We eat exotic food and drink exotic wines until we reel with merriment. We spar between the tents, dancing over the guy ropes. We make love clumsily, desperately, and it's not like it was before.

As we ride to Azmai my turmoil grows. I dreamed of an army, and all we have are a few ceremonial guards and a coven of politicos. Worse, the enemy rides with us. They speak in their own tongue and laugh when they catch me watching them.

The noon sun blazes above us when we reach my family's lands. Sally and I are arguing.

"What makes you think they'll honour the treaty, not turn Azmai to their side and scorch us all? You don't know what they're like."

"I haven't forgotten what's happened to your family. The decision to trust the Hostis isn't yours, nor mine. It is the Empress', and the council's. We must do our duty to Amitsa."

"A child and a flock of old women! How can *this* fulfil our duty?"

"We must trade, or starve. Do you want me to bind every spirit in every stone, every grove, every stream in Azmai? I could bury all my bones and not bind a tenth of them."

"All I know is that if I could do it myself, I would do it, a thousand times. You are a *blood-mage;* what's the good of that if you won't defend your people?"

"We have no divine right to Azmai, no more than we did the rest of the Empire. We will survive."

"Your grandmother bought us the right."

That night, I follow Sally down the track between the thorn bushes. She's heading for the shrine to our valley's Loaram. Why is she sneaking off? Why has she let me suffer, thinking she didn't care? I keep my distance, walking softly. I know every turn in the track, every hiding place.

She stops at the shrine, looking up at the twisting, ferny figure. The carving is beautiful and menacing; wolf-like teeth snarling, ears pressed back against its head. Sally clenches her fists, rubs her palm against the stone. She steps back, hands on the hilts of her swords. The carving shifts and the black eyes glow violet. The teeth shine and the gums glisten red.

"Loaram of the valley," says Sally, bowing her head. "I come on behalf of one to whom you have done great harm. He cannot rest until that harm is redressed. The ghosts of those you killed cannot rest. His people cannot walk this valley but in darkest dread."

"His people are strangers to me," it growls.

"They have dwelt here for three generations."

"They drove out *my* people, who yet fear and love me. Who yet pray, and burn offerings; they cross the abominable border and keep me alive. I will not abandon them."

"Alive, in hatred and resentment."

It smiles, all teeth and eyes.

"The settlers were prepared to love you," she says. "They love the valley. They fear you because of what you have done, but even now, they do not hate you."

"You lie."

Can it feel my hatred? Sally spreads her hands, palms up. "Soon your people will return. The Amitsans will withdraw and return the mountain to the Hostis. Does this comfort you?"

"Will justice be done to those who drove out my people and cut the ground with cold steel?" The spirit sneers. "You know it will not."

"I'm sorry. I must bind you now. It would have been best to do so with your heart at peace."

"I will rend you limb from limb and defile your corpse, necromage! You have no sacrifice; you have no power."

"I'm not a necromancer. I'm a blood-mage. I will lock you beneath the earth."

Sally draws her short swords. The wolf-thing lunges at her. Her blades whirl. The spirit snaps at her throat. Its teeth click, inches short but all too real. An image of of Sally ripped and rent, broken and lost, pushes into my head. *You won't do to her what you did to my mother,* I think, forcing myself only to watch, and not to move.

At first her blades slice clean through the monster, but as they turn black in the moonlight, blood running down the grooves in the metal, they begin to bite. Her dancer's balance and agility are little use against this foe. There's force behind its attacks, but it isn't bound by mortal physics. Again and again it drives forward, wrapping her limbs in indigo fronds, fangs seeking flesh. It slashes at her, never finding a purchase, but she's tiring. Her thrusts are slowing, her chest heaving. Eventually its jaws close around her forearm. She hacks at its neck with her free sword, but it doesn't let go. I leap into the clearing, my knife drawn-!

"No Kodju!" she shouts. "You can't help!"

I plunge my knife into the thing's back. My blade passes through it and buries itself in the ground. My knees hit dirt. I let go of the knife and roll forward, past Sally's booted feet. Blazing pain lights up my shoulder. Immortal fangs pierce my leather cuirass and my skin, lodging against my bones. I scream. I can't see anything, but I feel Sally wrestling the monster, trying to wrench it off my back.

When I come to, she's standing over the prone Loaram. Its head has disappeared between its fronds. It whimpers. Flat red ropes, like bloodstained bandages, bind it tight.

She pulls off her left gauntlet, wincing as the spurs tug her wounds. She holds up her bare hand, regards it briefly, then in one swift motion slices her little finger off: it drops to the ground. Ignoring my cry of horror, she presses the flat of her blade against the stump. When she takes it away there is no bleeding. She pokes the severed finger with the toe of her boot.

The finger sinks into the soil. Three white spikes emerge. She takes each one and bends it across the body of the monster, creating a cage. She passes her injured hand across her eyes, mutters something. The cage and its contents drop, as if in quickmud, until nothing can be seen. She stops to light a cigarillo, before she comes to tend to me.

IV. Osalma

THE HOSTIS OUTNUMBERED us seven to one, but they had no blood-mage. Like countless other tribes across the world, they'd never met a force like ours. The dragon-god was formidable, but they had not the lore or power to bind vir fully. Still, many of our warriors were scorched to embers before I gathered the strength to call vir down.

I stood on my trisk's back. Her bright feathers were sticky with blood; mine, hers, friends', foes'. The Swords of Light whirled around me. The Whale fought at my back. Ve had lost vir trisk, yet vir head was still as high as mine. My eyes were gummy with blood. My mouth was copper-full, my body a simple meat shell for a being made of light and pain. The Whale held vir amulet high, vir scent mingling with the scents of gore, burnt mountain grass and cooked flesh. The Swords were bright and sharp, more real than real, the bodies they sliced into were mere shadows. Shadows shot through with ruby; ruby that melted and flowed into pools on the ground. The power I drew from the ebbing lives of all those warriors – quickly, quickly, before their blood cooled – washed away the boundaries of my mind and I touched the essence of the dragon-god.

"Loaram Azmai," I whispered.

Ve lashed vir tail, dove towards me, wings folded. I recalled the Swords from their butchery and arrayed them above my head, points directed at the dragon's plummeting heart. They shimmered: coruscating fire. The swords in my hands were things of the earth, and they drew blood viscerally, their blades an unbroken line from my will to my arms to the throats of my enemies. The Swords of Light were something else; they danced and sang for love of blood alone: sought it, smelt it, spilled it and rejoiced. I could direct them only as one directs a falcon. By their quivering obedience I knew they desired the blood of Azmai.

At the bottom of vir stoop, ve tilted and stretched, talons gleaming, eyes bright as the sun in winter.

Ve dipped vir head and belched fire. The Whale threw one arm into the air, and as Azmai landed, vir flames were driven back by a dank miasma, as of sea-caves when the tide has flowed away.

"Azmai," I said. "My people will take this mountain, the range beyond, and all the land about. I must bind you. Will you be bound?"

The answer was No. I was shaking with No. I would be blown to nothing and the Amitsan army too. The Empire would dwindle and vanish. Azmai would rule a blasted land before ve bowed vir neck to my binding.

The Swords pounced. The dragon-god knocked two of them back, and three buried themselves in vir feathers.

A jolt threw me sideways. I arced through the air, thumping to the ground. The Whale had pushed me from the back of my trisk. A spear passed through the space I had occupied. The sky was black with ash, the sun blotted out.

The Hostis had not fled when their god came to earth. They rallied, and swarmed over us. The world was nothing but the clash of steel on steel, the cries and groans of the dying, blood, guts and the reek of death.

V. Skylla

BEFORE THE GATHERED dignitaries, atop the bone-strewn plateau, I face the entrance to the tomb where my grandmother once bound the Loaram Azmai to the earth. My mind is numb. *I can't do this. This is not my place. This is not my destiny.* Dancing the role of Osalma in a circus show has not prepared me to take on her mantle on this wind-scoured mountain. The stump of my missing finger throbs in agony with every beat of my heart.

"Blood-mage?" says the Hostis priest, vir hand on my arm. I can feel vir apprehension. I want to shake my head and put an end to this charade, but I nod, and raise my hand. Guards heave the slab aside. Inside is utter darkness.

It's a little like standing on the platform high in the circus tent, ready to step into space and descend on my invisible wire. But there is no wire. Nevertheless, I step forward, because everyone is watching me and that's what they expect me to do. The priest grabs at me, and together we pass into the rock-walled tomb. My throat thickens with – not soil, but the idea of soil, the memory of soil, of rock, of captivity.

A clicking of flints, and the priest holds a lit candle. Trembling, I squeeze my fist. Five drops of blood, five ersatz Swords of Light. Though false, they glow. The priest hisses, does not blow vir candle out.

"Azmai?" ve asks.

Before us is a cage of bone and within it lies the dragon-god. Ve is grey, as though carved from the rock around us, but when I reach between the bars I feel soft feathers. My hand comes away streaked with dust. So many, many bones, to hold this half-dead god against the earth.

A deep groan comes from all around us. The chamber shakes.

The priest falls to vir knees, muttering in Hostin. A bulky shape materialises beside me.

"Whale."

"Skylla."

A moment of silence, then: "You must speak with your grandmother."

"She's dead, Whale."

"She's here. So many died that day. She was so strong. When she . . . passed—" Vir gaze becomes unfocused. "—she remained in Ap'da. You must enter the world-beside."

Ve grasps my hand in vir huge one. I feel like a child again, putting my trust in vir to lead me. "We will not swim deep," ve says. Releasing my hand, ve takes a pouch from within vir cloak. When ve opens it, there's a strong smell. "The salt weed of the rocky shore beside the shrine to Mysticecia. It's a long time since I made pilgrimage – I have only a little, but it should be enough." Ve dips vir hand into the pouch and brings it out dripping. Three passes and my head and face are soaked in vile brine.

The Whale puts vir arms around me and the world shifts. The chamber grows brighter, Osalma's bone cage whiter, the dragon-god's feathers shine, and the Whale's eyes grow dark and limpid. The Hostis priest becomes a shadow of virself.

The Whale presses my injured hand against the bone cage. I bite my lip; the stump is hidden in my gauntlet. I don't want sympathy.

The bone-cage shudders and brightness swirls away from the structure and coalesces into a glimmering image of a woman – it is like looking into a mirror at myself after a performance. Her skin is taut, her eyes intense, her mouth a hard line of pain.

"Osalma," says the Whale. "Preshka."

"Whale." The spirit hisses, a susurrating whisper. "My *deliverer*."

Tears roll from the Whale's rock-pool eyes. "You gave everything."

"Does the Empire thrive?"

"We cannot hold Azmai. We must make a new peace, for the sake of trade. This is your granddaughter, Skylla. We are ordered to undo the binding and return Azmai to the Hostis."

She turns her awful gaze to me. "Isman lives?"

The Whale speaks for me. "Your daughter died valiantly. I raised a carved monument amidst the salt marshes. Her memory lives."

Osalma's ghost lets out a chilling moan and lunges towards the Whale. "I left her in _your_ care."

"Ap'da!" The voice of the priest, startled, triumphant. "Rana'a mi carulin va-sha Azmai!"

We turn to see the priest blowing a fistful of golden sparks into the bone cage. A small fire blazes behind vir.

"Not yet!" says the Whale.

"What?" I ask. "What's happening?"

"We are ordered," repeats the Whale, speaking low and urgently, "to release the dragon-god to the Hostis. This priest is pledged to bind Azmai in vir own fashion."

INSIDE THE CAGE, the feathered god twitches. Ve struggles and flutters. Looking past Osalma, I see the true Swords of Light, driven through vir wings and tail, pinning them to the rock.

"Free me!" Vir command reverberates inside my chest.

"Never!" Osalma cries.

"Priest," I say to the Hostis, who appears crazed with delight at vir success. "You must ready your bindings before I break this cage."

"Break the cage?" screeches my grandmother's ghost.

The priest stops capering and nods eagerly. "Bindings ready."

I look to the Whale. Ve sniffs the air. "There is powerful fire magic here, but – Azmai . . ." Ve shrugs. "We have given our word to the Empress."

Osalma screams in fury and snatches at my arms. I ignore her, leaving her to the Whale, who wraps vir arms around her and holds her close. There are a thousand things I want to ask her. I want to know her, to hear her story in her own words instead of from the untrustworthy mouth of the Whale, but there's no time. I clench my fists until the spurs grind against my bones. I let the blood run down onto my hands, then place them against the nearest bar of the bone-cage. I'm surprised when the bone responds to my touch. I concentrate my power. The bone starts to dissolve. Somehow it's dissolving *into* me. The stump of my lost finger throbs, and joint by joint I feel it growing back. Though Osalma still rails against me, I start to feel a connection with her, with the power she wielded in life. I move around the cage weakening the bars, until, with my swords, I can slice through them.

Meanwhile, the gazes of the priest and Azmai are locked together. When the last bone strut falls, the dragon-god rears up vir head atop the long, sinuous neck. The priest exclaims: "I will, Loaram!" Ve is holding a bag of vir own, and from it ve draws a pigeon, feet and wings bound. It struggles just as Azmai did. The priest twists its neck, throws it to the ground and smashes the body with vir heel.

The ground shudders and heaves. The walls of the chamber are blasted away and the light of the plateau pours in. The delegations and the pretty guards in their pretty uniforms are showered with shattered rock; they cower and cry out.

"This is no binding," says the Whale. I have never hear vir sound afraid before.

Terrified, I rush the priest and knock vir down, straddle vir and shove a blade against vir windpipe.

"What are you doing?" Ve shakes vir head, straining to turn vir face to vir Loaram. I push the blade a little deeper. "Tell me."

A thundering of trisk feet shakes the ground around me. "I told you we couldn't trust them," rasps Kodju, high above us. "Kill this vermin. Look to Azmai."

The priest stares into my eyes. I have no idea what ve's thinking. Is ve mad, a zealot? Would ve rather die than co-operate? Azmai roars inside my skull, the anguish of a god in chains. I yank the priest to vir feet, my sword against vir side.

More trisk shadows fall across us where we stand amongst the shattered rock of Azmai's tomb. A hundred yards away, the Hostis delegation huddle. Some of them are gesticulating wildly. All are shouting.

A small, clear voice says: "If you slay the priest, sword-dancer, we lose this chance at peace. The renewal of the Empire is at stake." A sudden, fragile moment of calm holds us all still.

Kodju gestures to the Whale, who helps him slide down from his trisk. He stands beside me and addresses the Empress.

"Majesty, how can we make peace with these murderers and necromages? How could we trust them to let our trade caravans pass along their roads? They hate us and we hate them."

The Hostis priest lets out a stream of invective in vir own tongue, then says, "*You* murderers. You kill my people, and the spirits of our land. We will drive you from the mountains and follow you onto the plains and then—" ve lapses into Hostin again, hissing and spluttering.

One of the Empress' advisers leans across to her and whispers. With a flick of her wrist she sends her guards to accompany the adviser over to the Hostis delegation. Kodju continues pleading, but nobody's listening. The calm has passed, and all eyes not fixed on the dragon-god are now on the Hostis.

The Hostis and Amitsan guards have drawn swords and voices are raised in anger. One of the trisk rears up and wheels around, startled, and tramples a Hostin woman under its feet. The Whale leaps onto Kodju's trisk and gallops over. The Empress and her entourage follow.

My attention has strayed from the priest. Sloppy. Ve hurls virself from my blade, and crouches over the dead bird.

"You're not the only necromage here, Amitsa."

A tremor moves the mountain again, and, from the hard black ground, Hostis warriors rise. Dead Hostis warriors. They rise up. And walk. And wield spears in their fleshless hands.

I had thought all my muscles were as tense and ready for battle as they could be, but I find a new level of tension, an acute sense of my own strength, position and potential. A skeleton closes with me, spear ready. I strike off its head. The skull falls and bounces beneath the feet of another skeleton, sending it stumbling to the ground.

"Betrayed! Raise the Amitsan dead, or you will be overcome."
Osalma's ghost wraps her hands around my head, making it
hard to see the enemy. "You must come fully into Ap'da, you
must release your power."

"What power?" I shout, striking away a bony finger reaching
for my eye socket – why can't everyone keep their hands off
my *face*? – and smacking my fist into its owners rib cage. It falls
back, but there are two more behind it.

"The blood," Osalma moans. "Reach into the blood . . ."

Rivulets of blood run down my wrists where my gauntlets
pierce my flesh, stinging wounds unhealed from the previous
night. I feel the tug of the shade, drawing me deeper into
Ap'da – I don't want to go, but I don't want to die here, either.

"It's not enough," she sighs.

"How much blood do you think I have in me? Should I slit
my own throat? What then? *What then*?"

"Oh, these dry dead things, already drained, already
used . . ."

Suddenly there *is* blood. I smell it, close beside me.

"Go on," urges Osalma.

"I can't—"

"You can."

Shame burns me.

He's not dead, but gore covers his legs and the ground
beneath. A sickening hunger flickers in me. His eyes meet
mine. I lean down, put my hand to his chest. I'm no healer; I
don't know if he can be saved. He says nothing. His eyes roll
back in his head.

"Kodju . . ." I hadn't even seen him fall.

A glancing blow from behind knocks me off balance and
I sprawl across him. Twisting, I find a dead warrior grinning
down at me, spear poised above my breastbone. The dirty
bones wear tattered cloth and an amulet bearing a likeness of
the dragon-god. Behind it, the true Azmai flails against the
Swords that pin vir down.

I roll away from its thrust. The spear impales Kodju. His last breath sighs out inches from my ear. Pushing myself to my feet, my left hand sinks through torn flesh, into my lover's squelching guts. I call the blood up. Strength flows into my limbs like a torrent of lava. I rise and snap the skeleton's head from its neck, cast it down and stamp on it, cracking it in two.

The priest has returned to Azmai. I close with vir, and am caught in a cloud of sparks blown from his fire. With a dizzying rush, I slip fully into Ap'da. Instantly, Osalma's shade is before me, face so awfully like my own.

The world reels. Shadowy weapons slash at me and I fight them off mechanically.

The priest shrieks joy, and the dragon-god stretches one freed wing into the air, beating it hard, stirring up ash and dust. Osalma cries "There!" Two bright streaks jig across my retinas before resolving into the shapes of swords, above Azmai. "Take them."

"You do it." *I wasn't meant to be here. I'm not really a blood-mage. I'm a dancer, just a dancer . . .*

She presses close. "I'm dead, child. Listen. The Swords are singing." I hear – feel – the chord ringing my nerves. "Sing back. Not with your voice. Inside."

I think of the Whale's mystic voice, how it emanates from inside vir. I find a silent note. The air pulsates with psychic dissonance.

"Now, a target."

The Swords flash down to the priest, and jab at vir throat. Ve vaults the remains of the bone-cage, rolls under the protection of the dragon-god's wing.

The sounds of the battle are faint beneath the song of the Swords, but I hear my name called. I spin around, to see the Whale slapping a trisk's great rump. The trisk gallops towards me. On its back, barely visible above its raised mane, is the child Empress. The Whale is surrounded by Hostis warriors; the living kind. The trisk tramples skeletons as it runs. I swore I wouldn't fight for the Empire, but I can't untwist my fate from hers now. I send the loose Swords into the skeletons. They resist; they want blood, not dry bones; but they obey.

A powerful gust blows over me. I turn. Azmai has torn both wings free. Loosed, glowing feathers tumble in the draught of vir wingbeats. Ve rears up, talons thrusting against the ground, more than willing to tear vir tail feathers out to get into the air. Ve breathes fire. I leap back, clear of the flames, almost landing beneath the ponderous feet of the Empress' trisk.

TWO MORE SWORDS dance in the air. I know I have to stop the priest from removing the last one. I bite my lip as four Swords lance towards the little Hostin, and, as one, pierce vir body and nail vir to the ground. Vir blood-stink reaches my nostrils. My power surges. I can taste victory, but the Empress calls out: "We're losing, Skylla! Do something!"

Me, do something? I am not Osalma. But why is it so important to me, not to be Osalma? Suddenly I don't know. I have the talent. I have the skill. I have the taste of god-blood at the back of my throat. I drag the Swords back to the skeleton horde, force them through their undead ranks, hacking and slashing with something like grace and something like glee, until the tide of battle turns. Azmai's roars grow deafening. The beat of wings grows stronger.

"*Bind vir,*" says Osalma's ghost.

A god should not be caged. The thought reverberates. Azmai is a beautiful, terrible, powerful god; a Loaram fit to straddle the world and the world-beside.

"Ve will destroy us."

My life is balanced on the edge of not one blade, but seven. I feel split into pieces already: here, in my hands, and leaping through the fighters, biting bone after bone.

"Quickly. You know what to do."

I do. I call the Swords back: they hurtle over. I call the Whale, and ve begins to wade through the battle towards us.

The Swords accept their target.

When they slice into my flesh, despite my exultation, I scream in terror and agony. I see my feet chopped out from under me and sent flying through the air, arterial blood pumping scarlet around them. When they take my hands, I become pure pain, and pure power. We whirl, the Swords of Light and the severed parts of a sword-dancer, around the dragon-god. I have enough spirit to recite the incantation, to command my bones to rise. When I am scattered in a ring around the dragon-god, my head on the ground next to the corpse of the priest, Osalma's face swims before mine, my own face, an image of joy and sorrow.

"Close the cage, Skylla," says the Whale, weeping.

Ve picks up my head and presses it against a newly grown bone-spike. *I want to live.* Let the god go free, let vir glory, and mine, stay in the world.

A moment's weakness. My spine extends from my neck, vertebra by vertebra, reaching for my head.

Azmai's wings flap. Vir feathers brush my face. With a wrench, ve breaks free and launches virself upwards between the spikes, up, into the glimmering dusk.

Vir fury is beyond all mortal rage and promises fire and ruin. No human hand will touch Azmai again. No human foot will walk the high plateau, or the valleys beneath. The Empire will remain undone. No sacrifice can bring glory to Amitsa or Hostis.

For the last time, the mountain shakes, and my dying eyes, clinging to Ap'da, witness the world turn vermilion, the volcano consuming the shape of Azmai, like a phoenix whose wingspan covers the earth. It dazzles white, then gold, then red. All falls into darkness, and drops away.

ARCHER 57

Lou Morgan

YOU CAN LEARN a lot crawling through a tunnel. A lot about yourself, a lot about the world you live in, a lot about what collects at the bottom of a tunnel. And I've crawled through a *lot* of tunnels. You'd think more people would use them: once you know your way through them, you can get anywhere, and quickly. There are no checkpoints down here, no snipers or mines to dodge – just grenades. It takes a while to learn to navigate them, true – especially if you're used to the grid system above ground. There are no maps for the underworld: Orpheus could have told you that, stumbling along in the evernight. The tunnels work in circles; they're a coil of snakes swallowing their own tails, looping round and round under what's left of the city.

I know there are others like me, slipping through the shadows and the junk. I hear them sometimes; hear echoes and footsteps and what could be voices in the distance, or could just as easily be the wind over a vent. They call us rat-runners, up above. I've heard it through gratings, down ventilation shafts and from the other side of grilles. They laugh when they say it. Did I, when I was in their place? I don't remember. I don't remember thinking about who might be down here at all. Maybe nobody was, back then. Sometimes, they'll throw a firecracker down a manhole. Sometimes they'll throw a bomb. They don't care if we're on their side or the enemy's: Loyal or Adverse, we remind them of what they could become. They don't care what we are now – but they can't look past what we were; where we came from and how we got here. Maybe that's why they enjoy killing us.

I don't remember what the city looked like before the war. I'm not sure I ever really knew what it looked like before. We seem to have been at war forever. It's always been said that the Steel Wars would be the wars to end all wars. They've ended a lot of things, I suppose, but not war. And in those early days as the fight raged on and the bombs fell and one by one, the men either volunteered or were conscripted, or were, finally, rounded up in cattle trucks and shipped to the front, the world Before crumbled. This is all that's left. War and ruins and bones. Perhaps this *will* be the last war – because it will only end once we're all dead.

Once the men were gone, they came for the boys. Teenagers, at first. Then down to ten. Seven. Six. Five. They took my son on his fourth birthday, throwing open the door to our home and dragging him away. I could hear him screaming in my head for days. I still can, if I listen hard enough to the silence. For a while I couldn't tell whether the screams I heard were his or mine: was I walking the streets in the dark, stepping between rubble mounds and screaming? And were my screams any different from the screams of every other mother, every other woman who had lost someone, had someone ripped away from her?

When the screaming stopped – his, mine, ours – and my head cleared, I knew what I wanted. And within a month I was being walked to my new bunk in the barracks. With every new war a new weapon, a new way of fighting emerges – and this one is no different . . . except this time, we have not looked to the future. We looked to the past. Not to the drones or the rockets or the death from afar dealt by our forefathers, no. In this war, archers are the new-old weapons of mass destruction, and I was one of the best. I was one of the best because I had nothing to lose. Or at least I thought I didn't.

There is always something more to lose.

To an archer, a fight is personal. We stand, we pick our target and we keep them. If we miss once, we aim again. We pick out a man, a woman we have never met, and we make them carry the burden of the whole war. We promise them, promise ourselves, that we will not stop until they are dead. And when they fall, we look for the soldier beside them.

I ran sorties. I ambushed whole companies of Adverse. I ambushed them and I did not stop killing them until my hands and my face were red and I could barely remember my name. I lost myself in death, because I had already lost so much else. My arrows found their mark and I showed no mercy, seeing in each and every face not Adverse, but the Loyals who had taken my son, my husband, my life, my world. I killed without thought and without hesitation because I was killing my own.

*

I WAS EXPECTING them to kill me when they captured me. They slaughtered the rest of my squad where they stood – kicking what was left of them, one by one, into a pit. Why they didn't do the same to me, I don't know. I was ready for it. Instead, they took the first two fingers of my right hand and they threw me to the wolves; the ones who had been handing me medals two days before. An archer who can't shoot is no use to anyone, and a useless soldier is just another mouth to feed. The fall from archer to rat is a short one: it's no greater than the width of two fingers under a blade.

I don't remember the pain. I don't remember how I got back to barracks, only waking up in a sweat-soaked bunk surrounded by ghosts and empty beds. The dead walked from mess hall to shower block to training ground, and I was the only one of us wounded. Maybe they thought I was a spy. Maybe they thought I was a coward or a traitor, or both. Maybe they suspected what had driven me all along: that I hated them as much as I hated the enemy. More. Maybe it didn't matter. I no longer had a purpose, with my shooting fingers gone. I had no purpose, and no place. And that could only mean one thing. The tunnels.

The darkness is so thick here that you can touch it. You can wrap it around you like a blanket. It has a weight, a feel, a smell. You can taste it; mould and cordite and sewage and something a lot like fear. You measure time by the explosions overhead: the dull rhythm of a bombing raid means night, the sharp prang of a mine means day. To begin with, I drifted in and out of sleep to the sound of explosions or trucks rumbling overhead. The Adverse had stitched my hand to keep me from bleeding out before they handed me over. The Loyals, my own side, my own enemies, ripped the stitches out. I couldn't stop the blood in the dark, so I tumbled through the tunnels until I found a boiler duct – clay now, not steel, but still hot. There are enough of them, if you know where to look. The world may be in tatters, but Loyal commanders still sleep in feather beds and take hot showers.

I pressed my hand against the hot clay of the pipe and I bit my lip so I wouldn't scream. When it was done, I spat out a mouthful of blood and it still didn't hurt as much as the day they took Adam. There are wars that topple buildings, wars that topple empires and dictators . . . and there are the small, all-devouring, all-destroying wars that begin with something as simple as a door kicked in. Their war is not my war. It never was. The tunnels are full of life, even if you don't see the humans. Cats, dogs, rats – they all came down here when life on the surface became too hard. The rats are the most dangerous: their teeth are sharp and their bites are deep and full of poison. Not long after I landed in the tunnels, I thought I saw one that glowed in the dark, but I was sure it couldn't be real. It was a fever dream, a hallucination. A nightmare. I found a handful of broken arrows – useless to anyone and thrown away, like an archer with missing fingers – and I made them useful again, short enough to swing and stab within the curving walls of the tunnels. They've kept me alive. With them, I've been able to hunt and to defend myself from things with teeth in the dark. As my strength returned, I was able to venture further down the tunnels, looking for something I could use. I'm not looking for a way up, a way out: I could open any vent and climb out onto the street, but to what purpose? The Adverse would cut me down on sight, and the Loyal would take one look at my hand, one look at what's left of my uniform, and know where I had been.

If you need to get out of a sinking ship, you follow the rats – but what do you do if you want to sink one?

You look for the rat that shines.

It took me weeks to find it: the place that sings in the dark. I circled the tunnels, searching every branch, every dead end, until I found it. An old storage space, long abandoned. Once, there was steel here; thick sheets fixed to the walls of the tunnel, doors wider than my whole body. Long gone – taken by Loyal or Adverse or god knows who. But so few of the soldiers know their history, and the commanders are too busy sitting on their cushions feasting in front of open fires to care where their men find the last few scraps of steel. Some rooms should never be opened. Some doors are meant to stay shut.

I knew I was getting close when living rats gave way to dead. Hundreds of them – thousands, hundreds of thousands and nothing left but their bones. They crunched underfoot and the tunnel became a door, and the door became a room like a cathedral. The walls soared up and curved into a dome, lost in the darkness, and I knew what I had found. Spaces for turbines, pumps, a place that once held water. The rats came to drink from it. The rats came to die from it.

This is how they made their power, this place. This is all that's left. The structure above ground has been reduced to rubble, the metal below stripped away. There are dirty marks on the walls where cutters have ripped through sheet steel, goggles left abandoned to rot. A set of wooden rollers here. Something yellow with a spiked, circular symbol on it. It collapses into splinters under my touch. There is sickness here, in the air. Decay. Danger. There is everything I need.

The tunnels run beneath the whole of the city. Whoever built them is long gone, long dead, long dust, but they may as well have made them just for me. It's the work of a night to collect what I need, dragging it through the tunnels as bombs thunder overhead. I can hear the officers laughing over their dinner, hear them discussing their plans, their schemes. They don't expect to die. They have soldiers for that: men, women, children. They expect to grow fat and rich, sending their orders out from behind thick concrete walls.

When the sickness comes, they'll think it's something they ate. When the headache and the fever come, they'll assume it's a virus and take themselves to the sick bay. And it will be too late, because by banishing me to the tunnels, they gave me what I needed to end this. I found their water supply. I found the old power plant. I found fuel rods still standing to attention, silent in the dark, like an army. My army.

And they will do what neither Loyal nor Adverse have managed. They will end this war. You learn a lot about yourself when everything you loved is taken away, and you're forced to crawl through tunnels.

But most of all, you learn how hard you'll fight.

The Runaway Warrior

Dolly Garland

THE TEMPLE BELL thundered. Shivani was the first to roll out of her pallet. Her ebony hair, wavy from constant braiding, swept across her face. She tucked it behind her ears, and hurried out of the nearly empty dormitory; most of her fellow warriors were away performing the ritual to renew their strength and appease Kali with days of meditation, hunting and prayers. Shivani crossed the courtyard to the temple. The main doors were shut for the night, hiding the idol of Goddess Kali. On the steps outside, Heena still pulled the rope, ringing the bell.

Seeing the High Priestess' personal servant, Shivani realised the situation must be urgent, and increased her pace.

"Heenaji." She bowed respectfully.

Heena stopped ringing the bell, adjusted the pallu of her white sari over her head. "The High Priestess will see you now," she said.

As they walked away, two other warriors approached the temple. Heena shook her head at them. "The goddess has chosen," she said.

The warriors bowed their heads and returned to their dormitory. Shivani followed Heena. This was the way things were done. The warriors did not choose the tasks. The tasks chose them.

*

THE HIGH PRIESTESS' chambers were behind the temple. Shivani had never entered them alone. Because traditions mattered. Too much, sometimes.

She straightened her charcoal tunic, smoothed the creases of her dhoti, and stepped in.

The chamber was bathed in soft candle light. The High Priestess, Nandita, sat cross-legged on the floor; a holy necklace of red beads in her right hand.

Nandita was older than anyone Shivani knew, yet her thin grey hair was the only obvious sign of her age. She had been in the service of Kali since she was a young girl, and this lifetime of wielding the magic of the Goddess had left a powerful imprint. Her voice was soft, usually calm, but when she commanded, one heard the voice of Kali in her mouth.

"Namaste, High Priestess," Shivani said, pressing her hands together in respect.

"I've received a message from Belapur. Apparently, demons have been attacking the town for months. The townspeople and the local guards were fighting them, but now the situation has worsened. They attack every night now, burning houses, even setting people on fire. They have taken all the valuables, and most of the children of the village. So many have died, the townspeople can't perform proper funeral rites. They have to pile the bodies together and burn them."

"What about the zamindar? He must have guards."

"He's in league with the demons, I'm told. They promised him power and riches beyond imagining." The steel in Nandita's tone – edged with the power of Kali – told Shivani what must happen to the zamindar. "The king has promised to send his men and assign a new zamindar. But until they arrive, the townspeople need our help."

Shivani waited. They were Kali's servants, not rulers of men. They did not get involved in political problems. So there had to be more.

"You have been chosen."

Shivani bowed. "On Kali's command, High Priestess."

"The people of Belapur want to perform the Kali-Kavach yagna."

The Kali-Kavach yagna was an extremely demanding ritual that had to be performed from sunrise to sunrise for three consecutive days. If it succeeded, it would protect the town from harm. If it failed, it would invite the anger of the goddess. Only the bravest, or most desperate, chose this ritual.

"You must protect the town while the villagers complete the yagna."

"As you command, High Priestess." Shivani felt a burst of excitement, and silently admonished herself for such an inappropriate reaction. But the past month had been tedious, staying within the temple boundaries, performing simple duties that left too much time for thinking. She was relieved to be given a task that required more of her.

"With most of the warriors away, I cannot spare anyone else. You must do this alone," Nandita said.

Shivani bowed her head in compliance.

"May Kali's grace be with you."

Shivani touched the High Priestess' feet for her blessings and withdrew.

*

BELAPUR WAS A broken shell of a once prosperous town. Every building was damaged. Debris lay everywhere. The townspeople gathered as Shivani rode her white mare into the square. Their faces were ashen, their clothes dirty. If the town was a shell, its residents seemed like ghosts. They looked at her clothes and weapons, and recognized Kali in her. Some pointed and grumbled; others called out greetings and welcome.

The bodies had been cleared. Shivani breathed in the stench of the mass cremations; her nostrils flared at the rancid smell. She sat on her horse, staring down at mounds of ashes. Mixed in with the ash were fingers and bits of skulls, bones that hadn't burned away.

Tearing her eyes away from the horror of the bones, Shivani turned to the nearest villager, a stooped, elderly man. "Tell me sahib," she said, "where does the zamindar live?"

"At the end of the lane that goes past the temple, warrior." He pointed behind her, "You can see his mansion from the road."

"Have you come to help us?" a woman asked. Her yellow sari was mud-streaked. The sleeve of her blouse was torn. Tresses of hair had come loose from her braid. Shivani stared at her, finding it impossible not to imagine what horrors she had seen each night. Did she have children? Did the demons have them now?

"What's your name?" Shivani asked.

"Devika."

"Devikaji, I'm going to take care of the zamindar, and then I'm going to make sure you can complete the Kali-Kavach yagna without interruption." Shivani touched the gold pendant around her neck. The pendant bore three eyes, for Kali's omniscience. It hung on a black thread, and it was the most valuable thing she owned – her connection to the goddess.

Devika nodded, tears brimming in her eyes. Others nodded too, but the old man stepped forward, waving his staff. "You? Alone? Where are the warriors?"

"I'm a warrior."

"You may be Kali's warrior, but you are one, and the demons are many." He turned away from her, shaking, perhaps with fear as much as anger.

Some people looked apprehensive, but no one tried to stop her as Shivani rode past them. The temple hadn't escaped unscathed. Part of the spire had fallen off, leaving a stub of stone at the summit. Two steps led to the porch, forming a corridor between the cracked pillars and the main body of the temple where Goddess Durga's idol sat, allowing people to perform the circumambulation ritual.

By contrast, the zamindar's mansion stood untouched. Even its expansive grounds were lush with greenery, though the fragrance of flowers did not disguise the lingering smells of death and destruction.

As she approached, Shivani spotted an old man and a boy tending the garden. They looked wary. The old man's eyes lingered on her clothing and weapons, recognizing her status, and he glanced towards the trees bordering the path leading to the mansion. Shivani followed his gaze, gave a quick nod, and continued on her way. She had travelled barely five feet when a trio of armed guards stepped out from behind the trees, blocking her path, and pointed their lances at her.

"What's your business?" the fattest of the guards demanded, eyeing her legs.

"I'm here to kill the zamindar."

The fat guard laughed, and his companions joined in heartily. "Be gone, woman."

"Let me pass." Shivani nudged her horse forward.

The guards edged closer. One of them grabbed her horse's reins.

"You are under arrest," he declared. He clutched her arm and tried to pull her down.

Shivani wrapped her fingers around the pendant and felt the goddess rise within, as if stretching after a slumber. Kali's power surged through her veins like adrenaline.

Sliding her foot from the stirrup, she kicked the guard hard in the chest, throwing him backwards. She pulled a sword from the scabbard at her waist and the blade caught the fat guard in the neck as he stabbed at her with his lance, missing her by inches. He spat blood, and collapsed with an inhuman gargling sound.

The guard she had kicked staggered to his feet. The two survivors advanced together, wary now. Shivani took a swing at the second guard, but his companion caught her left thigh with his lance. Shivani howled in pain, smacking him a ringing blow on the head with the hilt of her sword. He fell as if his legs had turned to water. The second guard dove forward, his lance aimed squarely at her horse. Shivani's sword lunged out, and neatly pierced his heart. The third guard rose, stumbling, took one look at his friend twitching his last on Shivani's blade, and fled, shouting for reinforcements.

Shivani wiped her blade on her horse's flank and slid it back into her scabbard. In almost the same, fluid movement, she grabbed her bow and an arrow from the quiver attached to her saddle, aimed, and fired. Her arrow drove into the guard's back. He pitched forward on his face, and lay still.

The boy in the garden cheered. The old man hushed him, pulling him away, out of sight amid the greenery.

Shivani passed through the well-tended gardens, past verdant lawns and honeysuckle and ivy climbing up marble pillars. Everything here was healthy and beautiful, as if in mockery of the burned and violated town.

The brass doors of the mansion stood closed. Shivani jumped off her horse, and hammered on the door with her sword hilt.

A bald servant in blue livery opened the door, and scowled at her. "Sahib isn't accepting visitors at the moment," he said. "He's waiting for his son to arrive."

As he moved to shut the door in her face, Shivani jammed her foot inside the frame, shoved him backwards and gestured with her sword. "Where is he?"

The servant's eyes bulged with fear. He stepped back, mouth agape, and pointed to a door at the end of the corridor, his eyes never leaving the blade in her hand.

She found the zamindar, adorned with pearls and gold and gems over his rolls of fat. He looked up from his ledger with the surprise of someone unaccustomed to being interrupted, and scowled at Shivani as if she was something stuck to the sole of his bejewelled slippers. Before he could demand anything, or order her to leave, one neat slice of Shivani's sword obeyed Kali's command.

The zamindar's turbaned head rolled across the marble floor. His surprised eyes stared up at the ceiling.

*

AT DAWN, THE Kali-Kavach yagna commenced in the town square. The last four priests of Belapur sat around the purifying fire. Except for the few men standing watch on the edge of town, everyone joined in the prayers, palms together, heads bowed.

Shivani stayed close to the fire. The daylight hours passed without incident, but when dusk fell, the sentries blew their horns in warning. She heard the beating of wings. It sounded like the very air being torn into pieces. Or perhaps it was her nerves. The rhythm of the demons' wings, disconcerting and heavy like muffled footfalls, seemed to increase the tempo of her heartbeat. A shadow loomed over the town, as a horde of demons flew across the eastern sky. The villagers shouted warnings to each other. Several men started shepherding the women and the few remaining children to the shelter of houses that were still standing, while others ran to protect their priests. Shivani saw the desire on their faces to run, to get away, but they stayed, clutching their odd assortments of weapons, and she felt a surge of pride for her race. For these humans who would stand against an enemy far stronger than them, and more brutal than they could ever be.

The demons were bigger than the humans, uglier too, adorned with necklaces and rings of bones and teeth. Their demented laughter whirred through the air. Their foreheads were coated with ash. They hovered above the yagna fire, and over the townspeople.

Fighting down her fear, Shivani focused on the goddess, touched her pendant. She felt the power filling her heart and mind, as the spirit of Kali consumed her, driving out fear, filling her with rage.

She notched an arrow, readied herself.

Then, she fought.

Arrow after arrow flew from her bow, faster than any human eye could follow. Most of them hit their mark. Demons howled in pain as they plummeted to earth. Their companions screamed with rage. Shivani's hands were sore from using the bow. Her arms ached and her tunic clung to her sweat-drenched skin. The rising dust from the mayhem all around her coated her throat. The yagna fire created a steady stream of smoke, and its smell, mingled with the dust clouds, stifled the air.

The demons were relentless. They had noticed her, singled her out as the main threat. A stocky demon lashed out with a whip and pulled Shivani's feet from under her. She crashed onto her back, and the bow slipped from her hand.

The demon unsheathed his sword, ready to plunge it through her heart. Shivani rolled away. Jumped up, and whirled around, kicking him in the gut. Before he had a chance to recover she grabbed his hair, and elbowed him under the chin. She heard the crunch of breaking bones in his jaw at the impact.

Instead of going down, the demon snarled in pain. His fist lashed out, punching her with such force that she staggered back, ears ringing.

Shivani bellowed Kali's name into the darkness beyond the fire. She lunged at the demon with her bare hands, clawed at his eyeballs with her nails. He howled in pain as Shivani ripped the inside of his eyelids. Kali's rage swam through Shivani as blood dripped from the demon's eyes and coursed down his cheeks. He pushed her away, blindly flinging his arms. A swipe caught her across the mouth. Shivani spat blood. She snatched up the demon's own sword, and sliced his head clean off, watching it arc high to shatter on the ground near the fire.

More demons were on the ground, attacking wildly, pillaging all around them without discrimination. The villagers had mostly abandoned their attempts to fight, instead intent on avoiding being maimed or killed as much as they were able. Several women had run out of the shelter to aid their husbands and sons. Their defiant screams, and their attempts to fight – brave, but futile against the demons – added to the chaos.

Shivani snatched up her bow and started shooting. It was difficult to see anything clearly through the smoke and dust. Difficult to distinguish the people she was supposed to protect from the demons. But she concentrated, let Kali guide her aim.

Demon after demon fell.

The priests continued chanting.

Shivani's arrows kept flying.

She did not miss a single target. She did not let her arms fall until every single demon was dead.

A hush descended from the empty sky, broken only by the sobs and grunts of the wounded and the wailing of the bereaved. Shivani stood poised, waiting for more demons to fall on the village, to finish what they had started. In that sudden quiet, the priests' voices gained focus, growing louder, more forceful. Their chant had never broken, not under the fiercest assault, and Shivani felt a surge of pride.

She remained on guard duty.

Exhausted now.

Waiting.

*

JUST AFTER SUNRISE, when Shivani thought it might be safe for her to rest a little, she heard the rattle of wheels. She turned to find a lone carriage approaching the square, preceded by four horse-guards in gold armour and helmets. She hastened down the road to block its path.

The guards pulled up, and behind them, the carriage came to halt. "What is the meaning of this?" the guard captain demanded.

"The Kali-Kavach yagna is in progress," Shivani told him. "You cannot pass through the town."

"Get out of the way, woman. Do you know who this is?"

"It could be the king himself, and I still wouldn't let him disrupt the yagna," Shivani said.

"What's going on?" A man stepped down from the carriage. He was young, on the cusp of middle age. His silk tunic stretched tight over his pot belly.

"You cannot pass until the Kali-Kavach yagna is complete," Shivani repeated.

"My father rules this town." The plump man spoke in a tone which implied there was no more to be said.

Shivani's lip curled. "You are the zamindar's son?"

"Yes, I'm Prakash Dayal. I can assure you he won't be impressed that you've kept me waiting. My wife has had an uncomfortable journey. She needs to rest."

"Your father is dead."

Prakash opened his mouth, closed it. Opened it again. He looked like a fish gasping for water. He tried to speak, but no words came out.

There was a rustle of fabric, and the curtains of the carriage parted once more. A woman stepped out, awkwardly holding her heavy belly. As she moved, the pallu of her sari slipped a little, revealing her face.

Shivani's heart leapt wildly. A sob rose in her throat. She bit her lip, and swallowed hard.

"What's the delay?" the woman asked Prakash.

"This woman," Prakash said, gathering himself and gesturing towards Shivani, "is claiming preposterously that my father is dead. Get back into the carriage, Nalini. I will sort it out."

Nalini turned. Her eyes met Shivani's, and she gasped. She stumbled back, leaning against the carriage, looking sick.

"You've caused my wife distress," Prakash said, not moving an inch to help her. "If my son is harmed, I'll have your head."

"The only way your child is going to be affected is if you do something stupid." Shivani moved towards Nalini, an involuntary movement, quickly arrested. "Sit down. The women of the town will help you."

"Get away from her," Prakash barked.

Shivani shot him a steely glance. "You have a choice. Wait quietly until the yagna is complete, or turn back now. Either way, your wife is staying here until the midwife says she can travel."

Prakash opened his mouth to argue, but Nalini put a hand on his arm. "I need to rest," she said softly. "Your son is kicking too much."

"I want to know what happened to my father," Prakash said, turning and marching towards the town square. He stopped, looked back at the guards. "Bring the valuables, and make sure no one steals anything from the carriage." He stormed off, without waiting for his wife, or looking to see if she followed.

*

SHIVANI WALKED ALONGSIDE Nalini, stealing sideways glances at her every chance she got. Nalini's amber eyes were lustrous. Her glossy hair was tied in an elaborate braid, half-covered by the pallu of her sari and kept in its place with a jewelled pin. She had put on weight, and she looked tired. But still so beautiful.

All the feelings Shivani thought she'd buried three years in the past came flooding back, as intense now as the day they had parted, no less glorious and painful.

"What are you doing here?" Nalini asked.

"I'm here to ensure the yagna is successful," Shivani said, looking straight ahead. Now they were talking, she could not look Nalini in the eye.

Nalini frowned. "I don't understand," she said. "You have weapons, and your clothes . . . you are wearing men's clothing."

"I joined Kali's order."

Nalini smiled. A ghost of humour, a reminiscence of the past. "I should have realised that." The smile disappeared. "You ran away."

The accusation in her voice stung deeply. "I didn't want to see you get married."

"I didn't have a choice."

"You could have run with me."

"And then what?" Nalini asked hotly. "It would have been no different somewhere else. The rules are the same all over the country."

"You could have run," Shivani repeated.

"You should have stayed."

"They were going to marry me off to an old man."

"They would have waited for someone else, if you had behaved a little more—"

"—guilty?" Shivani demanded. "Is that the word you were looking for?"

"We were in the wrong. We had to be punished." It sounded like Nalini was repeating a mantra she had taught herself.

"Do you believe that?" It was the question that had haunted Shivani for three years. Was she guilty, or not guilty? Did love have to stay within proscribed boundaries? When the heart transgressed, did it become a crime? On some days, she felt certain she had done nothing wrong. On others, she felt equally certain she was a sinner, and deserved to be punished.

"Yes, I do," Nalini said, without conviction.

"Is this your first child?" Shivani asked, changing the subject.

"The second. I have a daughter. She is with my parents in Sundarnagar. She loves it there."

"Or is it that your husband isn't happy with a daughter?"

Nalini's averted eyes told her enough.

"Everything will be fine, once my son is born," Nalini said firmly.

She sounded normal. The way a woman was supposed to be. Talking about things a woman was supposed to want. But as Shivani stole another glance at Nalini, she wondered if the Nalini who had once dreamt of their life together was still there.

"Are you happy?" Shivani asked.

Nalini caressed her belly. "I'm content. I've done my duty to my family. I can hold my head high in society. That is more important than happiness."

*

THE RESIDENTS GRUMBLED as Prakash and his guards made their way into town.

"What is he doing here?" Devika demanded, standing with her hands on her hips, proud and stubborn.

"His wife is with child," Shivani said, gently pushing Nalini forward.

"If he causes any trouble – " One of the men glared at Prakash.

"He won't." Prakash was too much of a merchant, she judged. He would want his guards to keep his property safe, not take on a fight with the whole town. She didn't doubt he would demand his inheritance, but not without more manpower.

A middle-aged woman came forward, gave Nalini a reassuring smile. "Come, beti. Sit down. We don't have much, but we can share our food."

"We have food," Nalini said, and Shivani realised that the Nalini she had loved wasn't entirely lost.

Nalini looked at her husband. "It would be bad luck for our son to take food from those in need," she said pointedly. "He would be in their debt, and I do not wish my son to be born in debt."

Prakash understood that. It took lifetimes to pay off karmic debts, and an unpaid debt could bring ruin to a family for generations.

"Bring food," he ordered the guards.

Shivani watched as Nalini naturally fitted in with the women. She talked about her pregnancy, about the daughter she had left behind. She talked about their journey, and spoke to them as if she was one of them, and her husband's father hadn't caused their current plight.

"Where do you live? I haven't seen you before," Devika asked.

"Sundarnagar. My husband has business there."

"Sundarnagar is a beautiful town," another woman said wistfully.

"So was ours, until the demons attacked. And all because your father-in-law made a pact with them," Devika said to Nalini.

"It's not her fault." Shivani spoke without thinking. All the women looked up, surprised. She was there to guard them. They didn't expect her to express opinions.

Shivani turned away, pacing the yagna fire, making herself busy. She watched the sky and the roads for the demons' arrival, ready for battle. She did not look at Nalini again.

*

As THE SUN set on the second day, the sentries' cries rang out, warning the village of the oncoming swarm. It was a larger group this time, and so bedecked with bones and teeth, Shivani wondered how they could fly with such weight hanging from them, and how many they must have killed.

Too many, she thought.

Shivani looked at the townspeople, lessened by the losses of the previous night. Their pale, gaunt faces stared up at the demons. Some clasped hands, and she heard their fervent prayers.

She touched the pendant, steadied her resolve, and connected with the goddess.

Her first arrow skimmed a demon's ear.

"You missed." His voice rumbled, a bass ripple in her belly.

"That was a warning." She hoped she sounded braver than she felt. "Leave this town alone."

The demons laughed harshly and started to land, fanning out amongst the villagers. One grabbed the loose end of a woman's sari, pulling her to him. Shivani's arrow punctured his heart.

His eyes widened at the arrow poking out of his chest, and he fell, dead before he hit the ground.

The others launched into their onslaught. These demons were not here for sport. They were here for revenge. One snarled; Shivani could only watch in horror as he reached out, taking hold of a villager and snapping his neck like a dry twig before flinging him carelessly aside. The man's body clattered on the ground, inanimate, broken.

This casual viciousness spread the terror even wider. Shivani saw it on the villager's faces. Her face, she hoped, did not show the fear she felt in her heart.

"Protect the yagna!" Shivani shouted to the townspeople, as they gathered themselves to fight back. She spotted a huge, hairy demon, shaking one of the priests like a rag doll, and put an arrow right through his forehead.

Another lanky demon lunged towards the same priest as the man dropped to his knees. Shivani notched another arrow, but as she took aim she heard a scream. A voice she could tell apart from any other in the crowd. Her breath caught. Her heart ricocheted in her chest. This time, it was a different kind of fear.

Nalini.

She turned. A demon clutched Nalini by the hair as she twisted in his grip. Nalini was screaming and struggling, her hands wrapped around her belly in a futile effort to protect her child.

Shivani hesitated, looked from the priests she was sworn to protect to Nalini, the woman she loved and had lost everything for. The power of Kali, surging inside her, urged her towards the priests. As did her duty. But her heart, faithless little traitor – or faithful, depending on the viewpoint – urged her towards the woman she loved. Shivani defied the goddess, firing instead at the demon attacking Nalini.

Shivani swung back immediately, another arrow at the ready, and saw the priest's head fly into the yagna's holy fire.

The townspeople wailed.

The purifying fire of the yagna went out, plunging the square into sudden darkness. Shivani blinked, her eyes swiftly adjusting to the moonlight, able to pick out the remaining priests' silhouettes as they sprang to their feet, crying over their dead colleague and the ill-luck an interrupted yagna might bring. The townspeople remained frozen, fearful of Kali's anger. But Shivani didn't have to wonder about that. The moment the fire went out, the rage rose inside her, hot and piercing.

Rage at herself.

The Goddess' rage for being disobeyed.

The bow fell from her hands.

Shivani clutched her head. It felt like it was splitting from the inside. Tears of pain ran down her cheeks. In the distance, there were echoes, but they seemed too far away.

The rage, burning, turned her vision red, even with her eyes closed.

It consumed her, and instilled such bone deep fear that Shivani felt as if she would never stop being scared again. As if she'd always been afraid.

The rage subsided. She understood it was a temporary respite. Kali hadn't forgiven her, but there was still work to be done.

She opened her eyes. Blinked. There was light. Not moonlight. She was on her knees, dizzy and confused. Several of the villagers were holding lit torches, using them as weapons. Shivani struggled to stand, dragging her bow out of the mud.

The townspeople were fighting with whatever they could grab hold of, but there were so many more dead in the moments Shivani had retreated into herself. How much time had passed?

The demons continued their rampage. Their object seemed to be to destroy everything, and take pleasure in it. They did not just kill, but viciously mutilated bodies. A huge demon grabbed a young man, swung his body around overhead to gain momentum and flung it as far as he could. A few of his comrades joined in, as if it was a sport.

Struggling back to her feet, Shivani fired arrow after arrow. Firing through tears of shame. Firing till her fingers bled.

Arrows whipped through the air, sizzling, thudding into bodies, knocking demons out of the sky.

She had never fought so fast, or so well. But it was all too late.

*

THE VILLAGERS GATHERED the bodies of their dead in one pile, and the demons in another. The demons would be burned first, quickly and without ceremony.

When Shivani moved to help, one of the women shouted in her face. "Don't touch my husband! It's your fault he died in vain."

Everyone was staring at her. Accusing. Angry. Despondent.

"It wasn't her fault. They were too many," Devika said, in a hollow voice.

"She chose to save that woman. The zamindar's daughter-in-law. She cost us the lives of many more. She should have saved the yagna. That's what she's here for."

"Maybe the zamindar's got to her too? How do we know she is not in league with them?" another woman wondered aloud.

Shivani said nothing. She moved away from their dead, and started stacking the demons' bodies instead. These were the only bodies she'd earned the right to burn.

"She made a mistake, but the woman is with child. Would it have been less of a sin to let a pregnant woman die?" she heard Devika say.

The reply was muttered, intermittent. Hostile.

Once the funeral pyres were lit, most people went to find shelter in the few houses that did not look on the verge of collapse. Many of them would have to rebuild their homes, alongside their lives. If they survived.

Others sat, watching the flames, witnessing their loved ones reduce to ashes.

Shivani sat apart.

Alone.

Between the two fires.

Her eyes stung from the smoke. The thick smell of ash filled her lungs. She sat, and watched both fires.

Devika came and sat next to her. "They want you to leave," she said, without preamble.

"How will that help?" Shivani said dully. "The demons will only return."

"They think you brought ill-luck by not protecting the yagna. We will hide until the king's men arrive."

"You can't hide when demons are burning down your houses. More will come, once the news of these deaths reaches their brethren." She waved a hand towards the fire, the pyre of twisted demon-corpses.

"Why did you do it? I thought Kali's warriors were used to making tough choices, for the greater good."

Shivani stayed quiet, but the throbbing in her head began anew. Kali knew the answer, and she wasn't pleased that she had been defied for personal affection.

"It was because of the child, wasn't it?" Devika asked, misinterpreting the silence. "Yes, it would have been a hard choice. But babies die every day. So do pregnant women."

"I will make amends," Shivani said, with a determination she didn't feel.

Yes, you will, and you will pay a price for your disobedience, came a thunderous voice from within her.

She had to make amends. Not just to the people, but to Kali. If she did not, she would never know peace again.

"The only way to make amends is to start the yagna again, and see it through to completion," Devika said. "But three of the priests are dead, and there aren't enough supplies. We can't do it."

"It will be done," Shivani said. "Get some rest, Devikaji. The demons won't return again tonight. It's almost dawn. Tomorrow, we will start the yagna again."

*

IT WAS NOON before Shivani returned to the village. She noted the surprised looks on people's faces. They must have assumed she had run away. The truth was confirmed when she saw Devika's relief.

"Where did you go?" Devika asked "Four people have fallen ill. The goddess is angry, and now we will suffer for it."

Shivani jumped down from her horse. "What happened to those people?" she asked.

"They collapsed with a high fever. Our physician's dead, too."

Shivani untied the pack hanging from her saddle. "I bring supplies for the yagna," she said. "Three more priests are on their way, following in a carriage with an armed escort. They will be here before sundown. Tomorrow at sunrise, they will start the yagna once more."

"How did you manage that?" Devika asked.

"Tomorrow at sunrise," Shivani repeated. There was no need for anyone to know the price she'd paid, selling the only thing that mattered to her.

She left Devika to distribute the supplies. The goddess would be appeased. There wasn't much else she could do right now. She had made a choice. But even now, she wasn't sure if she had done the wrong thing. As the thought occurred to her, the hot rage flared in her mind. Kali had no doubts about the wrongness of Shivani's actions.

While the remaining priest prepared for the second yagna, the townspeople cleared and cleansed the land, so it could be used again for the ritual.

Shivani sat between the two fires, now burned to smouldering ashes, and watched the skies. She was jolted from a fitful doze when someone touched her shoulder.

It was Nalini.

"You saved my life," Nalini said. "You were so brave. But then, you were always brave."

"I ran away."

"You ran away and became a warrior."

Shivani didn't know what to say to that.

"I know it's selfish of me, but I am glad you saved me. I was so scared. I don't want to die."

Shivani looked at her. At the beautiful, earnest face, amber eyes filled with tears. She had defied the goddess for Nalini. It wasn't a conscious decision. It just was. Like breathing.

"Go inside, Nalini. This isn't the place for you."

"Eat something," Nalini said and offered her a bowl of rice. She squeezed Shivani's shoulder, and walked away.

*

THE CEREMONY RESUMED at dawn. It was a more muted event than the previous attempt. There was plenty of work to be done for the town to be rebuilt, but for now, all hopes were pinned on the Kali-Kavach yagna.

The day passed uneventfully, but Shivani wasn't surprised by that. It was dusk she was waiting for, and dusk she feared. More demons would come, and she was afraid she might make another mistake. There would be no more chances. The yagna had to be completed this time.

As the darkness approached, she told everyone who couldn't fight to gather in the temple. The demons couldn't step onto consecrated land, even though they could burn it or throw weapons inside. But people could not live there permanently without defiling the temple with their bodily functions, and so it became a temporary refuge.

Shivani was relieved to see Nalini in the temple, amongst a handful of women and children, the village's old men, and Prakash, who had refused to fight.

The rest of the villagers remained near the priests. They would protect the yagna at all costs. The greater good took precedence over individual safety.

As the sky darkened, Shivani stood ready with her bow.

The sentries cried out.

The demons were coming once more.

A tense silence filled the courtyard, broken only by the priests' rhythmic chanting. The horde flew in from the west. These demons weren't gleeful. They saw the piles of ashes, the discarded bone necklaces. They smelled the blood of their brothers, and they screamed for revenge.

A gravelly voice came out of the shadows, "We'll burn this town to the ground." This demon stood taller than the rest. His teeth, sharp as an animal's, were bared in a feral smile.

Shivani didn't waste time on warning shots. Her first arrow penetrated the leader's heart. But he didn't die. He pulled the arrow from his body as if it was a twig, and snapped it between his fingers.

Shivani's grip tightened on her bow. Her strength alone wasn't enough. She needed Kali. Her hand reached for the pendant, but there was nothing to hold onto. She'd sold her only tangible connection to the goddess. She tried to focus, tried to find Kali.

Please, Kali Ma. Don't abandon me now.

Nothing.

The demons circled the priests as their chants wavered. Some threw pieces of bones and birds they'd plucked from air and killed, to defile the holy fire.

Shivani fired, fervently calling to the goddess.

She screamed Kali's name.

The speed and power of her arrows caught all the vile objects before they could touch the yagna flames. Her arrows shot out, piercing demon after demon, made unstoppable by Kali's power.

The army of demons was reduced by half, and those that survived snarled in anger and frustration. They attacked the people, who fought back with scrounged swords and clubs and sticks. The villagers were a pathetic band – merchants mostly, and some Brahmin. Not one was trained in combat, but they fought for their lives, with everything they had. Shivani saw an old Brahman, trying to stab a demon with a kitchen knife.

She knew what she had to do. Kill the leader, and the rest of the band would fall apart. But the leader wasn't interested in the havoc his underlings were causing. He was headed for the priests.

Shivani intercepted him.

"Oi, you!" she shouted with as much insolence as she could muster. "Are you just here to fight unarmed priests, or can you beat a warrior of Kali?"

The leader of the demons stopped in his tracks, and turned. His scrutiny told Shivani he wasn't stupid. He didn't disregard her just because she was a lone woman. He realised that she was responsible for the deaths of many of his followers.

"You first then." The demon started towards her, teeth bared.

Shivani notched an arrow, aiming to bring him down before he could reach her, but he was faster than she'd expected. With one massive leap, he was on her. He snarled, backhanded her with his massive hand, and sent her flying to crumple against a low wall. Her bones cracked at the impact.

Shivani struggled to her feet.

Part of her felt the pain, but another part of her, fuelled by the goddess' magic, didn't break focus. She used it to channel her anger. She ran headlong towards the demon, pulling out her sword. And she swung.

He spun away, unhurt.

She went at him again. In another hand, she held a knife. They danced back and forth, in a graceless battle.

Her eyes were focused on him. He had to die.

Inside her, the goddess approved of this determination.

She swung and nicked his shoulder. Enraged, he plucked a curved blade from one of the dead demons, and blocked her next blow.

His blade scraped her torso. She reached out, kicked him in the knee, and charged again.

Shivani was drawing more and more magic. It was no longer her in control. Kali directed her body, so that she was faster, stronger and more tireless than humanly possible. But she was also helpless, carried along with the fight.

She almost had him, when a voice screeched, "You killed my father! You bitch, I will kill you!" Prakash ran out of the temple, Nalini at his heels, pleading for him to stop. Prakash was aiming straight for Shivani, heedless of everything around him. A demon intercepted him, grabbed him by the neck, dangling him as if he weighed no more than a child.

Nalini collapsed on her knees, holding her belly. "Shivani!" she wailed.

The leader of the demons regained his ground, pressing in on Shivani once more.

Another crossroads.

A thought emerged in her mind, but she pushed it down, fighting for control. Her body did not delay. Her blade swung, her aim was true, and it separated the demon leader's head from his body.

Blood splattered her face.

Shivani wiped her eyes, and snatched up her bow. She ran towards towards Nalini, who was cradling her husband's body. The twisted position of his head confirmed that his neck was broken.

As the demons saw their leader die, they fled shrieking into the sky. But Shivani's arrows spared none. There was no mercy.

In the background, the priests still chanted. Their voices swelled and fell back in a cadence, calling out to Kali.

The townspeople started to gather. The women and children who had been hiding emerged from the houses, looking at the destruction around them with numb expressions. People sought for their loved ones amongst the injured and the dead. The cries of children mingled with the wailing of adults. There were some reunions, but mostly all Shivani saw around her was pain and death. Eventually, the townspeople gathered themselves enough to begin to clear the corpses. Once again, they lit two pyres to burn the dead.

Nalini protested as she saw her husband's body dragged along with others, to be burned with them. "He should have a proper funeral," she insisted. "He is my husband."

"So should everyone else," Devika snapped, and turned away, leaving Nalini alone with Shivani.

Shivani knelt at her side, and put an arm on Nalini's shoulder.

Nalini's tear-filled gaze reproached her. "You should have saved him."

"I had to save the yagna. There would have been no more chances. The survival of the whole town depended on it."

"You should have saved my husband. He died because of you. He died because you murdered his father."

"Nalini – " Shivani felt her slipping away all over again.

"You let him die on purpose. You were jealous that I made this life. That I chose to marry him, instead of running away with you."

Shivani flinched. "Nalini, please . . ."

She broke off, unsure what to say. She understood grief and anger, and she wanted to believe it was just that. The shock of Prakash's death, the shock of her situation, was making Nalini say these words. But as Shivani looked into the eyes of the woman she loved, the only one she'd ever loved, she only saw rage.

Shivani rose, and with one last long look at Nalini, she walked away. She returned to the priests, and in the holy fire of the yagna, she added a contribution of her own. Her past, and the remnants of her feelings. Memories she would carry forever.

There would be a price, the goddess had said. Kali always kept her promises.

Fire and Ash

Gaie Sebold

T EN."

It was too much of the money she had left. Riven knew that. But it was that, or another night without sleep. She put the coins on the counter and picked up the jug.

Movement in the corner of her eye. Her elbow shot out, and something flew backwards, a stool tumbled, skidded away and lay, legs up, like a dead beetle. Next to it a young man sat on the floor, rubbing his chest, gasping with shock.

Riven's heart pounded, sending white shivers around the edges of her vision. *Stop. Stop it. Calm down. Stop it.*

"What do you think you're doing? Crazy bitch!" the young man said.

"Sorry." *What am I doing? I don't know.*

"You've got your beer. Get out," the alewife said. More customers were standing in the doorway, gaping and muttering. Riven felt their eyes like crawling things on her skin as she pushed past them.

Now she would have to find another place to buy her beer. That might be a good thing. This one was too close to the apothecary. She'd passed the place often enough, in the last months, walking the streets in a dazed fog hoping to tire herself enough to sleep through the night. Until now, she'd not gone in.

"Hey! Hey!"

She'd barely noticed the gaggle of youngsters, eyeing her from the other side of the street. Now one broke off, a boy, maybe seven. Gap-grinned, eager, hair a red flurry.

"You're a soldier, right?"

She'd kept wearing her armour and carrying her sword. The places she'd been staying it wasn't safe to leave anything behind, not if you wanted to find it when you came back. And she felt better, safer, with it on. "I was."

"You were in the war, weren't you?"

"Yes, I was in the war." She picked up speed, but the boy, limber with youth and full of energy, kept pace easily. "Did you kill lots of people? Have you got lots of scars?"

"Move yer arse, kid."

"Were you at Crishnak? When the gods won the war for us?"

The name flicked her on the raw, it always did, no matter how many times she heard it. "Fuck off."

"But were you?"

"Nishi, Nishiii, come on . . ."

"Your friends are calling you."

"But . . ."

"Go. The fuck. Away." Riven was sweating, her heartbeat a cold drum.

She wanted the beer in the jug, badly, now. But it was still light, would be for another four hours. She tried not to drink while it was still light. Come winter she'd be in a stupor before most people had taken supper.

No. Come winter, she'd be under the care of the clericals, or dead.

"Get away from me, boy. I'm warning you." Her hands tightened into fists without her will. She felt her arm-muscles jump. *Don't hit the boy. Don't hit the boy.* He was nothing but an underfed street-brat, if she punched too hard she'd break him.

The boy heaved a sigh. "Bet you weren't even there." He stuck his tongue out and ran off.

Riven just about made it to her crappy little hired room before the shakes hit. The hell with sunset. She drank the jug and stared at the walls. It got dark. She didn't light the lantern – she hadn't used it since she got here. She listened to people come in and slam doors and argue and fuck, and all of them were so many miles away beyond the thin, badly-painted walls. She wasn't drunk enough. She wished she had some more beer, all the beer, enough to drown in.

*

TWO NIGHTS LATER she was at the River Run, one of the town's cheapest inns, nursing a pint, trying to make it last, trying to summon up the energy to ask the landlord if she could sleep in the stables tonight, or at least lie down in them. She'd been thrown out of her room that morning, because even in those lodgings, a naked screaming woman running down the corridor with a sword in her hand and hell in her eyes three times a night was more than the other customers could stand.

It was worse, now, and it was all that fucking kid's fault.

She'd been at Crishnak all right. The rest of her company, the Dancers, had been wiped out.

And every night she was back there.

Back against the cliffs, a bad situation, yes, already, some idiot's fucking stupid idea to pull them into this valley with stone behind them and steep slopes to either side, the Kashtin troops piling in after them, their young commander at their head, yelling them on, and a half-grown boy straight off the farm, swinging at her, no technique, then, the roar, the sound like a million swarms of bees, a blur of darkness rising, the boy distracted, she'd killed him, but the roar, so loud, and the valley suddenly all one dreadful rage of fire. Soldiers, horses, shrieking and rearing and flailing and burning. Flags, threshing insanely in the hot wind like dying birds.

The farmboy, shocked wide-eyed by death, sprawled at her feet, his shirt and hair smoking, then flaring.

To her left – Kathje, her comrade-in-arms, all those fights survived, no-nonsense Kathje with her loud laugh, screaming, burning, crumbling away. To her right – Ordel with the sweet mouth and musician's hands, howling, turning to her as his eyes melted, one hand reaching, the flesh blistering, peeling from the blackening fingerbones, tumbling. And all the others. There were hundreds of them trapped in the valley, but the ones she heard, and saw, and smelled the awful choking stench of their death, they were her company. Kathje, Ordel, Lod, Marthe, Brack, Tunning, Big Jashy, Dark Jashy, and young Tenshin. Their voices, their names, burning. The flame, the wall of flame, closer and closer, Riven standing with her sword in front of her as though it would help, her back to the cliff, watching her swordpoint begin to glow, feeling the heat start to poison her armour, too late to take it off, nowhere to go.

In her dreams, the flame didn't wink out, leaving her sweating and alive, in a smoking ash-heap, powdered with the remains of every friend she had.

In her dreams, the cliff opened behind her and she ran, ran over the blackened crying remnants of friends and enemies, only to find the flame in front of her at every turn.

In her dreams she burned in the gods' fires.

She counted her coins again. Enough for another drink and a night in the stables, if the landlord was feeling generous.

But that wouldn't leave enough for the apothecary. He'd sell her what she wanted, and tell her to use it wisely, and not to take too much, and she'd find somewhere and take it all and sleep without dreams.

There was no-one to miss her. The Dancers had been her family, and they were gone. She'd sent messages to Kathje's people, a couple of others that she had names for. There were no loose ends.

Kathje, Ordel, Lod, Marthe, Brack, Tunning, Big Jashy, Dark Jashy, Young Tenshin. The only loose end was Riven.

Why was she even thinking about finding somewhere to lie another night? She'd spend it in hell. What was the point?

She went to the apothecary.

He emerged from the cluttered, reeking rear of the shop as she came in, muttered the usual warnings, counted the coins with stained hands, and disappeared again.

Well, she thought, *that was easy.*

Are you really going to do this, Riven? After all you've survived?

Why not?

She'd had a place picked out for some days. She didn't want some do-gooding clerical on their rounds finding her, and having her dragged to the nearest sanctuary before the thing was done. She didn't see why some poor bastard should find her in their stables. With practicality that might, once, have been tainted with a kind of mordant humour, she'd chosen the graveyard. She didn't leave things unfinished. That had never been her way.

As she walked she was suddenly aware of guilt. She should have kept back a couple of coins, as payment for whoever found her. *There's still your sword, Riven. And your armour.*

Oh, yes, she still had those. But still – her hands dug in her pockets, rummaging. This would be almost their last task, she thought. Maybe they just wanted to keep themselves occupied.

There was a hole in the left pocket, and something caught below the gaping seam. Her fingers went on feeling at it even as she looked for somewhere secluded to lie down.

It wasn't a coin. Coins didn't catch on thread. She tugged, not sure why she even cared, and the thing came out of her pocket. She stared at it.

It was a ring. A heavy, red-gold piece with a black stone carved with some design she couldn't make out. It had belonged to Tenshin, the new boy. He'd joined them less than a month ago, taking the place of old Garl who'd caught it in the last fight with the Kashtin.

Tenshin was young, sparking, full of angry energy. Clear blue eyes and sleek blonde head, all of nineteen if he was a day. They'd been suspicious, they always were at first.

"So why the Dancers?" Kathje asked him. Take him to a tavern and sound him out, it was what they did with the new ones.

"You know why," he said.

They did, too. They had a reputation. Good but clean, the Dancers. No looting, no rape – Kathje and Riven would have castrated any man caught at that, and they weren't the only ones.

The Dancers were good. Maybe the best. Tight and fast and lethal. They got the hard duty, because they could do it, but they cut clean.

The boy wasn't the first who'd pushed for a posting with them. The Dancers checked them over, and then they watched how they were in the line. Liabilities didn't last. An unfortunate training accident – not lethal, just enough to invalid them out – a transfer, and they were someone else's problem.

Sometimes, of course, they just got themselves killed. That was the way of it. The Dancers watched each other's backs, but you didn't earn that until you'd proved your mettle.

"Where'd you get your training?" Kathje said.

"Trewater."

"Trewater!" The rest rolled their eyes at each other. Ordel laughed aloud. "Officer school, eh?" He looked languid and bardic, did Ordel, and he played the fiddle like a demon in heat. That and his sweet dark eyes kept his bed full – men, women, he liked them both. On the field he was cold, slick, efficient.

"Could be worse," Riven said. "Not much, but it could be worse." Officer school it might be, but Trewater didn't turn out complete idiots.

"So what are you doing getting yourself in among the infantry, boy?" Kathje growled. She wasn't drunk, not yet, but her temper was always on a short leash. Fierce, loyal, a roaring terror in the line, a rowdy, unsinkable friend.

"If I'm going to be an officer I need to know what it's like in the line, right? I know what you think," Tenshin said. "Officer-whelp, out to get his hands dirty and get in the way. But even if I *am* supposed to lead, one day, how can I do it if I don't know what it's like for those I'm leading? How do I know if I even *can?* I can't learn that up on a hill, watching the action through an eyeglass, can I?"

This time the look the rest of them shared was a touch more thoughtful. They'd all survived commanders with no more idea of life in the line than a newborn babe. Sometimes not by much.

"Well, good for you, then," Riven said, and the boy had grinned as though she'd given him a present. They'd all drunk a fair bit and Tenshin had shown them the ring. "Pa gave it to me. Gave me a lot of stuff about it being my granda's and to remember who I was and never take it off – he said it so often I'm surprised he didn't have it welded to me. I think he thinks if I see it every time I use my hand, I'll remember who I am and come to my senses, take up the post I was meant for." He sighed. "But the wretched thing rubs when I use a sword, so . . ." he retied the cord it swung from, and slung it around his neck.

He'd acquitted himself well enough. Sharp, skilled, a fast learner – and, like Ordel, he was a sight tougher than he looked. By the time Crishnak came along, he was well on the way to being a Dancer.

There had been rumours for weeks. They'd found a halfway decent tavern and piled in, the whole company. The innkeep had looked scared half to death. But they were the Dancers. They drank hard, but no-one made trouble. It became their tavern, in the nights before the battle.

That last night, they'd known something big was coming, the next day. They got a little noisy. Ordel brought his fiddle. Tenshin proved to have a pleasant tenor, Riven could carry a tune, and the pair of them sang duets, the songs going from cheery to maudlin to obscene and back to maudlin.

Lod and Dark Jashy got into a conversation about magic swords, Lod swore he'd actually used one, once. Dark Jashy said the damn things were a liability. "Can't put your trust it," he said. "People start relying on the magic, they don't use the blade like they should."

Big Jashy and Tunning were feeling each other up, not very discreetly, under the table. Marthe was trying to teach Brack a new card game. "Every time you play Kings, you get screwed. Every fucking time. You gotta learn another game."

"I like Kings."

"You like losing money?"

"Kathje, tell him."

"What are you putting him off Kings for? You've been paying for your drinks out of his losses for a year . . ."

"I was hoping he'd learn. He ain't learned. It's embarrassing. Makes us look bad."

Eventually Tenshin declared himself hoarse, and drunk, and made off. He wasn't that drunk – none of them were, not even Kathje; they'd been doing this too long to risk thick heads and shaking hands the next day. Riven found the boy's ring on the floor when she scrabbled under the table for her coat, and picked it up to give it back to him. But the next morning had been a scramble and then they'd been in that fucking valley.

She closed her eyes at the last memory of that bright blond head, shining against the darkening sky. The ring felt cold and heavy in her hand.

I should take it back.

Riven had sent Ordel's fiddle to his sister, hardly able to bear touching it. Kathje's spare sword went to the only name she had for her, some man. A brother, a son? She didn't know. She'd not sent messages with them. She had no words. The things she wrapped and sent away had no meaning, or too much, now that the people who'd borne them were ash on the wind. She wondered if the summer growth had covered the blackened cliffs by now. It seemed impossible, even obscene. In her mind the place was scorched lifeless, and should remain so. After all, it had been the target of the gods' hatred, hadn't it?

And now there was this damned ring.

I should take it back.

Her weariness dragged at her. She wanted nothing more than to lie in the long grass under the trees, and stop. Stop fighting, stop jolting at every shadow, stop shaking so badly when she tried to light a lantern that she'd given up bothering, stop revisiting that fucking valley every night . . . someone would find the wretched ring, and take it to the boy's family, or sell it, and what business was it of hers? She couldn't even recall his last name, he'd been that new. Brassen? Brishen? They'd know it at the barracks.

If you don't take it there, his family may never get it back.

What of it? They'd never get their boy back, either, and that, presumably, mattered more.

Whoever finds it will think I stole it from him.

Who cared?

She didn't. No, she didn't. She couldn't.

That's all that will be remembered of you. And not just of you. The only one of the Dancers not to die at Crishnak, a thief?

Oh, she was so tired. The grass looked soft, a good place to rest.

Is that what's to be left of the Dancers' reputation?

What did it matter, now?

But the Dancers were ash on the wind, and who would guard their memory if she did not?

*

WHEN RIVEN TURNED up at the barracks, the place echoingly empty; half the troops disbanded, now the war was over; she felt the whispers before she heard them. While she waited for the record-keeper to finish shuffling papers, sitting on a hard chair in a small room that smelled of dust, she heard footsteps in the corridor. She knew they were making excuses to pass by so they could look in at her. Last of the Dancers.

She knew what she looked like. Skinny, flesh scoured away. Her thick dark curling hair, that she'd always been proud of, always washed when there was water to be had, now rough and dry and streaked with grey.

But she'd washed it, before she came here. In a horse-trough, but she'd washed it. And she'd cleaned her armour as best she could.

The record-keeper huffed and muttered. "Wait here."

Riven folded her arms and sat. She should have just left the damn ring and gone. Once there was paper in it, you were in for hours of waiting. She should have remembered.

It wasn't the record-keeper who came back. An older woman, thickset, scarred. Eyepatch and officer's marks. "Follow me."

"Ma'am, I just want to return a keepsake to the boy's family. I'm not . . ."

"Yes, you are."

Riven, sighing, followed, thinking of the long grass under the graveyard trees. Another room, neat, empty of everything but a table and two chairs, a jug, tankards. An open window letting in the crisp air from the hills and echoes of drill from the practice ground. Surely they weren't going to ask her to re-enlist? She'd served her time and more. She felt a vagrant flicker of pride.

The officer sat, gestured her to do likewise. "All right, soldier. Tell me about this ring."

"Ma'am, I told the records-keeper. The last night, in the tavern, I found it after the boy went to bed. I was going to give it back to him the next morning, but . . ." she shrugged. "They rousted us out in such a hurry, I didn't have a chance . . ." her throat dried.

The officer shoved a tankard at her.

Riven drank. Water. A pity. "We were on the field, then. And after, I forgot. I found it in my pocket this morning."

"You didn't try and sell it, then?"

"Sell it? I didn't know I *had* it, till this morning."

"That can be checked."

Riven felt anger, sick and hot, pushing up through the weariness. "You think I'd have *sold* it?"

"You signed out. From the look of you, you need money."

"I'm a *Dancer*, Ma'am." Riven stood up, shaking. "If you know who the boy's family are, I'll thank you to get the ring back to them." Stupidly, furiously, she said, "*I'll* check." She turned for the door.

"Sit down, soldier."

Habit was so strong, she almost did. Then she said, "I'm not a soldier anymore."

"You just said you were a Dancer."

"Yes. I was. But the Dancers are gone."

"Yes," the woman said. "Yes, and it's . . ." she sighed. "Look, I can only give you advice. You're no longer under my command or anyone else's. But the ring will get back to Lord Braish. And you'd best not be here when that happens."

Riven, her hand on the door, stopped. "I wasn't planning to be," she said.

"That's it, is it? Yes, I thought you had the look. What, you don't think I've seen it before? You're not the first, girl, not by a long way. War doesn't always end when the fighting's over. Take my advice. Go back."

"Ma'am?"

"Go back. Go to Crishnak. Look the place over. Yes, I know it's the last thing you want. But it'll cleanse you. And then, keep going. Find another town. Another profession."

Riven heard herself make a strange noise, like a crow trying to laugh. "Like what?"

"You're young. Right now, you feel old, but compared to me, you're a stripling. You're healthy, or will be if you start eating more than you drink. And there were no fools in the Dancers. You'll do, but you need a new start, and you'll best get it by going backwards."

The woman stood up, and held out a purse. "Back pay."

Riven took the purse. "Thank you."

"You're dismissed."

"Ma'am."

She went.

Crishnak.

She looked up as she left the barracks, up to where the hills jabbed the sky. Three days' walking would take her there.

No.

But her feet would not move back towards the graveyard.

She stood until a shout from the practice ground made her jump, spilling the purse. Coins tumbled into dust. Riven picked them up, one by one, brushed off the dirt. Why had she taken it? She wasn't owed any back pay, she'd always kept track. Like she'd always paid what she owed.

Not thinking, purposefully not thinking, holding her mind like a cup of dark liquid she dared not spill, she bought water, food. A flask of the local spirit that tasted of bitter flowers. The weather was easing towards summer. It had been winter, in the valley, she realised, laughing that strange crow laugh again and shocking the boy who took her money so that he too dropped coins, ringing on the countertop. Winter, it had been winter. Snow had melted and run down the rocks, hissing, in the brief terrible heat. Then she forced her mind quiet again, liquid, its surface reflecting only emptiness.

Locked in silence, she started to walk. Her footsteps trod out their names.

Kathje, Ordel, Lod, Marthe, Brack, Tunning, Big Jashy, Dark Jashy, Young Tenshin.

Out of the town, not looking back. She slept in a barn, the first night; the second, another farmer offered her a bed. An empty room, kept neat. A rag doll with open arms sat in the worn chair. A son, a daughter, lost in the war? She didn't ask. He was a slow-moving man, face harshly used by weather, time, and grief. "It's cold yet to sleep out," he said.

"I've done it before. And I . . . talk, in the night."

He snorted. "If my wife's snores couldn't wake me in forty years, that won't."

Screams might. She couldn't bring herself to say it, or much else. She was tired. She let him make up the bed. He stewed rabbit for supper, served it at the big scrubbed table with room for six. When Riven dropped her fork, she bent to fetch it and saw a woman's dusty slippers, waiting under a stool by the door for their owner to kick off muddy boots and ease her feet into comfort. The dust was thick as fur.

Riven crept out to the barn with the blankets, once the farmer was abed, trusting a soldier's habit of early waking to get her back indoors before he rose.

The dream changed that night. Young Tenshin stood next to her, where Kathje had been. "I can't go home," he said. "They're angry because I changed my name."

"You have to. Go home," she said, knowing that he had to leave, had to get out of there, because the fire was coming. "If you go home they all can."

"But they won't let me," he said, and his voice was full of dreadful mourning, and then the fire came.

When she woke, half out of the barn door with a scream still raw in her throat, the chained dog barking like a maniac, she thought, *He didn't change his name, I just couldn't remember it.*

Of course, farmers rise early too. He made no comment when he found her in the barn, but gave her a hearty breakfast, and refused payment. "Ah, I always make too much, the food'll only go to the pigs and they're fat enough."

He pushed a greasy parcel into her hand as she left, and turned away before she could thank him. He looked small and old. *I should have slept in that room he offered,* she thought, as though one night could change the house's emptiness.

That day the road rose into the hills. Water ran in trickling rills through a greening landscape; birds flickered and peeped in the low bushes. She caught the scent of burning, and nausea rose in her throat, but it was only a campfire.

The road that had led to hell had become ordinary. Farm carts. A small girl riding a donkey, kicking dirty heels. Dogs. Daily life. Not her sort of daily life, not what she'd known since she was eighteen, but . . . daily life. She let it pass her, nodded if someone greeted her, held the bowl of her thoughts steady.

But her hands were shaking. The liquid in the bowl rippled, shuddered with broken images. She thought about stopping, opening the farmer's greasy parcel of food, but her throat was too tight for eating and she knew if she sat down she wouldn't move, would stay seated at the side of the road until she turned to stone and the moss grew over her.

Kathje, Ordel, Lod, Marthe, Brack, Tunning, Big Jashy, Dark Jashy, Young Tenshin.

She heard Kathje's laugh from a passing couple. Big Jashy grinned at her from the back of a cart.

I should go back now, before I go completely mad. That'll be the end of this.

You've been mad for months, Riven.

Her feet kept moving.

There were yellow flowers in the grass the exact colour of Young Tenshin's hair. A bird sang like Ordel's fiddle, ridiculously cheerful.

There was the narrow pass, the stone throat that had swallowed them. The ground was green between the stones, speckled with bright colour, here and there something shining. Nature had thrown an embroidered cloth along the valley, hiding death.

Burning.

But there was no smell of it.

The rocks were streaked with black. She touched one of the streaks with a shaking hand. It didn't stain her fingers – not ash, not after all these months of rain and snow. The rock was scarred.

It had been magical fire, she'd always known that, but somehow the marked rock confirmed it. Hot enough to scar stone, and she'd survived. How?

The cold hill wind hissed and shook the feather-headed grasses, made the little bright flowers tremble.

Screams.

But there was only the hissing of the wind and the high far call of a bird circling, up against the blue.

Riven, her legs numb, walked towards the back of the valley. Between the grasses, the earth was black. Ash was good for growing things, her farmer mother had told her, many years ago. This ash must be rich. No wonder there were so many flowers.

Something gleamed. A strange, smooth stone, with a streak of coppery brilliance across its surface.

Metal. Metal melted into a puddle, here on the valley floor. Something had scraped across it, cutting through the dulled surface, leaving that gleaming line.

The fire was hot enough to melt armour. Melt weapons. There, and gone. Gods' fire.

I should be dead. Why aren't I dead?

The question had occurred to her more than once, but now, it had gained an extra weight.

She rose, walked on. Her legs shook. *Come on, Riven.* She didn't know why she was doing this but it felt necessary that she should stand where she had stood. The valley seemed endless, and then, at once, there she was, facing that same rock wall.

Riven turned. Leaned her back against the stone. Looked down the valley. It was empty of everything but sunlight, birds, the breeze hissing in the grass.

The tears came without warning, grabbing her up and shaking her as a dog shakes a rat. She sank to the ground and wept. And screamed. And raged. And wept again.

When the sun was dying bloody behind the ridges, she got up, and began to walk. Her face was stiff, her limbs felt as though they belonged to someone else. She left the valley as it filled up with shadows.

*

SHE FOUND THE Braish house easily enough. The windows were draped with blue mourning silks, like a hundred others

– though down in the town real silk was rare. There you'd see any cheap stuff, dyed blue, or a treasured dress or shirt, ripped up for grief and memory.

Why are you here, Riven?

The door opened. A servant, cold-eyed. "Yes?"

"I'm here to see Lord Braish."

"And why would he want to see you?"

"It's about a ring."

"Wait here."

The house was big and cold, and echoed with silence.

Lord Braish was waiting for her, standing against a high window that looked out over sweeping grounds.

"You," he said. His face was carved away, like hard stone from which all the softness had been worn by a scouring wind. "Why are you here?"

"I was told I should leave," Riven said.

"You should have. *Thief.*"

She ignored that. "See, that got me thinking. That, and other things. Because I should be dead. Everyone else is. But I'm not, and I think it was because of the ring. I didn't steal it – he was wearing it on a cord around his neck, because he couldn't use a sword right with it on. Did you know that? Damn thing was too big and clumsy. So he tied it around his neck, and the cord snapped, and I found it where it fell. I'd have given it back to him, if he'd survived the day. What with one thing and another, I forgot I even had it."

He watched her, silent, one side of his mouth twitching as though something were trying to burrow its way out. His eyes were raw, dry, full of hate.

"It wasn't just any ring, was it? It was magical. It was meant to protect your son. And that means you *knew.* You *knew* what was going to happen. They said it was a sign from the gods, that the enemy's best troops were there, their leader was there, and then the fire came. But I don't think the gods had a thing to do with it. I think someone found a way to make the fire. But it wouldn't work unless the enemy were trapped in that valley, and so, well, someone decided to draw them in. Tell me, did he tell you he was going to join the Dancers?"

"*Hah.*" An explosion of disgust. "No."

"But he did. Because we were the best."

"A *line* company! You worthless scum, you murdered my son!" He slammed his hands on the heavy table, his lips drawn back from yellowing teeth.

"No, she didn't, Harna. *You* did."

Riven hadn't even seen the woman come in. Slight, straight, holding herself like a bow drawn almost to breaking. Even with that bright hair gone grey, her resemblance to Young Tenshin hit Riven in the gut, forcing out a grunt of pain. The woman barely glanced at her. All her attention was on her husband.

"The ring was meant to protect him," she said, "because Harna knew, whatever company Tenshin joined, he was likely to want the thick of the action. Want to *prove* himself. He never had to prove himself to me."

"He'd have lived if this bitch hadn't been carrying the ring!"

"Yes, perhaps. And then what? What if he had, Harna? What if he'd seen all those around him fall, do you think he wouldn't have realised, do you think he wouldn't have known that only his father's wealth had saved him? Do you think he'd have accepted that? Do you think he'd have been *happy*?" She looked at Riven for the first time. "He mortgaged the estate, to buy that ring. And now he can sell it again. But there's no-one to inherit, now, of course." That brutally held control faltered. "You knew him."

"Yes Ma'am, I did. He was a good boy," she said. "He'd have been a good officer."

"I never wanted that for him," she said. "War and death, what life is that? But the family name was made in war and must be carried like a banner, isn't that right, Harna? It was because you were the best, you know," she said to Riven. "He might despise line regiments, but they all knew."

"Ma'am?"

"The Dancers. Harna told me, after. They put the Dancers in there because they were the best and they knew it, and so did the Kashtin. Does that make you happy? Even the Kashtin had heard of you. They made sure the Kashtin leader knew where you were. Another boy with something to prove," she said. "He's dead. They all are. Girls, too. Go, now, please."

Lord Braish snarled. "Don't you move, I'll see you hanged."

"No, you won't," his wife said. "It's *over*, Harna. It's all over." She looked at Riven. "Please go away."

"I'm sorry," Riven said. And she was sorry. There was a terrible sorrow everywhere, all through her, and all over everything like ash.

She shut the door behind her, and stood in the street. To the west, the hills. To the east, the town and the barracks. Nothing there for her, now.

*

THE FARMER OPENED the door with a look of mild surprise. "Thought you were headed out."

"I was. Wondered . . . if maybe you wanted some help around the place. I grew up on a farm. Haven't forgotten everything."

He glanced down at her bundle. Armour. A sword. Looked back at her face. "I could use it," he said, slowly. "But you'd best look at the place in daylight first. I haven't kept it up as I'd like."

Fruit trees by the back door sent a scurry of petals through the air, like fleeing spirits on the breeze. Small green spikes pushed through the earth of two fields, neat rows of spears, an invading army of corn. Another field lay fallow, scattered with blood-bright poppies.

"Those fruit trees need replacing," the farmer said. "Too much work for my back."

"I can do that," Riven said. There would be new trees, next year, scattering their petals on the wind. She would plant nine of them. *Kathje, Ordel, Lod, Marthe, Brack, Tunning, Big Jashy, Dark Jashy, Young Tenshin.*

About the Authors

Anne Lyle

Anne Lyle was born in what is popularly known as "Robin Hood Country", and grew up fascinated by English history, folklore, and swashbuckling heroes. Unfortunately there was little demand in 1970s Nottinghamshire for diminutive swordswomen, so she studied sensible subjects like science and languages instead. It appears, however, that although you can take the girl out of Sherwood Forest, you can't take Sherwood Forest out of the girl. She now spends practically every spare hour writing – or at least planning – fantasy fiction about dashing swordsmen and scheming spies, set in alternate pasts or imaginary worlds.

She is the author of the Night's Masque Elizabethan fantasy trilogy: The Alchemist of Souls, The Merchant of Dreams and The Prince of Lies, and is currently working on a new series set in the same world as her 2013 short story A Thief in the Night. She lives in Cambridge with her family, two neurotic cats and enough fountain pens to last several lifetimes.

Juliet McKenna

Juliet E McKenna is a British fantasy author who has loved history, myth and other worlds since she first learned to read. She has written fifteen epic fantasy novels, from *The Thief's Gamble*, beginning *The Tales of Einarinn* to *Defiant Peaks*, concluding *The Hadrumal Crisis*. In between novels, she writes diverse shorter fiction, reviews for web and print magazines and promotes SF&Fantasy through blogging, attending conventions, teaching creative writing and commenting on book trade issues. She's currently exploring opportunities in independent digital publishing, re-issuing her backlist and bringing out original fiction. Learn more about all of this at julietemckenna.com

Nadine West

Nadine West is a prose writer, poet, spoken word performer and English teacher. Her first novel is nearing completion, and she lives in Manchester with her husband, Adam, and her wayward cat, Cleopatra.

Fran Terminiello

Fran writes secondary and first world fantasy where fighting often plays a part, and has contributed stories to several anthologies, including: Tales from the Nun and Dragon, edited by Adele Wearing; the Fox Pockets series; and Tales of Eve, edited by Mhairi Simpson. She is currently finishing a coauthored novel written with David Murray.

Now running two historical fencing clubs - School of the Sword and Waterloo Sparring Group - she has studied swordplay since 2010, with an emphasis on rapier and Renaissance sword arts. Fran is also a founding member of Esfinges, an international organisation for women in Historical European martial arts.

Living in Surrey with her family, Fran is also parent to a growing collection of swords.

Joanne Hall

Joanne Hall lives in Bristol, England, with her partner. She has been writing since she was old enough to hold a pen, and gave up a sensible (boring) job in insurance to be a full time writer, to the despair of her mother. She dabbled in music journalism, and enjoys going to gigs and the cinema, and reading.

Her first three novels, which made up the New Kingdom Trilogy, were published by Epress Online. Since then she has had to move house to make more room for books. Her short stories have been published in several anthologies, including "Dark Spires" and "Future Bristol", as well as a number of magazines. A collection of short stories, "The Feline Queen" was published by Wolfsinger Publications in April 2011, and her latest novel, "The Art of Forgetting" was published by Kristell Ink in two volumes in 2013/14, and the first volume has been longlisted for the 2014 Tiptree Award. With Roz Clarke, she has co-edited two anthologies, "Colinthology" and "Airship Shape and Bristol Fashion."

She is also one of the founders of Bristolcon. Her blog can be found at www.hierath.co.uk, and her twitter is @hierath77. She's always happy to hear from readers.

Kim Lakin-Smith

Kim Lakin-Smith is a Science Fiction and Dark Fantasy author. Kim's short stories have appeared in numerous magazines and anthologies, including *Interzone, Black Static, Celebration: 50 Years of the BSFA, Behind the Sofa: Celebrity Memories of Doctor Who, The Mammoth Book of Ghost Stories by Women, Solaris Rising 2, Resurrection Engines, Best British Fantasy 2013, Sharkpunk, The Mammoth Book of Dieselpunk*, and more. Her short story, 'Johnny and Emmie-Lou Get Married' (Interzone, Issue 222) was shortlisted for the 2011 British Science Fiction Association award and her novel, *Cyber Circus*, was shortlisted for both the British Science Fiction Association Best Novel and the British Fantasy Award for Best Novel 2012. The Guardian described Kim's crossover novel, *Autodrome*, as 'an off-beat mystery adventure like no other.' She is also the author of *Tourniquet*, a gothic science fantasy, and the YA novella, *Queen Rat*. Kim lives in 2/5ths of a Victorian Gothic mansion house with her wolfgirl of a daughter and dark lord of a husband. Kim is represented by the Andlyn Literary Agency, London.

K R Green

K. R. Green writes fantasy novels about winged creatures: falcons, corvidae and dragons alike. Her writing process involves a lot of herbal teas, list-making, video gaming, star-gazing and reading. When she isn't painting pictures with words, she works in the mental health sector in Hampshire, tweets at @K_R_Green and writes blogs at www.krgreen.co.uk.

K T Davies

KT Davies writes about herself in the third person, sometimes practices historical European martial arts and sometimes plays MMORPGs. She also reads comics and books, lots of books.

Interesting, but pointless fact (unless you're madly interested in pointless facts in which case, fill yer boots): She once fell down the highest mountain in south east Asia and then had to walk back up the damn thing. It was quite tiring. She thinks she's funny and a mistress of understatement.

Sophie E Tallis

S.E Tallis is a published author, freelance illustrator and a full member of *The Society of Authors*. She was born in Bristol but grew up in a sleepy village dreaming of dragons and wild adventures, and currently lives in the Cotswolds with her family and four white wolves. She was a full-time teacher for 16 years and now works in a library, a dream job surrounded by books all day! She is a writer, poet, painter, illustrator and confirmed nerd, with a BA (Hons) Degree in Fine Art and a Post-Grad in Education. She has illustrated 9 books to date. Her epic illustrated fantasy, *White Mountain*, was re-published in 2014 by Grimbold Books, and she is currently writing the sequel, *Darkling Rise*.

S.E Tallis has also written short stories for the charity anthology, *A World Of Their Own* (published September 2015 by Kristell Inklings); dark fairy-tale anthology, *Shadows of the Oak*, (soon to be published by Tenebris Books); and is writing dark fantasy novel, *Ravenwing*, which she wrote 50,000 words of, for her first ever Nano in November 2015.

Danie Ware

Danie runs the social media profile of cult retailer Forbidden Planet, and has organised their signings and events calendar for more than a decade. When not at work, she remains geek and gamer, warrior Mum, outward-bound cyclist and fitness freak.

She went to an all-boys' school (yes really), studied English Literature at UEA in Norwich, then joined a Viking re-enactment group and spent her twenties fighting, writing, and rolling certain multi-sided dice. At thirty, she made an attempt to grow up and didn't like it much; at forty, she spends her time with her son, in the gym, or making up for missing the battlefield by writing epic stories about it. Author of the Ecko series, published by Titan Books.

Julia Knight

Julia Knight is married with two children, and lives with the world's daftest dog that is shamelessly ruled by the writer's obligatory three cats. She lives in Sussex, UK and when not writing she likes motorbikes, watching wrestling or rugby, killing pixels in MMOs. She is incapable of being serious for more than five minutes in a row.

Kelda Crich

Kelda Crich is a new born entity. She's been lurking in her creator's mind for a few years. Now she's out in the open. Find Kelda in London looking at strange things in London's medical museums or on her blog. Kelda's work has appeared in *The Lovecraft eZine, Journal of Unlikely Acceptances, Dreams from the Witch House* and in the Bram Stoker Award winning *After Death* anthology.

Roz Clarke

Roz Clarke is a specfic writer and editor. She's a graduate of the Manchester Metropolitan Creative Writing MA and the Clarion West writer's workshop. She's had short stories published in various magazines and anthologies, including the story 'Haunt-Type Experience', which was first published in Black Static and was recently reprinted in the acclaimed anthology *Stories for Chip: A Tribute to Samuel R. Delany*. Roz moved from Manchester to Bristol in 2007, and has been a member of the BristolCon committee since its inception in 2009. She is delighted to have come to rest in that peculiar, inspiring city, and is a member of both the wonderful Bristol Science Fiction and Fantasy Society, and the North Bristol Writer's Group, with whom she helped produce the *North By*

Southwest anthology and is currently leading a collaborative novel project entitled *The Sealed Room*.

Roz occasionally blogs at www.firefew.com, and you can twit her at @zora_db, where she likes to talk about books, dogs and bicycles.

Lou Morgan

Lou Morgan is an award-nominated adult and YA author. Her urban fantasy *Blood and Feathers* books are published by Solaris, while her first YA horror novel *Sleepless* is published by Stripes as part of their Red Eye series.

Her short stories have appeared in anthologies from Solaris Books, Jurassic and NewCon Press, amongst others, and she is a long- and short-list reader for the Bath Novel Award.

Dolly Garland

Dolly Garland writes fantasy that is bit like her - muddled in cultures. Having lived in three countries, and several cities, she now calls London her home, though the roots of her fantasy have returned to India, where she grew up. You can chat to her @DollyGarland on Twitter, @DollyGarlandAuthor on Facebook, and www.dollygarland.com

Gaie Sebold

Gaie Sebold was born rather longer ago than seems reasonable. She has written several novels, a number of short stories, and has been known to perform poetry. Her debut novel introduced brothel-owning ex-avatar of sex and war, *Babylon Steel* (Solaris, 2012); the sequel, *Dangerous Gifts*, came out in 2013. *Shanghai Sparrow*, a steampunk fantasy, came out in 2014 and the sequel, *Sparrow Falling*, is due in 2016. Her jobs have ranged from till-extension to bottle-washer and theatre-tour-manager to charity administrator. She lives with writer David Gullen and a paranoid cat in leafy suburbia, runs writing workshops, grows vegetables, and cooks a pretty good borscht.

Her website is www.gaiesebold.com and you can find her on twitter @GaieSebold.

A Selection of Other Titles from Kristell Ink

Cruelty by Ellen Croshain

Once a year, in the caves deep below the house, the Family gathers to perform a ritual to appease their god. But Faroust only accepts payment in blood. Eliza MacTir, youngest daughter of a powerful Irish family, was born into fae gentry without the magical gifts that have coursed through the Family's veins for millennia; she was an outcast from her first breath. Desperate for freedom, Eliza's flight from rural Ireland is thwarted by the Family's head of security. The only weapon she has to fight her captor is her own awakening sexuality. Drawn into the world of magic and gods, Eliza must find a way to break free, even if it means breaking the hearts of those she loves, and letting her own turn to stone. Cruelty, it runs in the Family.

In Search of Gods and Heroes by Sammy H.K Smith

Buried in the scriptures of Ibea lies a story of rivalry, betrayal, stolen love, and the bitter division of the gods into two factions. This rift forced the lesser deities to pledge their divine loyalty either to the shining Eternal Kingdom or the darkness of the Underworld. When a demon sneaks into the mortal world and murders an innocent girl to get to her sister Chaeli, all pretence of peace between the gods is shattered. For Chaeli is no ordinary mortal, she is a demi-goddess, in hiding for centuries, even from herself. But there are two divine brothers who may have fathered her, and the fate of Ibea rests on the source of her blood. Chaeli embarks on a journey that tests her heart, her courage, and her humanity. Her only guides are a man who died a thousand years ago in the Dragon Wars, a former assassin for the Underworld, and a changeling who prefers the form of a cat. The lives of many others – the hideously scarred Anya and her gaoler; the enigmatic and cruel Captain Kerne; the dissolute Prince Dal; and gentle seer Hana – all become entwined. The gods will once more walk the mortal plane spreading love, luck, disease, and despair as they prepare for the final, inevitable battle. In Search of Gods and Heroes, Book One of Children of Nalowyn, is a true epic of sweeping proportions which becomes progressively darker as the baser side of human nature is explored, the failings and ambitions of the gods is revealed, and lines between sensuality and sadism, love and lust are blurred.

Fear the Reaper by Tom Lloyd

All Shell has ever wanted was a home, a place to belong. But now an angel of the God has tracked her down, intent on using her to hunt the demon that once saved her. The journey will take her into the dead place beyond the borders of the world, there to face her past and witness the coming of a new age.

A stand-alone novella from the author of The Twilight Reign series and Moon's Artifice.

www.kristell-ink.com

Lightning Source UK Ltd.
Milton Keynes UK
UKHW04f2036211018
330933UK00001B/5/P